PRAISE FOR JOHN D. NESBITT

"Nesbitt is a true artist…"

— WESTERN AMERICAN LITERATURE

"John Nesbitt knows working cowboys and ranch life well enough for you to chew the dirt with his characters as this tale unfolds."

— TRUE WEST

"Nesbitt has a nice turn of phrase and creates characters so real, you can hear them talk if you close your eyes."

— ROUNDUP MAGAZINE

"Nesbitt demonstrates himself a skilled wrangler of detail and character."

— PUBLISHERS WEEKLY

BROKEN HORN

ALSO BY JOHN D. NESBITT

Western Short Story Showcase

West of Dancing Rock & Other Western Stories

Ridin' with the Pack

Across the Cheyenne River

Don't Be a Stranger

Justice at Redwillow

Boy from the Country

Jess Delaine Series

Lost Canyon

Dunbar Series

Dark Prairie

Death in Cantera

Destiny at Dry Camp

Dusk Along the Niobrara

BROKEN HORN

JESS DELAINE
BOOK 2

JOHN D. NESBITT

WOLFPACK
PUBLISHING

For Janet Homer

BROKEN HORN

1

DELAINE GAVE HIS HORSE REIN TO LET IT MOVE AT ITS
own pace, a fast walk. Out of habit, he watched where
the horse put its hooves, and as the ground moved
beneath his gaze, he recognized the first flowers of
spring. Some were white, and some were yellow. They
all had five petals and grew in low-lying clumps, with
delicate blossoms smaller than a dime. Carpet flowers.
He had seen them every year when he lived in
Wyoming before, and here they were again, making
their appearance after the prairie had lain like a dry
crust through the winter.

As he approached the edge of town, he noticed a
group of four boys kneeling on the ground near a
frame house with peeling white paint. The boys
formed a small circle, and they were laughing and
jeering as they poked short sticks at something. Closer,
Delaine saw that they had a young rabbit trapped.

Delaine stopped his horse, and a couple of the
boys looked up. "Why don't you let the rabbit go?" he
asked.

A pug-nosed, squinting boy with ginger-colored hair said, "We're not hurting him."

"You don't think you are. But what if someone did that to you? Don't you think you'd be scared? And why do you want to be poking at him with sticks?"

"Just somethin' to mess around with."

Another boy said, "No law against it."

"Think about what it feels like to him." As Delaine heard his own words, he imagined they were just that, words on the air. He reverted to his first question. "Why don't you let him go?"

The boy with reddish hair said, "We will."

Delaine rode on. He could not remember at what age he learned to take into account how other creatures—human or otherwise—felt. He thought he was younger than these boys, who were about nine or ten. People learned those lessons at different ages, he understood. Some people never learned them at all, never developed a sense of how others suffered. He had heard that some men who committed serious crimes against other humans had started out being cruel to animals—crueler, he imagined, than poking at a rabbit with a stick.

His mind cleared as he rode toward the Sweet Auburn café. He took it as a good sign that no other horses were tied in front. He stopped at the hitching rail, swung down, and wrapped the reins. Leaving the brown horse to bask in the sun, he went in.

As he had hoped, no other customers were present. As the doorbell finished tinkling, a dark-haired woman in a blue dress and white apron came out of the kitchen. Her face relaxed, and she smiled.

Rachel. As her name went through his mind, he smiled in return.

She arrived at his table as he took a seat and set his hat on the next chair. "Out and about this morning?" she asked.

"Same as before. What time is it? About ten thirty?"

"About that."

"I went out to another ranch to see about work. Still nothing."

"It's early yet. Mid-April." Her rich-colored skin had a shine as she smiled again and said, "Coffee?"

"Please."

He watched as she walked to the kitchen and came back with a coffeepot.

As she poured a cup, she said, "Weather looks nice."

"It is. I'd like to get out and work in the sunshine and fresh air. Not that I mind the job I have. It's kept me through the winter." He had an image of the interior of the livery stable. "I think Hiram Fitts wants to come back, now that the new owners of the Lost Canyon Ranch have taken over. He worked at the stable before, and of course no one owns a job like that, but I think Kent, the stableman, would like to have him back. He knows I'm looking for ranch work, and he asked me how soon I might find something. All I could say was I don't know." Delaine took a sip of coffee.

Rachel gave a light shrug. "I might know of something."

Delaine met her eyes. "A job?"

"Something like it. The bad thing is that it would take you away."

Delaine frowned. "What is it?"

Rachel set down the coffeepot and brushed her

hand against her apron. "There's a family here, and they haven't heard from the father who went away to another town."

"What's the town?"

"I believe it is called Harrow."

Delaine drew his eyebrows together. "I think I know where it is. A couple of days' ride from here."

"Sounds like it."

"Did he go there to work?"

"No, there was another relative there who died. This one went to see about the inheritance or to— what do you call it, settle the estate."

"I think that's what they say in English. Is it a Mexican family?"

"Yes. The family here is named Sandoval. The man who died was named Luna—José Luna, I think."

"Are they relatives of yours?"

"No, just friends."

"Not that it matters. I just like to know." Delaine drank from his coffee cup. "And they want someone to go see about the relative they haven't heard—from— this Sandoval?"

"Yes. Robert Sandoval."

Delaine studied her. "Did you recommend me?"

She pursed her lips. "They mentioned it first. They said you did a good thing when you helped find the missing girl last fall, and they thought you might know the kind of people in that town."

Delaine nodded. He formed an image of a typical frontier town here on the northern plains, with almost all White people. "I can understand that they'd be concerned if they hadn't heard from him. How long has it been?"

"About a month, I think."

He pondered. "I can't say for sure that I'll do it, but I can talk to them."

Her face brightened. "That's good. I'll let them know. What would you think about coming by my place at about seven, and I'll take you to them?"

"I'll do that."

———

LA SEÑORA SANDOVAL, wearing a charcoal-grey dress and shawl, received them in her living room. She appeared to be of early middle age—not quite plump but no longer slender, and beginning to grey. Her dark-brown eyes expressed worry. When she had her guests seated, she offered them coffee. As she served the coffee, she said in English, "Something else? A brandy?"

Delaine said, "It's not necessary."

"Just a little," she said, making a gap with her thumb and forefinger and giving a nod.

Delaine smiled. "All right."

A fourth person joined the group, a boy of about sixteen or seventeen, scrubbed and combed and wearing a clean white shirt. He sat in silence as his mother spoke, sometimes in Spanish and sometimes in English.

The uncle, José Luna, used to live in the town called Harrow. He had a business like a hotel, or guest house, and he did not have a family. It was believed that he had money in the bank, and he had written letters to Roberto Sandoval, who was the son of Mr. Luna's sister, may she rest in peace. When Roberto received news of Mr. Luna's death, he went there.

"And you haven't heard from him?" Delaine asked in English.

"Not a word," said the señora, also in English.

"And you'd like me to go look for him."

She nodded. "If you can."

"Could you tell me what he looks like, or do you have a picture?"

The lady looked at Rachel, who converted the question into Spanish.

The answer came in Spanish. The lady did not have a photograph or a painting. Her husband was a good-looking man, about like her son here, a littler darker than herself, with dark hair and brown eyes, good teeth. Not as tall as Señor Delén but not short, neither slender nor fat. He was wearing clean work clothes for travel, and he had a blue suit in his valise.

"And a hat?" Delaine asked in Spanish.

"Oh, yes, a hat. Of grey felt."

"And how did he travel?"

"*Por diligencia.*"

Delaine looked at Rachel.

"By stagecoach," she said in English.

Delaine nodded at the señora and continued in Spanish. "Oh, yes. I believe I will go on my horse."

"Then you will go?" Creases showed at the corners of her eyes.

Delaine looked at Rachel and said, in English, "I guess so. It seems as if these people need my help."

La señora Sandoval spoke to Rachel in Spanish. "And there is a matter of money. We have to give him something for his expenses, and this is work, like any other job."

Delaine winced. He did not want to take money from these people, who might be facing difficulties that would make an inheritance seem unimportant. But he had to be realistic and businesslike. In English, he said, "I've thought about it, and I think I'll need about a dollar a day for expenses and a dollar and a half a day for my work. If it takes me ten days, that's twenty-five dollars. And so on, if it goes longer than that. I have no way of knowing, of course."

Rachel directed her attention to the lady, who spoke in English.

"I understand. I think he should take fifty dollars." She spoke two syllables in Spanish to her son, and he stood up and left the room.

He came back with a handful of five-dollar gold pieces and handed them to his mother, who rose from her chair. She held the coins with her hands together and extended them toward Delaine.

He stood up and received them into his two hands, counting them by habit. Ten. "Thank you," he said. "I hope I don't have to use it all."

The woman replied in Spanish. "May God bless you. Thank you for your help. May God help you to find our beloved Roberto, come what may."

Delaine put the money in his pocket and sat down. In Spanish, he said, "Thank you. Is there anything else I should know? Did you tell me how old Mr. Sandoval is?"

"Forty-two. Young and in good health. Strong. Hard-working."

"*Con bigote*," said the boy. With a mustache.

Still in Spanish, Delaine said, "Maybe one other thing. Do you know the name of the hotel or guest house of Mr. Luna?"

The mother looked at the son, whose voice changed as he spoke in English. "The Blue Iris."

Delaine smiled and said in English, "Thanks. I'm glad I thought to ask."

The boy smiled in return, and a brief silence hung in the air. The hostess nodded toward the brandy, and Delaine took a sip. He felt the family's hope and optimism, but he sensed that an alternate fatalism was not far away.

"I hope I can find him," he said in Spanish.

"*Si Dios quiere*," said the señora. If God wishes.

———

DELAINE HAD his bag packed and tied onto the back of his saddle when he stopped at the café to take leave of Rachel.

"I hope I'm not gone too long," he said, "and it goes without saying that I hope I have positive results."

"Of course I hope so, too. This is a very good thing you are doing."

"It seems like something I should do. It's bigger and more important than my own little concerns."

"I hope you don't have to be gone too long."

He allowed himself a glance at her full figure and brought his eyes back to hers. "Whatever it takes. I can't guarantee anything, but I'll find out what there is to know."

———

DELAINE REACHED THE EAST–WEST road in the afternoon of his second day of travel. The trail north through Hartville took him through country he had not seen before, rolling plains of hills and buttes with the Laramie Range to the west. The north–south trail met the more-traveled east–west road at Glenrose, a town with a water tower and a train stop. This route, like the one Delaine had been traveling, was new to him, though he had heard of the railroad being built when he lived in Wyoming before. From the map he had studied before he set out on this trip, he knew that the railroad and the wagon road went along together, with towns about five to ten miles apart. Kent, the stableman, told him that the railroad had been in for about ten years but none of the towns along this stretch were much more than a signal stop.

Delaine had the sense that he should not tell people right away about his purpose, and he did not like to ask unnecessary or conspicuous questions, so he turned west at Glenrose without stopping in.

The afternoon grew warm, and he did not push his horse. After an hour an a half, he came to a small town on the left or south side of the road. A sign at the railroad stop confirmed that the place was called Willett. On a hill in back of the town, a schoolhouse faced east. The town itself consisted of a coal business, a post office, a general store, a livery stable, a feed and grain business, and a saloon set off by itself so that it resembled a roadhouse.

A few horses were tied in front of the saloon where Delaine dismounted and tied up as well. The day being Sunday, and the horses all dry and dozing as if they had been there awhile, Delaine reminded himself to be wary of Sunday drunks, men who were on a jag from the night before.

Inside, half a dozen men stood along the bar, and voices floated on the air. As Delaine moved to the bar, the slam of a leather dice cup on the bar top was followed by a gravelly voice.

"Puppy paws. See if you can beat that."

Delaine pictured two fives as he glanced down the bar and saw the ivory-colored dice, too far to read.

As a rule, he preferred whiskey to beer and even more so in out-of-the-way places where the beer might be warm or homemade or both, but the long ride and the warm sun had given him a thirst, and a couple of other patrons had glasses of beer that looked clean.

The bartender was a middle-aged fellow with a bristly mustache, spectacles, and a high, balding forehead. He swiped the bar in front of Delaine and said, "What'll it be?"

"I think I'll try a glass of beer."

The bartender turned his back and drew a glassful, scraped the foam off the top with a strip of wood like a ruler, and set the glass in front of Delaine. "Fifteen cents. Pay now."

Delaine set a quarter on the bar.

The bartender gave him change and pointed at the far wall, where a temporary table was made up of pine boards set across a pair of trestles. A metal tray held a heap of friend food that Delaine did not identify in the dim light. "Help yourself," said the barkeep.

"What is it?"

"Lamb fries."

Delaine raised his eyebrows. "Is someone docking and castrating lambs this early?"

"Somebody is. Castrating, at least. These came in fresh in a bucket today." The man cast a glance at the fries. "On the house."

"Thanks. I might, a little later."

The bartender raised his voice. "That goes for the rest of you. Help yourself to the fries."

Delaine took a drink of beer. It was not cold, but it was not bad.

The dice cup slammed down again. A yelp caused Delaine to look in that direction. A man with a needle nose, close-set eyes, and stringy hair spoke in a Southern accent. "Boxcars. Now see if you can beat that."

Two men who were not shaking dice moved to the makeshift table. The taller of the two had a forward-leaning posture and rounded shoulders. He wore a black hat that had been discolored by the sun, a red shirt, and a dull-black, loose-hanging leather vest with silver rosettes. His holster was slung a little lower than the average cowpuncher's, and he had large-roweled spurs. He picked a lamb fry off the tray and put it in his mouth.

His companion was not very tall but had a sturdy build, with light-colored hair, a thin, light mustache, a dull brown shirt and vest, and denim trousers with cuffs. He sampled a fried prairie oyster as well.

The taller one turned toward the bar and called out in a deep voice. "Hey, Dill, these things are cold."

"Should've tried 'em sooner," said the bartender.

The man with the Southern voice said, "Baick home, we have 'em fer breakfast. Pig balls. Hot off the stove."

The tall man gave a sour expression. "Eat these, then."

A man in the drab-colored clothes of a traveler, who had been drinking beer by himself, stepped away from the bar. He was a large man, a little taller than average with a heavy build, a broad face, squinty eyes, fleshy lips, and a sallow complexion. For a man his size, he had light steps as he moved toward the table. He ate one oyster and then a second one. "Not bad," he said. He licked his fingers.

The taller man said, "They taste greezy to me. But some people'll eat anything."

The heavy man shrugged, and with a small wave of the hand, he said, "If you don't like 'em, don't eat 'em."

The taller man drew himself up straight. Still in his deep voice, he said, "I don't like the way you said that."

"All I said was—"

"I know what you said. I didn't like the way you said it."

The heavy man took in the comment and turned to walk away.

"Don't turn your back on me when I'm talkin' to you." The man in the dark hat stepped forward, into better light. He had a round nose, large eyes with shadows beneath them, and a rounded area above his upper lip.

The man with the broad, sallow face stopped and made a slow turn. He wore a pistol high on his hip, but he did not hold his hand anywhere near it. He faced the antagonistic fellow and said, "What's your purpose?"

"My purpose. My purpose is to get some respect from the likes of you."

The large man seemed to be taking measure of the situation. He said, "Why don't we just leave things the way—"

"Because I don't like it. I don't like some tub of lard gettin' smart with me."

The larger man's chest rose, as if something came

up before he could control it. "You don't have to," he said, in a quick voice.

The man in the red shirt lunged forward and landed a fist on the other man's jaw. He stepped forward and hit him two more times, left and right. The heavy man backed up, stumbled, knocked the boards from the trestles, and regained his balance as the tray of lamb fries spilled to the floor.

A rapping sound on the bar brought everything to a standstill. Dill, the bartender, had laid a single-barreled shotgun on the bar and had slapped the bar top with a smooth black stick that looked like a truncheon. His voice barked. "That's enough of that, Jim." He settled down when he had everyone's attention, and he continued. "Everyone knows I don't put up with that in here. So, Jim, you can just leave, and don't come back until you can keep your hands to yourself."

The man named Jim was settling his faded black hat onto his head. "I guess I will. I'll finish my drink first." He stepped to the bar, tossed down the rest of a drink of whiskey, and nodded to his pal. Jim's spurs jingled as the two of them headed out the door. A few seconds later, drumming hoofbeats sounded as the two rode away.

The heavy man returned to the bar and his glass of beer.

The bartender spoke to him. "I don't know who you are, mister. I could see Jim picked that fight, but I always say it takes two. So if you move along after you finish your drink, that would be all right. Come again some other time, that would be all right, too. But that's it for today."

The bartender put away the shotgun and the billy club. He craned his neck and watched as a hound-like dog ate the fried pieces scattered on the floor. He turned to Delaine. "Ready for another beer?"

"I think one is good enough for me today. How far is it to Harrow?"

"About ten miles."

The sun was moving into the latter half of the afternoon when Delaine set out. He wondered if he would see any of the three riders who left ahead of him, but all he saw was a pair of ravens sitting on the railroad track, about a hundred yards away from where he rode on the trail. They watched him. Magpies, crows, ravens—they had learned the white man's range and how to stay just beyond it.

2

DELAINE FOUND THE TOWN OF HARROW ON THE NORTH side of the tracks, with the main street running north toward open rangeland. The two largest buildings were the general store on the right and The Brookfield Hotel on the left. Smaller buildings, also with false fronts, housed The Shamrock Café, north of the general store, and the Diamond Horseshoe Saloon, north of the hotel. Delaine did not see The Blue Iris right away, but he did not think it would be hard to find. For the time being, he was interested in finding something to eat.

He tied his horse in front of the café and went in. A row of tables ran along each side of the center aisle, and a dark green shamrock the size of a dinner plate hung on the wall behind the counter. Only one person sat at a table, a slender, greying man who was reading a newspaper. As Delaine chose a place and sat down, the man rose from his seat and approached Delaine's table. He was wearing a dull white shirt and a pair of grey wool pants, both garments worn but not yet shabby.

The man folded his hands together and lowered his head. "Good afternoon. Almost evening. What would you like to order?"

Delaine did not see a menu posted, and the waiter did not offer him one. "What is there?" he asked. "Is the evening meal ready?"

"I don't think so. People start to come in for that between five and six. I believe there's ham left over from noon dinner, and there might be some potatoes that are still warm."

"That sounds all right. Can I have a cup of coffee to go along with it?"

"Of course." The man gave a perfunctory smile and turned away.

The Shamrock Café seemed like a casual place, but Delaine reflected that it might just be at low ebb, late on a Sunday afternoon.

The coffee arrived in a tan crockery mug, followed by a matching plate with odd pieces of ham and a pile of fried potatoes not quite yet congealing.

The waiter said, "I hope this is all right. Most of our business on Sunday is at noon. This food was pretty good at that time."

"I'm sure it'll be fine now. What would I have gotten if I had waited for supper?"

The waiter twisted his mouth, and with a droll expression, he said, "As a matter of truth, the cook doesn't get up a separate meal on Sunday evening."

"How about the people who come in between five and six?"

The waiter smiled. "That's during the week. On

Sunday, whenever we run out of what we had at noon, we close up."

"Then I was lucky to get what I did."

"I would say so, considering the alternatives. The hotel has a dining room, but it is more expensive. This plate is only thirty cents, coffee included."

As the man shifted his weight onto one foot as if to turn away, Delaine held him with a question. "Could you tell me of an inexpensive place to stay?"

The man stood up straight and gave Delaine his attention. "I can. There's a place called The Blue Iris. It's a kind of lodging house. I don't think they serve meals at present. The man who had it for a long time died, and even when he was alive, I think they had mutton stew half the time. The fellow who has been trying to get it back on its feet doesn't have enough business for him to keep food in stock."

"I see. How are the rooms?"

"All right, I guess. I haven't heard of any ghosts or bedbugs."

"And where can I find this place?"

The waiter pointed to the north. "It's on a cross street, two blocks up, facing this way."

"And it's called The Blue Iris."

"Yes. I believe that was the name from before. The old gent didn't bother much with flowers. He was pleasant enough in his own right, though."

"Well, thank you for the information."

"Glad to be of help, if I am." The waiter paused. "Are you passing through, or—?"

"Depends on whether I can find work."

"Of course. I believe this is the time of year when work starts up."

"I do ranch work."

"Yes." The waiter glanced over him. "Well, I'll leave you to your meal. I'll be right over here if you need anything."

"Thanks."

———

DELAINE FOUND The Blue Iris without any trouble. It was an older two-story building with peeling light-blue paint, the one concession that seemed to be made to its name. No flower beds or shrubs or lawns were visible. Some of the taller weeds near the house had been bent over by hand, as he had known people to do when hoeing or pulling weeds was too much effort, and the lot in general looked as if it could benefit from having a few sheep graze it down. Delaine walked on a worn pathway and up two steps to knock on the front door.

He heard footsteps on the wooden floor inside, and the door opened halfway. A man with a round upper body filled the space. He had light-brown hair, balding on top, and pale brown eyes. He wore a brown three-button pullover shirt with no collar, plus a pair of loose trousers held up by a pair of green suspenders.

"Yessir," he said.

Delaine met his eyes. "I'd like to have a room if there's one available."

"There is. Come in." The man stood aside and opened the door wider.

Delaine walked into a sitting room with a low table in front of a couch, a couple of stuffed chairs, and a sideboard. Above one of the chairs, a plaster of Paris painting of The Last Supper hung on the wall. Delaine recognized the kind of art, as he had seen several examples of the same style in New Mexico, painted in different colors by different artists. This one had bright garments of blue, red, and yellow, plus a shiny brown table in front and a greenish-brown wall in the background. The colors seemed a bit garish for the subdued tones of the northern plains, but they were common on art objects favored by Mexican people. In New Mexico, it had been normal to see chickens, burros, flour bouquets, and angels, all in plaster of Paris and bedaubed in bright colors.

"Are you the owner?" Delaine asked.

The man tucked his chin and smiled. "I'm the manager. Name is Steven Reed." He held out his hand. As they shook, he said, "They called me the Slender Reed when I was younger. Ha-ha."

"Jess Delaine."

"Do you want a room for just one night, or more?"

"I think I should take it one night at a time. I hope to find work on a ranch."

"Sure. But if you want to take a room for a week, it's a little better. Forty cents a night, or two-fifty a week."

"Room only?"

"No meals, if that's what you mean. But there's a bath. Once a week is normal. More if you need it because of your work. Men who deliver coal, for example. Are you a range rider?"

"When I can find that kind of work."

"I used to do it myself, when I was lighter on the hoof."

"Uh-huh." Delaine cast a glance around the room. "The fella at the café said the last owner died."

"Luna." The manager pronounced the name so that the second syllable died in the throat. "I think they expected a relative to show up by now, but no one has, so a man named Mr. Melworth is handling the business for Mr. Luna in the meanwhile. They were friends. So I'm managing the place. Mr. Luna had a cleaning woman, but the place went into decline when he died, and the woman went to work at the hotel. I hired another woman who comes in when we have lodgers, but we're not up to offering meals until we have more trade. We're trying to build up."

"It seems adequate to me. Just to be clear, I'll take a room one night at a time."

"You bet. And if you end up staying the whole week, I won't charge you the full amount on the seventh night."

"I'm not worried about that."

"Neither am I."

"Well, then, I think I'll take my bag and rifle scabbard in, put my horse up at the livery stable, and be back before dark."

Reed smiled. "I'll be here."

———

THE AIR COOLED as evening set in, and Delaine had a pint of whiskey in his coat pocket when he knocked on the door again.

The Slender Reed opened it and stepped aside. "You made it."

"I did. Getting cool out there."

"It is. If it gets any colder, I'll have to light a fire."

"I brought provisions." Delaine lifted the bottle so that the top of it came into view. "Don't know if you care for a nip."

Reed's eyes widened. "Sometimes I take one. For

medicinal purposes, of course. If you want to take a seat, I'll fetch a couple of glasses."

Delaine sat facing The Last Supper, and the host sat facing him. Delaine poured two generous drinks of whiskey and left the bottle on the low table. They lifted their glasses in a salute, and each of them took a sip.

"Nothing wrong with that," said Reed.

"Not at all." After a moment of silence, Delaine said, "That's quite a painting."

"Oh, that." Reed gave it a glance. "Mexican art. I don't care for it myself, but it's worth something, and it goes with the place."

"Did Mr. Luna collect other kinds of art?"

"Not that I know of, except for things he wore. They had value. He wore gold-rimmed glasses and a large turquoise ring. They're on hold for whoever inherits his property." Reed took a drink.

"What kind of fellow was he?"

"Luna? To tell you the truth, he wasn't the kind of fella I'd be natural friends with. He had a bit of money, and he was kind of smug. I think he enjoyed having his ring and his gold spectacles on show."

Delaine said, "Like they say, you can't take it with you. I guess some people are buried with their valuables. By the way, what did he die of? I hope that's not a bad question."

Reed shrugged. "Nothin' to me. They think he died of apoplexy or gout. He didn't look like he was in the best shape. Kind of like a soft-boiled egg."

"That's too bad."

"It is. And they say he died with a good sum of money in the bank, which no one has been able to touch."

"Maybe an heir will show up. Someone for the inheritance."

"No one has so far, but I would expect someone, sooner or later."

"So you work for Mr. Melworth?"

"I think in a technical way I work for Mr. Luna, but Mr. Melworth has taken charge of things, so I do what he tells me."

"Don't they have a lawyer for that in most cases, or at least an executor? Is that what he is?"

"I don't know that he's an egzegator par say, but he's handling things. He was a friend of Mr. Luna's."

"You mentioned that before. It's none of my business anyway. I shouldn't ask so many questions."

"No harm at all."

"I hope not. By the way, if you don't mind my asking, why did they call you the Slender Reed?"

"Well, I was thinner in those earlier days, as I said. But the other reason was that I was known to bend with the influence. Women and whiskey, in that order, back then."

"Things change with time," Delaine said.

"That's right. Women are a distant second these days. But if one came to sit in my lap right now, I would bend. Ha-ha." He swirled the liquor in his glass and drank most of it.

"Let me pour you a little more," said Delaine.

"I don't want to drink all of your liquor."

"You won't," said Delaine. "I've been known to bend with the influence a little myself."

———

THE SAME WAITER was working in the café when Delaine went in for breakfast. He was wearing a dull-grey tweed jacket that had seen some years, but he had shaved, and his hair was combed.

"What would you like to order?" he asked.

"What are my choices?"

"Eggs are expensive right now, but we have some. For twenty-five cents you can have bacon and hotcakes or bacon and fried potatoes. Coffee included."

"I'll have the bacon and hotcakes."

"Good choice. But they're both good."

The waiter returned with a crockery mug of coffee. "Be a few minutes. He's mixing the batter."

"No hurry. I don't have a job to go to yet."

"A thought occurred to me, in the watches of the night."

"What was that?"

"There's a fellow named Leo Rawlinson, has a small ranch north of town. I think I heard that he might be looking for help."

"That's good to know. Could you tell me how to get there?"

"I don't know the country out that way, but it's called the Six Mile Ranch, and I believe it's—" he held his finger in the air—"six miles out."

"I'll give it a try."

———

THE ROAD CURVED as it followed a dry creek bed. A line of bare hills on the left reached northward, and the land on the right rolled away in grassland beginning to show green between the patches of grey sagebrush. Delaine's horse had rested, so it moved at a fast walk, and the countryside flowed by.

The rolls in the land became tighter, with more sagebrush. Dry washes appeared, along with occasional hills with sparse pines and cedars. A creek alongside the road began to show small cottonwood and cedar trees.

Four grey sheep came into view, grazing on the side of a gully.

The land opened up again, with cedars dotting the hills of the grassland. In places along the creek bottom, bright green cedars grew with a few pale cousins, like junipers, among them.

The sun was not very strong through a thin haze, but between the position of the sun and his own sense of time and distance, Delaine estimated that he had ridden about six miles. He kept an eye out for a marker, and before long he saw a low pile of rocks with a grey cedar post lying across it. The post looked as if it had spent its career as a fence post until it rotted off at ground level and became too short to be used again. It was weathered and striated with the words *Six Mile Ranch* burned into it. A thin road led to the east. Delaine followed it.

After riding about a mile, Delaine topped a rise and came upon a huddle of ranch buildings. They had been built in the lee of the ground that rose on the west and north sides. He noted the ranch house, the bunkhouse, the barn, and a couple of sheds as well as a round corral for riding and regular corrals for stock. As he rode into the yard, a calf bawled from the confines of a boarded pen.

A man in work clothes stepped out of a shed and

closed the door behind him. He carried a crowbar in one hand and a hammer in the other.

Delaine swung down from the saddle so as not to be talking down to him. The man was lean and not tall, with straight brown hair, side whiskers, a bushy mustache, prominent cheekbones, and cheeks a bit sunken. He looked to be about thirty-five. As he drew closer, he moved his blue eyes from Delaine to the horse and back. In a nasal voice, he said, "What can I help you with?"

"I heard you might be puttin' on help, so I thought I'd drop by."

The man came to a stop. "Have to talk to Leo."

"Is he around?"

"Should be." The man walked to the weathered ranch house, dropped the crowbar and hammer by the door, and went in. He came out after a couple of minutes and lingered by the door.

A minute later, a man of about forty-five came out, putting a hat onto a head of light-brown, greying hair. He was of average height and average build, dressed in a lightweight grey wool shirt, a darker grey vest, and denim trousers. He had the stubble that a man who shaved on Saturdays would have on Monday. He walked right up to Delaine, held out a large hand, and said, "Leo Rawlinson. How do you do?"

"Fine, thanks. My name's Jess Delaine."

"This is Max Brundage, one of my hired men. The other one's around somewhere."

"Pleased to meet you both."

"Max says you're lookin' for work."

Delaine glanced at the hired man, who was tracing his finger along a horsehair watch chain that disappeared into his vest pocket. "That's right."

Rawlinson said, "Things are startin' to pick up. We've got fence to fix, and we need to get out, see where the cattle are, and maybe get an idea of how many we've lost."

"Did you have a bad winter?"

"I don't know yet. Things happen in winter sometimes, between the weather, and the coyotes, and some of these lone operators."

"Uh-huh." It was a familiar line, with cattlemen big and small, that there were always rustlers out to steal from them.

"You know, when you work for a man, you work for *him*."

"Oh, yeah."

"So we might do some of that. Go out and see what things look like." Rawlinson had a straight-stem pipe tucked against his left hip. He raised it and took a few puffs until he drew smoke. "In another month, we'll start spring roundup. In the meanwhile, we'll bring in the horses and get things ready. All regular work. I pay a dollar and a quarter a day for every day you work, plus bed and board. Sometimes the bed is on the ground. You ride my horses unless you want to use yours to keep him in shape." Rawlinson paused. "Let me see what else. Ah. Don't smoke when you're on horseback. Around camp, or when you get down to take a rest, or around the headquarters here, it's all right. Just not in the saddle. It's too easy to drop a hot match or a live cigarette stub."

"I don't smoke."

"So much the better." The boss gave a half-smile. "So are you with it?"

"I guess so. I need to go to town to get my belongings."

"Good enough. You can eat with us tonight and start work tomorrow." Delaine was about to turn away when the boss said, "By the way, where are you from?"

Delaine was conditioned to think that questions like that were a bit personal to begin with, but he had a straight answer. "I grew up in Wyoming. I worked in New Mexico for several years, and I decided to come back."

"You like the wind and cold, then?"

"I don't mind it." Delaine glanced at Brundage, who was looking at his watch. "Doesn't do any good to complain about the weather."

Brundage put his watch away. "That's for damn sure."

———

THE SLENDER REED was amiable when Delaine gave him the news that he was checking out.

"Man gets a chance to do better for himself, I'm all for it. 'Course, I'm back to zero again. But things change all the time, 'specially now with more things on the move. So you're goin' to work for Rawlinson at the Six Mile. That's not too far from Mr. Melworth's."

"Oh, does he have a ranch?"

"He sure does. Bigger than Rawlinson's. I 'magine you'll see for yourself."

"I suppose."

"If and when you finish out there, you can always come back here and stay. Might even have meals by then." Reed tucked his chin with a smile.

"I'll keep it in mind." Delaine shook hands, caught a parting glimpse of The Last Supper, and went on his way.

———

DELAINE RODE to the center of town before leaving for the ranch. He did not know how soon he would be back, and he thought he should send a message to report on the little he had done. With a penny's worth of paper and ink at the post office, he wrote.

RACHEL—

This is just a note to let you know that I made it here to Harrow. I haven't learned much yet, but I want to find out whatever truth I can, though at this point I don't know how much that will entail. Something tells me I should not ask direct questions right away. I have found work at a ranch, so I will have something to do as I wait to find out more.

Best,

Jess Delaine

HE HAD DASHED off the closing and the signature out of habit before it occurred to him that he could have used a more personal touch. As he read over the letter before folding it, the wording all seemed formal as well. But it was written, and the postal clerk was waiting. Delaine wrapped the letter with a blank sheet around it to form an envelope, then sealed it with a mucilage that the clerk had on hand. He addressed it to Rachel Valera, Overton, Wyoming, and put his initials for the return address. He gave the clerk a penny for the postage.

"Should go out tomorrow."

"Thanks."

Delaine walked outside, where the town sat quiet

under the midday sun. The sky had cleared, and a breeze came from the southwest. It occurred to him that he would have to keep some kind of a mental ledger of when he was working for the Six Mile and when he was working for the Sandoval family. The two seemed quite separate at the moment. He hoped it would not be too long before he had an occasion to come back to town. He was sure there was more to be known, beneath some surface somewhere.

SUPPER at the ranch consisted of salt pork, beans, and biscuits. The other hired man, Jerome Hall, did the cooking. He had dark hair beginning to grey, brown eyes, and a trimmed beard. He said he had been a knife sharpener in New York City before coming west, and sometimes he missed the smiling women who let knives down in baskets from upper-story windows. Most things were on one level here, and there were not many women.

Brundage called him Carter. Hall explained that Carter Hall was a pipe tobacco.

After supper, Brundage was in charge of the dishes, and Delaine helped. Brundage used the lingo of the cowhands and called the work "pearl diving."

"Gets my hands clean once a day," he said.

Rawlinson sat smoking his pipe. He had finished reading a newspaper and had passed it across the table to Hall.

Brundage's nasal voice rose on the air. "What's in the news?"

"Just gettin' to it," said Hall. "Here's a story about a murder in Rawlins. No relation, of course." He went on to read the story about a hard case who had cut another man's throat after a night of drinking and had tried to hide the body in an outhouse that wasn't being used. The law caught up with him at Point of Rocks and took him back to Rawlins to wait for trial.

Brundage said, "You could use that in the story you want to write."

Delaine glanced at Hall.

The man relaxed the newspaper and said, "That's just a joke we have going about me writing a story about two cowhands named Justin Case and Oliver Sutton."

Brundage said, "Oliver Sutton, the cattle stampeded."

Rawlinson held his pipe by the bowl as he said, "No relation to Oliver Twist."

"No," said Hall. "But I've read that one. It's more like this story from Rawlins. It's full of danger and mystery and dark secrets, with a murder and an accidental hanging. Narrow streets, fog, spooky buildings, people obsessed with doing evil." He breathed out. "But that's London for you. I haven't been there, but I've lived in New York City, and I imagine a place like that is a magnet for that kind of people, who can go to a big city and disappear into a crowd where they can carry on their business."

The boss said, "You don't need to go to a big city to find people who prey on others or try to take advantage of 'em—or, as you say, do evil. Take that story you just read, or a hundred others that never make it to print because they haven't been found out yet. Like the missing witness to the Cattle Kate hangings. That wasn't too far from Rawlins, for that matter."

"That's true," said Hall. "People who have got

malice in their hearts thrive in all kinds of different places—some of 'em in the cover of a big city, and others in the midst of their neighbors, out here in the wide open West, where the eyes of the law are few and far between."

The boss said, "That's for damn sure."

Brundage's voice came up. "Are you talkin' about rustlers?"

"That's never very far away," said Rawlinson.

Hall said, "I was thinking about people who do more personal things."

"Like Big Nose George," said Brundage. "He was in Rawlins, too."

Hall said, "What he did, and then what they did to him. Way beyond reason on both sides. But the point I was making is that it could happen anywhere."

"Or any time. Big Nose George was fifteen years ago. And here they are, still doing the same thing."

Delaine wondered if Brundage was one of those people who liked to get in the last word. For his own part, he thought it was a good opportunity to keep to himself. If he kept his eyes and ears open, here and in town, something else might come to the surface.

3

———

Delaine rode east in a wagon with Hall and Brundage toward the road from town and then north. Hall explained that some of the Six Mule pasture was fenced but most wasn't, and the cattle and horses were on open range at present. They needed to repair a fence around a one-section pasture where they wanted to hold animals when they brought them in. A section was a mile square, so Delaine imagined they might be repairing four miles of fence.

The wagon carried half a dozen replacement posts that had been used before, two spools of barbed wire, a digging bar, shovels, a posthole digger, a crowbar, a hammer, a saw, two pairs of pliers, a bucket of staples, and a can of nails, plus rope, a folded canvas tarpaulin, three pairs of heavy leather gloves, food for lunch, and a water jug wrapped in burlap.

Brundage handled the reins. Hall talked about the poor living conditions in New York and the number of ragamuffin children who seemed to live on the streets.

When they arrived at the fenced pasture, Brundage

said, "There's a broken strand not far from this first corner." He drew the wagon to a stop, and the men climbed down.

The quiet of the rangeland set in. The air was still. The song of a meadowlark carried from a short distance and ended. Brundage leaned into the wagon and began pushing tools around. In his pitched voice, he said, "Wish we had three pair of pliers."

Working with barbed wire was laborious, as even the old wire wanted to curl. To splice a broken strand, the men had to tie a loop on each loose end, run a length of wire from one loop to another, and tighten. Tying each loop required two pairs of pliers, as did tying and wrapping the new piece that went between them. Wearing the leather gauntlets, Delaine and Hall each pulled a loop toward the middle of the open space, and Brundage, breathing hard through his nostrils into his mustache, wrestled with the splice.

"I don't care how careful you are, you always cut yourself," he said.

"Seems to be the rule," said Hall.

Delaine had felt one barb go through the thick leather already.

Brundage gave one last twist, and they let the splice go. It sagged.

"Son of a bitch," said Brundage. "I thought I had it tighter than that."

Hall said, "You don't want it to be as tight as a piano string. They say that when barbed wire is real tight, it snaps in the coldest part of winter."

"That's when you tighten it with a wagon wheel or some kind of a winch." Brundage glanced to his left. "We're close enough to the corner that we could take out the staples there and tighten it that way so it don't look so bad."

Hall said, "I don't think it's necessary."

"No, it isn't. But I don't like to start the day out this way."

Delaine had understood that the Six Mile did not have a foreman, but Brundage had worked there a year longer than Hall, and it was evident that Hall let him take the lead in small matters. Brundage reached into the wagon for the crowbar and the hammer, and the three of them walked to the corner brace.

Delaine held the two pairs of pliers while Brundage struck the hammer on the crowbar head to gouge out the staples. Hall held onto the strand so that it would not whip loose. With the staples removed, Brundage hooked the claw of the crowbar onto a barb, put the crook against the post, and pulled the wire.

"Hold this," he said to Hall.

With Hall pulling on the crowbar, Brundage hammered on the prongs of each staple, as they had widened coming out, and then he drove each staple into the post. He took a pair of pliers from Delaine and wrapped the loose end, which was coiled like a pigtail, onto the strand.

"That's better," he said.

They were working on the next break when the thud of hooves and the rustling sound of horses and saddle leather caused them to look around.

Four men on horseback had come to a stop on the other side of the wagon.

Brundage muttered something as he stood up straight and turned to face them. He brushed his leather glove down across his mustache and spoke out. "'Mornin'."

The man who seemed to be the boss answered. "Good morning'. I hope you know what you're doing here."

Delaine did not know the man, but he had familiar features. He was a little over forty, with lines in his face. He had hair and a full mustache of a color between brown and blond, with a few days' worth of stubble. His brown eyes bore down on the men who were on foot, and he had a hard set to his face. He wore a cream-colored cattleman's hat, a brown jacket of light wool, a matching vest, and a greyish-blue shirt, closed at the throat, with a full row of buttons. His brown wool pants had grey stripes, and his boots did not yet have the toes worn from much riding. As he moved his jacket to reach into his vest, the butt of a pistol on a gun belt came into view.

Brundage's voice rose on the air. "We're doin' what we were told."

The man on horseback drew out a sack of tobacco, troughed a paper, and shook grains into it. He rolled the cigarette and looked across as he licked it, then struck a match on the saddle horn and lit it. "You know, we don't like fences. They cut up the range, and they get in the way of the free movement of cattle. Not to mention close off water holes."

"This is Leo's land and Leo's fence. He paid to put in a windmill."

"I know. And you're just doin' what you were told. And we just came over to make sure you stay on your own land with all that nester stuff." The man moved his chin in the direction of the wagon where the fence-posts and wire lay.

A rider who had stopped half a length back rode forward, dismounted, and handed the reins to another rider. Delaine's pulse jumped as he recognized the man who had started the fight at the roadhouse in Willett. He was not wearing a red shirt, but his full-crowned dark hat and rounded shoulders were unmistakable. He turned his back on the group, and with something of a swagger, spurs jingling, he took about five steps, then went through the motions of a man unbuttoning his pants to make water. He snorted and spit off to the side as he went about his business.

The man who held the reins was new to Delaine. He was slender, with dark hair, blue eyes, and a clean shave. He wore a buttoned cloth vest that was the same shade of brown as his hat.

Delaine's glance moved to the fourth rider. He was the other one who had been at the roadhouse—light hair, thin mustache, sturdy build. He was riding a nondescript sorrel.

The man who had urinated came back, took his reins, and mounted up. His horse was a large bay, not shiny like some. He looked down at the workmen with his large, shadowy eyes, but he did not show any recognition when he swept past Delaine.

The boss took a long drag on his cigarette and blew away the smoke. He said, "For all that you put in fences and such, this is free range. Most of this land out here is public domain, and your boss uses it as much as anyone, so he knows as well as anyone does, what I don't have to tell you, and that's the trouble we have with fellas that throw the wide loop." His eyes settled on Delaine. "Are you new here?"

"New to this ranch, but I'm from Wyoming."

"Then you know what I'm talkin' about. Men come out here, they think they're a long ways from the law. They're not always right."

Delaine nodded. It seemed like another good time not to say anything. He noted the man's horse, which was like a buckskin but with a dark-brown mane and tail.

The man put on a pair of leather riding gloves, took another drag from his cigarette, pinched out the live end, and let the fragments fall to the ground. He said, "Keep an eye out for snakes," then turned his horse and trotted away. His three men followed.

When they had gone a quarter-mile, Brundage said, "That's Melworth. Always on his high horse."

"Oh," said Delaine. "Who's the fellow in the dark hat and big spurs?"

"That's his foreman. Name of Jim Rudy. The other two are Vick and Sorensen. Vick is the one that looks like a worm, and the light-colored one is Sorensen."

"A worm?"

"Seems like one to me. He's got kind of a squirmin' motion when he smiles."

Delaine said, "Has he got a big outfit, this Melworth?"

"Bigger than this one," Brundage said. "He's got more deeded land and more cattle. But he isn't much of a cattleman, I don't think, and I don't know how much he knows about managin' a ranch. Rudy's the one who runs it, in his rough way."

Delaine gazed at the horsemen becoming smaller in the distance. "He talks like other cattlemen."

"You can pick that up," said Brundage. "But the word is that he came out here and bought a ranch, a little over ten years ago. That's given him time to learn some of the ways."

"The familiar complaints," said Hall. "Fences and rustlers."

Delaine walked over to the spot where Melworth had stripped his cigarette and dropped it. No ashes or sparks showed. He stepped on the scrap of paper to be sure.

Brundage spoke. "That's neighbors. And he wonders why people build fences."

"Oh, he knows why," said Hall. "Anyone can see there'll be more fences to come, and men like him are one of the reasons. They want it both ways. They want to control the whole country, but they want the railroads so they can ship their cattle to market. But the railroads cut up the country in their own way, and they bring out settlers with barbed wire and plows. And they control more than anyone else ever could. Ask anyone who tries to fight 'em. As for the cattlemen and the other settlers, everyone wants the same thing, only some of 'em want it all and to hell with the others." Hall smiled. "There. I've said it, for all the good it does."

"Yeah," said Brundage. "Who knows who'll be here in another ten years. Maybe none of us."

———

WITH THE BUNKHOUSE and the kitchen area in the same building, the interior grew warm as Hall fried the pork and potatoes and then heated the dishwater. Rawlinson opened the front door and returned to his meal.

"Now we can hear better if someone rides up to eavesdrop."

Hall and Brundage had told him about the visit from Melworth and his men, and Rawlinson had waved it off. "No use getting stirred up," he said. But it was evident that he had paid attention.

As Brundage and Delaine were washing and drying the dishes, Rawlinson asked Delaine how long he had been back in Wyoming.

"About six months. I spent the fall and winter in and around Overton. I worked on a ranch for a short while, put in some time repairing the shipping pens, and then worked through the winter at the livery stable."

"Did you just get here, to Harrow?"

"I spent one night in town, at a lodging house called The Blue Iris."

"Oh, that place. I know of it."

"Not all that bad. Less than a hotel, and the manager's good-natured. Maybe a little talkative."

"I know him, too. Reed."

"Curious thing, now that I think of it. He said a Mr. Melworth was in charge of the place. Said the owner had died, and they were waiting for a relative to show up."

"I heard something like that, too. I don't know if Melworth is the executor."

"That wasn't clear. This fellow Reed said that Melworth and the recent owner, Mr. Luna, were friends."

"They may have been."

"You could tell that someone else had owned the place. The color of the building, and the painting of The Last Supper in the front room."

"I haven't been inside, but I've heard of the painting."

"It seems as if Mr. Luna may have been Mexican."

"I didn't know him, but I think he was. Either that or Spanish."

"I knew who he was," said Brundage. "I think he was Mexican, but he wasn't very dark. Pale, like he stayed inside all the time, and kind of soft. People said he had money. He wore gold-rimmed glasses and a turquoise ring set in silver."

"Reed said he thought he died of gout or apoplexy," Delaine put in.

Brundage shrugged. "He could've died of anything, the way he was, soft and pasty."

"It's too bad. I didn't get the impression that he'd ever done any harm."

"You never know." Brundage sniffed.

Hall, who had been reading a newspaper, spoke up. "Here's a story. About a cow that fell into a potato cellar and was trapped until they could get her out. Do you want to hear it, Max?"

"Might as well."

Delaine recognized a pattern or routine in which Hall read and Brundage listened. Rawlinson smoked his pipe and didn't seem to mind the repetition, as he had already read the paper. Delaine had not seen Brundage even look at a newspaper or anything else printed, like the almanac that lay around.

When Hall finished, Brundage said, "That's a good story. I'm glad they got her out. Must have been a lot of work to dig all them potatoes out from under her so they could lead her out the front door."

Rawlinson said, "I've gotten 'em out of mud before. Most of the time, they know when they're being helped."

"You can see it in their eyes," said Brundage. "Sometimes they seem smarter than some people."

Rawlinson puffed on his pipe, and Hall went back to reading the newspaper to himself. Delaine wondered if that was a pattern, too, to let Brundage have the last word.

———

DELAINE WAS STANDING by with the hammer and Brundage was stretching a strand of barbed wire with the crowbar when one of the wagon horses nickered. Delaine put a staple in place, hammered it, and straightened up. A quarter of a mile away, a thin cloud of dust rose from the road that ran parallel to the fence. A single horse was pulling a light buggy at a trot. As the three hired men watched, the buggy veered off the road and headed for the work site.

Two people were seated beneath the canopy. As the buggy drew closer, the figures became identifiable as a woman in light yellow and a man in brown.

"Fella from town," said Brundage.

The horse slowed to a walk for the last fifty yards and came to a stop. Delaine did not recognize the man. He was wearing a brown herringbone jacket and vest and a homburg hat of a matching shade. He had wavy brown hair, a light-brown mustache, a rosy complexion, and a leisured air about him. He raised a gloved hand and said, "Good afternoon."

"Afternoon," said Brundage, who had stepped forward. "Can I help you find your way?"

The man smiled. "Oh, I'm not lost. Just out on a drive." His brown eyes moved over the three men. "Do you fellows work for the Six Mile?"

"We do," said Hall.

"We've been staying in town," said the man, "and

the weather being so fine, we thought we'd take a drive and see the countryside." Silence hung for a couple of seconds. "Plenty to see," he added. He smiled again, took off the deerskin driving gloves, and set them in his lap. Reaching inside his jacket, he drew out a leather cigarette case, opened it, picked out a cigarette, and lit it. As he shook out the match and blew away the smoke, the woman next to him shifted in her seat.

She must have nudged him with her foot, for he said, "Pardon my manners. This is Miss Capps."

The three hired men shifted their attention and took off their hats. Miss Capps gave a half-smile. She was blonde and blue-eyed beneath a straw hat with dyed red and blue feathers. She wore a custard-colored jacket and a dress of matching color. Delaine guessed her age at about twenty-five, maybe twelve to fifteen years younger than her escort.

The man spoke again. "My name's Edward Cunningham. I've been staying in town, sort of looking around, as they say. Plenty of opportunity here."

"There is," said Hall.

The man tapped his cigarette so that the first fragments of ash fell inside the buggy. With his free right hand, he reached across his body, picked a bit of dried grass off his left coat sleeve, and flicked it out to fall on the ground. He smoothed the fabric where he had picked at it, as Delaine had seen men do when they looked after their Sunday best.

Delaine shifted his glance to the young woman, who seemed to be holding herself stiff in her new clothes. The set of her face suggested that she might be more comfortable in the clothes of a woman who washed or cooked for a living. Her expression changed, and she raised her chin. Delaine felt as if he had been caught looking at her and she needed to let him know they were not on the same level.

"How's the country?" said Cunningham. "Did it come out of winter all right?"

"Seems to," said Brundage.

"Does it look like a good calf crop?"

"Hard to tell. The cattle are still scattered out. We'll know more as we go along."

"Of course." Cunningham gazed away, as if he was adding to his own understanding of the country. He raised his cigarette and took a thoughtful drag.

Delaine noted his clean hands and trimmed fingernails. He wore a gold ring with a dark-blue stone, less rounded than the point of a .38-caliber bullet but about the same diameter.

"Had a good snowfall?"

"Normal," said Brundage.

"That's good," the man continued. "What's the annual precipitation here—sixteen inches?"

Hall said, "A little less, I think."

"You can use every bit of it, can't you?"

"Unless we get too much at once."

"Sure." The man looked down at his clean shirt front and brushed a speck from it. "Well, we should move on. Don't want to keep you men from your work."

"Pleased to meet you," said Brundage, casting his glance at both people in the carriage.

"The pleasure's all ours." Cunningham smiled, put the cigarette in his mouth, and took up the reins. "So long."

The men put on their hats as the buggy rolled

away. Brundage said, "I wonder what it takes to get an Easter egg like that."

"Two things that I don't have," said Hall. "Money and charm. But they were quite pleased to meet us."

"How long has he been in town?" Delaine asked.

Hall said, "A few weeks, at least. He stays at the hotel. He has the air of someone on a vacation, but I've heard that he might be interested in buying property."

Delaine said, "He seemed to be practiced in the topics of conversation."

"Social grace," said Hall. "Didn't bother to learn our names, but it was a great pleasure meeting us."

"Can't blame him," said Brundage. "If I had a gal like that, I wouldn't want her to get too close to galoots like us."

Hall laughed. "Not much danger of that. What do you think, Delaine?"

"I think she knows how to keep her distance." Delaine smiled. "I don't blame her. She has to look out for herself."

Hall watched as the buggy receded through the sagebrush. "I think you're right. It's not easy for women, and even less so out here in the West."

———

RAWLINSON SMOKED his pipe as Brundage and Delaine made short work of the dishes after breakfast. He said, "Jess, I'm going to have you go out on your own today. I want you to ride north about five miles and then west about the same. It's just about all open range. You'll see cattle of different brands. What I want you to look out for is Six Mile cattle. You know the 6M brand by now."

"That's right."

"I'm not lookin' for a count as much as I'd like to know if there's many cows without calves. You know what I mean?"

"I think so. Caws that haven't had calves, and cows that might have lost their calves or had them taken from them."

"That's the idea. I want to have some notion of what to expect. We'll know better as we round 'em up, but I've heard other cattlemen talking, and it's eatin' on me a little bit."

"I can take a look."

"Max will show you what horse to ride. Plan to be out most of the day. Poke around in the places where cattle like to hang out—draws and canyons and breaks."

"I'll take along something to eat, then."

"I would." The boss took a puff. "Max and Jerry, you can keep on with the fence work."

———

DELAINE HAD a sorrel horse for the day, a sturdy animal with a blaze and front white socks. He led the animal from the corral and tied it to a hitching rail with a neck rope. With a hand on the horse's neck, he felt the animal relax as he brushed and bombed it. The horse had done most of its shedding for the year, but fluffs of hair fell to the ground on both sides. Delaine did not see any saddle tracks, and he did not know if the horse had been ridden yet this season.

He laid the double saddle blanket onto the horse's

back, then swung his saddle up and over and let it settle into place. The horse remained calm. Delaine reached under for the front cinch and drew the latigo through the ring three times. He laid his hand on the horse's hip, and the animal did not flinch. He reached for the rear cinch and buckled it.

He went into the barn and came out with the bridle. With his right hand between the horse's ears and his left hand holding the bit, he draped the headstall from the horse's nose to its eyes and guided the bit into its mouth. The horse took the bit over its tongue and into the corners of its mouth, and Delaine pulled the ears through the headstall. The bit made the horse smile, so the bridle did not need to be tightened.

Delaine untied the rope, gathered it, and tied it onto the right side of his saddle. Leading the horse by the reins, he walked out into an open area. He tightened the leather strap, put three fingers between the webbed cinch and the horse's brisket, and tightened it one more notch. After leading the horse a few more steps, he put his reins in place, grabbed the reins and the saddle horn, put the toe of his boot in the stirrup, and swung aboard.

As he settled into the seat and caught the other stirrup, he was prepared for the horse to buck. Nothing came, so he touched his right leg to the horse's side, and they moved out of the ranch yard.

With his mind clear as he rode out onto the range, he reviewed his work for the day. He was looking for cows and calves, not men with long ropes and running irons. He had turned down a job last fall because he did not want to be spying on his fellow punchers. Back from New Mexico, where he had done his share of mavericking over a few winters, he wanted to leave some of those habits behind. He also wanted to stay clear of that shadowy world where branding an unbranded calf was sometimes legal and sometimes not. He did not want to do that work any more, and he did not want to work his way into the company of those who did. So he drew the line for himself again now. If he saw something amiss on the range, or signs of it, he would tell his boss. But if the boss eased into asking him to spy on his own men, he would pack his bag. As hired men liked to say, he was looking for a job when he found this one.

Cows with calves. Cows without calves. On the open range, the cattlemen couldn't control the breeding or have a set calving season as they could in country that was fenced, so the calves could be of various sizes and ages. Some unbranded calves could be old enough to be separated from their mothers. Seeing cows by themselves, or cows with only young calves, could be an indication that calves big enough to be separated might have been spirited away. So would a cow lying dead. Delaine had known ruthless opportunists who would shoot a branded cow just to take the unbranded calf. He hoped he did not see any of that today.

The air warmed as he rode north. The hills in the west had trees now. The land in front of him opened up into broad basins and almost treeless grassland. He saw a buck antelope, unbothered, a hundred yards away as a hawk soared overhead.

He saw cattle, sometimes in groups of two or three and sometimes in groups of a dozen or more. Some animals were of the rangy, brindle and spotted varieties, such as those that had come up the trail from Texas many years earlier, while others, often of a reddish hue, had the more compact build of Durhams and Herefords that had been brought in in recent years. Delaine saw a little bit of everything—yearling heifers and steers, large bull calves, cows with calves, cows without calves, sullen bulls, and carcasses of cattle that did not make it through the winter. He kept a general inventory in his head. He did not see anything that caused him to be suspicious, but he knew he had seen only one part of the range.

He ate lunch on the western edge of the open country, in the shade of a large cedar tree. Back in the saddle in the sunlight, he began to feel drowsy. He yawned, blinked his eyes, and told himself he needed to stay alert. The sorrel horse had fallen into a slower pace, and he needed to be prodded as well.

Delaine followed his usual caution of not riding straight up onto a high point but rather taking it slow at the top and letting his eyesight clear the crest a little at a time. More than half the time, he saw nothing. On a few occasions, he saw cattle out ahead of him. On one occasion, he surprised a band of antelope that wheeled and took off running in a direct line away from him. On another, he stopped and registered what he saw. Two riders. He slid from the saddle, led the horse down the slope, and crept back up with his hat in his hand.

The land ahead of him came into view again, as did the two riders moving away from him on a diagonal. At this distance, the horses were more visible than the riders. He could not be sure, but one horse resembled the sorrel that Sorensen rode, and the other looked like the large bay, not shiny, that Jim Rudy used. The two riders were moving at a lope, so Delaine did not see them for very long before they went over a hill and out of sight.

4

———

THE MAIN STREET OF TOWN WAS LINED WITH WAGONS and horses, which Delaine thought was normal for a Saturday afternoon. He kept an eye out for children as he rode behind Brundage and Hall. As they passed The Brookfield Hotel, Brundage raised a hand in greeting at two people who sat on the porch. The hotel being on the west side of the street, the porch was in shade, but Miss Capps was easy to recognize. She was not wearing a hat, and her full head of light-colored hair, pinned up, was as bright as a paper lantern. She sat in a rigid posture with her hands in her lap, while her companion, Edward Cunningham, had a relaxed appearance, with one leg hiked over another, an elbow on the arm of his chair, and two fingers holding a cigarette in a dark cigarette holder. He was not wearing a hat, either. He was dressed in an oyster-colored flannel suit, which complemented Miss Capps's sea-green dress. Two glasses containing clear liquid sat on a low table in front of them, and Delaine wondered whether, to a person like Hall, the two people looked as if they were on a beachside veranda in New Jersey.

Brundage said, "I just remembered somethin'," and he turned his horse around.

Delaine and Hall followed. Delaine wondered if Brundage wanted to parade in front of Miss Capps again, but the lean puncher stood in his stirrups and trotted back to the Diamond Horseshoe Saloon, where he turned in and swung down.

"I'll just be a minute," he said. He draped his reins over the hitching rail and went in. He came out with a half-pint of whiskey and tucked it into his saddlebag. Mounting up, he led the way across the main street, took the cross street heading east, and turned south on the street that ran parallel with the main street. Half a block down on the left, he stopped in front of a building that had two doors and appeared to consist of two basement-level apartments and two upper-level flats.

"Come on in," he said to Delaine. "You should meet this fellow." With the half-pint under his waistband, he led the way through the door on the left and down a stairway. He knocked on the doorframe, and a minute later, the door scraped open.

A voice said, "Come in," and Delaine followed the other two into a casual-looking sitting room with a couch, a low table, a desk, and a chair, with light filtering in through a high window.

The occupant turned around, and Delaine recognized him as the waiter from The Shamrock Café.

"This is Delaine," said Brundage, standing aside.

"We've met," said the man. He held out his hand. "My name's Edwin Teale."

"Jess Delaine."

Teale returned his attention to Brundage, who produced the half-pint of whiskey and said, "A little somethin' for ya."

Teale's face lit up. "Why, thank you. That was thoughtful of you." He waved at the couch. "Sit down, sit down."

The three riders sat on the couch, with Brundage crowded in the middle. Teale sat sideways in the wooden chair at the desk. He reached for a small contraption with cloth and rollers that Delaine recognized as a cigarette-rolling machine. He poured in a measure of tobacco, put a paper into place, licked it, pulled the lever across, and produced a cigarette.

"Anyone else care for one?"

All three visitors declined.

Teale lit his cigarette. He was wearing a wool jacket more worn than the tweed he used for work, and his leather slippers had holes worn in the toes. He seemed at ease with his company, as he smiled and said, "Day in town, eh? What's new?"

Hall said, "We heard they found a sheepherder dead in his sheep wagon. They said he died of a broken heart."

Teale gave a faint smile. "Men have died, and worms have eaten them, but not for love."

"You don't believe in that, eh?"

Teale looked at his cigarette. "When someone is said to die of a broken heart, there's often a personal history of whiskey by the quart, or, in the case of some sheepherders, strong red wine by the gallon. When did this happen?"

Hall said, "A couple of weeks ago."

Delaine said, "What was his name?"

"McGill, or something like that."

Teale said, "What else is new?"

Hall shrugged.

Brundage said, "What do you know about the sweet dove that keeps company with this fellow named Cunningham?"

"Nothing more than her name. And it's all proper. They have separate rooms."

Brundage said, "She seems kinda uppity for someone who looks like she worked as a chambermaid."

Teale cocked an eyebrow as he took a drag. "Maybe she did, but at least she's not wasting her time on someone with no money, like myself. But it's not polite to talk about her that way."

Brundage said, "Do you think he has that much money?"

"He may. I heard that he either sold a business or received an inheritance and has regular allotments sent to him from a place called Rockford or something like that in Illinois."

Hall said, "Rockford is a town in Illinois."

"I've heard of it," said Teale, "and I think that's the place."

Brundage said, "Do you think he might buy something around here, like a ranch or a business?"

"Oh, you can't tell. He does seem like a duck out of water, but sometimes people act one way or another so as not to show their hand." Teale had set the half-pint on the desk, and now he set it a few inches closer to the wall. "My thanks for this. Did you come to have me write another letter to Hilda?"

In a joking tone, Hall said, "I thought it was Helga."

"That's the milkmaid in the story," said Teale.

Brundage, who had his shoulders drawn in, leaned forward and said, "I had somethin' like that in mind."

Hall stood up. "We'll wait outside. We just came in to say hello."

Teale remained seated with his elbow on the desk and smoke curling up from his cigarette. "I'm glad you did."

Outside, as they waited by the horses, Hall said, "Max is a little bit private about some things. I could write his letters for him, but he has Teale do it, along with sending and receiving them. Max doesn't want anyone in town to know if he gets a letter from a girl."

Delaine said, "I can understand. I've known of fellows who write to a girl they meet through a magazine, and they go to meet her when the work's all done in the fall, and she's not anything like they expected. Then their pals make fun of 'em."

"Max is all right. He wouldn't let on that he's anything other than what he is, but he knows that other people do. Send someone else's picture, things like that. And I think he's kind of shy about the boy-girl stuff, anyway."

Brundage came out after a short while and said, "That's all done."

"Shall we go have a drink?" said Hall.

"I could use one."

Delaine said, "I'll meet you there. I want to step into the post office and see if I've got any mail."

Hall said, "You could ask if there's any for the ranch, though I believe Leo checked in a couple of days ago."

Delaine found the post office, which he had seen before, adjacent to the general store. He did not expect anything romantic, but if he had a letter with anything pertaining to Luna or Sandoval, he wanted to read it alone. As it turned out, there was no mail for him or for the Six Mile, so he was back outside with the sun in his eyes in a couple of minutes.

As he stepped down from the sidewalk, a voice on the left caught his attention.

"Do you need any work done or any parcels moved?"

Delaine settled his eyes on a boy about five feet tall, maybe fourteen years old, who had a donkey on a hemp halter and a frayed cotton rope. The boy wore a cloth cap, a three-button work shirt that was too large for him, grey cotton trousers, and scuffed work boots. He had short, light-brown hair and light-brown eyes, and he squinted as he looked up at Delaine.

"I don't need anything done right now," said Delaine. He cast a glance over the donkey, an average-sized brown-and-grey burro with a cross stripe on his back and shoulders. "That's a nice-looking donkey. I don't see as many of them up here as I did in New Mexico."

"It used to belong to Mr. Luna."

"Is that right? What did he use it for?"

"Nothing that I know of. I think he just had it for company. But he died, and Mr. Melworth sold me the donkey for five dollars. I'm trying to make some money for myself by delivering parcels and messages and such."

"Good for you." Delaine looked at the animal again and saw the shades of color running along its neck and chest and shoulders. "What's his name?"

"Pete. Mr. Luna called him Pete."

"I see. And what's your name?"

"Dan. I don't like people to call me Danny or Danny Boy. Just Dan."

"Good enough." Delaine admired the animal's straight back. "Do you have a packsaddle?"

"I have an old riding saddle that I use to tie things onto, but I hope to get somethin' better. I need to make some money first."

"Sure."

"If you have any work you need done, let me know. I'm always around."

"I'll do that." Delaine reached into his pocket and took out a dime. "Take this for the time being."

"Thanks, but I didn't do any work."

"That's all right. Maybe I'll have something for you to do later."

"Thanks, mister."

"You're welcome. Take care of yourself and Pete."

———

THE DIAMOND HORSESHOE Saloon was humming as Delaine walked in. Hall and Brundage were engaged in conversation with three other men, so Delaine stood near the bar to order a drink by himself. He had been inside once before, when he bought the pint to share with the Slender Reed, but he had not taken much notice on that quick visit. Now as he waited for the bartender, he noticed the high ceiling, the large mirror, and the standard varnished wood columns with the ledge connecting them. A longhorn steer head hung on the wall on the left side of the mirror, and a shaggy buffalo head hung on the right. On the ledge over-head, a stuffed raccoon appeared to be stalking a prairie chicken. Livestock brands were burned into the wooden wall, including one that was larger than the others and had a horseshoe centered inside a diamond. A couple of sets of deer antlers hung at a height where men could hang their caps and mufflers and, from the looks of it, forget them. An antelope head with dull glass eyes was gathering dusk, and a splayed coyote pelt was tacked on the wall beneath it.

The bar ran almost the full length of the wall on the left. Tables occupied the middle area, and a piano sat against the right wall. Four men were playing cards at one table, and the other two tables were vacant at the moment.

Delaine ordered a whiskey, paid for it, and kept his place at the bar. A minute later, he was aware of a man standing on his left. He looked to see if the man wanted to order, but he had a drink in his hand. Delaine thought he might want to say something.

"Good weather," said the stranger.

"Can't complain."

"Been travelin'?"

"No. I've got work here. Just came into town. With a couple of other fellas, but they're in a conversation."

Something seemed unusual about the man until Delaine realized he was not wearing a hat. He had a full head of dark-brown hair, dark eyebrows, and a beard about two weeks old. His eyes were bloodshot, and a decayed spot showed between his two front teeth when he spoke.

"I've been on the road."

Delaine nodded.

"Don't suppose you've noticed a fella come through this way with a brown-haired girl about twenty."

"I've been out at the ranch."

"You'd know if you've seen her. Green eyes. Full body."

Delaine shook his head.

"She rides a horse, but she's not real good at it. She's with this guy."

Delaine had heard the word "guy" before, and it sounded common, like slang. Not wanting to give the man the silent treatment, he said, "What does he look like?"

"Not very good-lookin', as far as that goes. Brown hair, lighter than mine, straight. Brown eyes, I think. Average height. Not very strong-looking."

Delaine shook his head. "Doesn't sound familiar."

The man's eyes hardened as he waved his drink. "I don't care all that much about it. I'm calm and collected about it. I could walk away from it at any time. But I just want to know how I stand, and I want someone to tell me to my face." He raised a lit cigarette from his side, took a long drag, swelled his chest, and blew the smoke out of the side of his mouth. "That's all I want to know, is how I stand, and what the hell this other guy thinks he's doin'."

Delaine thought the man was wound up pretty tight. The glint in his eye suggested that he might want to have more than a calm conversation. Delaine recalled Hall's comment about people with malice in their hearts, and he thought that this fellow, in addition to having desperation coursing through his veins, might have some malice as well.

"I need to go join my friends," Delaine said. "Good luck. I hope you find what you're lookin' for."

The man raised his cigarette and paused long enough to say, "I will." He took a puff and said, "I'm leavin' after this drink. I think I'm movin' faster than they are."

Delaine noted the red tinge of the man's face, which might be from riding in the sun with no hat, keeping the boiler going, or a combination.

The man tipped up his drink, pressed his lips together as he swallowed, and set his glass on the bar. "You don't have to go anywhere," he said. "Enjoy your drink."

A man had sat down at the piano, and another man stood by. The man who was seated played a few notes of what sounded like "Red River Valley" and stopped. The two of them laughed. The man at the piano played the same few notes again and left off. He thrummed several keys together, rested, and ran through the first few notes.

A large man pushed up to the bar on Delaine's right and said, "Why don't they just play the damn song?"

Delaine recognized the voice and the broad, sallow face at the same time. The voice had a sarcastic edge to it and was a little higher pitched than one might expect from a man of his dimensions. Delaine saw no indication that the man recognized him from the roadhouse where the lamb fries had gone to waste.

The man spoke again. "My friend's sister was a schoolteacher. She said every teacher had to know how to play that song. That one, and 'My Bonnie Lies Over the Ocean.'"

"I don't think every school out here has a piano."

"That was in Wisconsin." The man called to the bartender. "I'll have a beer." Back to Delaine, he said, "Where are you from?"

"I grew up in Wyoming."

"Well, they've got country schools back there, too, but it's farm country where we were. People live closer together." The man gave Delaine a looking over and did not seem to recognize him. "You do ranch work?"

"That's right."

"Things are more spread out here. People live way the hell and gone out in the middle of nowhere. Not like farmhouses or even a cabin in the woods."

"They have lumber mills there, don't they?"

"Oh, yeah. That's where some of the lumber for pianos comes from."

"Do you not care for that kind of work?"

"Don't want to get an arm or a leg cut off." The man paid for his beer and took a drink. "My work takes me to different places."

"Is that right?"

"I look for missing people. Where there's a reward out. Not like a bounty hunter. I don't look for criminals. More like a reward hunter. Most often put up by the family."

Delaine noticed the pistol riding high on the man's hip. "I imagine you might cross paths with a criminal now and then."

"Not as much as you would think. But I don't mind seeing them put in jail. As far as that goes, sometimes my profit comes from someone else committing a crime."

"I think you said the family often pays for it."

"I did. I provide a service that someone wants to pay for. Sometimes it comes about because of a crime. If someone has done some something illegal and deserves to pay for it, and is found out and turned in, so much the better."

Delaine could see that he had it well worked out.

"My name's Milligan," said the man. He held a thick hand forward.

"Jess Delaine." On a hunch, he said, "Do you have any interest in the case of a man named Mr. Luna? He had a lodging house here and died."

Milligan shook his head. "Nah. I know who you mean, but there's nothing interesting about him. He's dead and buried. I look for people who haven't been found yet. Of course, some of them are dead and buried, too. Sometimes I'm on the lookout for as many as half a dozen people at the same time. It keeps me on the move." The man cast a sideways glance. "Hello, constable."

A man in a black hat and coat, white shirt, and string tie had presented himself. He had deep brown eyes and a full mustache. "Good afternoon. Almost evenin'. Say, have you seen a fellow who might be lookin' for trouble?"

Milligan laughed. "Who hasn't?"

"I had a report about a man who said he was lookin' for someone else, askin' questions in an aggressive way. Might have been someone who ran off with his woman or somethin' like that."

Milligan shook his head. "I just got back into town."

The man who was addressed as constable turned is attention to Delaine. "How about you?"

"I met someone who might match that. A fellow about thirty, with a flushed face, not wearing a hat."

"Sounds like him. Did you notice where he went?"

"No, but he said he was leaving town. Wanted to gain ground on whoever he was following."

"Well, good riddance. Thanks." The man turned and walked away.

"Who's he?" Delaine asked.

"Town marshal," said Milligan. "His name is Galen. The town hires him to keep the peace. Night watchman as much as anything else, I think. There's no bank or big business with a payroll here."

"Just stray animals and barroom fights."

"Regular stuff," said Milligan.

"Where's the rest of the law?"

"In Douglas. A deputy comes around, but not very often unless he's called for."

Hall appeared and tapped Delaine on the upper arm. "We're going to take a table," he said. "Come and join us."

"I will." Delaine turned to Milligan. "Good to meet you."

"Likewise."

Delaine joined Hall and Brundage where they sat at a table with the other three punchers. The man at the piano was banging out a tune, and it helped isolate Delaine as he sat at the edge of the conversation. He cast his memory back to one part of the conversation with Milligan, and he was satisfied that the man was not looking for Robert Sandoval. Whatever else he was looking for was his business.

The sound of the piano rose above the sea of conversation. Delaine recognized the tune, and the words ran through his head.

Buffalo gals, won't you come out tonight,
Come out tonight, come out tonight.
Buffalo gals, won't you come out tonight,
And dance by the light of the moon.

Those girls were far away in Buffalo, New York.

Delaine wondered if the man at the piano would play the tune about the sidewalks of New York, but the next song was "Oh, My Darling Clementine."

The man standing nearby chanted rather than sang, and he came down heavy on the lines "Thou art lost and gone forever, drefful sorry Clementine."

A prickly sensation rose from between Delaine's shoulders and ran up his neck. A man in a dark hat and a red shirt passing through his line of vision became the person of Jim Rudy. The round-shouldered man was walking next to his boss, Melworth, whose stolid face did not turn to either side. Behind them walked the smaller, slender man named Vick, smiling and clean-shaven as he looked to each side. Spurs clinked.

The three men passed behind Milligan, who held still and did not turn his head but may have seen them in the mirror. Delaine felt a tenseness but was relieved when the trio walked to the far end of the bar, near the back door, and found space for themselves.

One was missing. Delaine searched his memory. An image of a light-featured man came to mind, a man of middle height with a sturdy build. Sorensen.

The three men kept to themselves as they ordered drinks, smoked cigarettes, and chatted. They did not show an awareness of anyone else, and they were far enough away from the piano to pay no attention to it.

Delaine let his eyes travel along the bar to the spot where he had stood and talked to Milligan. The large man was gone. Delaine relaxed a little more. Milligan had struck him as being self-assured and abrasive, but he must have some good sense. He would have to, in his line of work.

5
———

Rawlinson was gazing past Delaine, in the direction of a sack of beans standing against the wall. "I want to send you out again," he said. "Range out wider and look into different kinds of places—canyons and breaks like before, but basins and valleys and anything you come across. My idea is for you to make a complete circle, between five and ten miles out. All the way around. I think you could plan to stay out a couple of nights. The boys will fix you up with a good bedroll. We're still gettin' frost, of course."

"Look for the same things as before?"

"Well, yes. Whatever you see. I want to know if there's anything to this talk about men picking off a few head here and there, maybe bunchin' 'em up in some out-of-the-way place, and either brandin' 'em or movin' 'em off to a farther range."

"If I meander or poke around, there's a good chance that someone will ask me what I'm doing."

"Tell 'em you're out lookin' to see where my cattle are. That's what you'll be doin'. And you'll be ridin' a horse with my brand. I'll give you a letter that says you're workin' for me. That way, there won't be any questions about the horse, either."

"I might as well get going, then. Two nights out. So I could expect to be back sometime late in the day on Wednesday."

"That's right."

———

DELAINE SADDLED the sturdy sorrel horse with a blaze and three white socks. He rode west until he came to the bare hills, then went north along the base. Pine and cedar trees began to appear, and the grass was growing well. The cattle he saw looked very much like those he had seen a few days earlier—a general mix, with nothing conspicuous.

He felt responsible in his work for the Six Mile, but with town behind him and growing farther away, he felt as if he was not doing enough to look for Robert Sandoval. He still thought it was wise not to state his mission outright, but he needed to find more occasions to dig up information. It was too easy to wait until the next day or the next opportunity.

He veered northeast and then east, along the edge of a broad basin. Everything seemed peaceful and in place. Cows with calves at their sides stood in grass up to their knees. Here and there he saw horses that did not turn and run like wild horses. Riding down through a swale, he came within seventy yards of a band of eight antelope—does and fawns and one buck —that walked away from him and did not seem spooked.

The air cooled when the sun went down, and he

made his camp in a small canyon that cut into a row of bluffs. He picketed the horse, laid out his bedroll, and sat down with his saddlebags next to him. For supper, he had cold beef and biscuits with a can of tomatoes to help wash things down. The night darkened, a coyote howled, and another answered. He imagined that life went on by itself every night when no one was out here—coyotes howling, sometimes an owl hooting, deer listening.

His thoughts went to Rachel, more than two days' ride away, in a town where people lived in houses with roofs and windows, where the sound of the train came through the walls.

He yawned. This was big country, and it seemed as if he was the only one out here. But he knew there could always be someone over the next hill, each of them unaware of the other's presence. He was satisfied that he was alone now, though, and he enjoyed the solitude.

———

HIS RIDE eastward the next day took him through sparser country. For a stretch of a couple of hours, he saw no trees. Rocks grew out of the ground. A jackrabbit with ears like broomsticks stared at him as if it had never seen a human before, then zigzagged away. At his farthest point east, before he began to curve to the south, he saw a herd of sheep a couple of miles away. He did not see a man or a dog, just a dull blanket of sheep on the stark plain.

He took his bearings from the Laramie Mountains to the west. When he veered around a broad rocky area with thin grass and no livestock grazing, he thought he was as close to Harrow as he would be on this circuit. His sense of obligation to the Sandoval family weighed on him, and with the thought that Rachel might have answered his letter, he rode straight west for a few miles. He kept an eye out for Six Mile cattle. Near the edge of town, two figures appeared on the grassland. An animal smaller than a horse or cow had its head down, and a medium-sized person stood nearby. The animal raised its large head, and Delaine recognized the sand-colored donkey. The person of proportionate size would be the boy named Dan.

Delaine nudged the ranch horse toward them. As he approached with the late morning sun at his back, the boy looked up and shaded his eyes with his right hand. With his left, he held the worn cotton rope. The donkey kept its eyes on the horse.

"How do?" said Delaine as he came to a stop. "Lettin' your pal have somethin' to eat?"

"Might as well. I'm not gettin' enough work to buy feed."

"Persevere," said Delaine. "Keep at it."

"Not much else I can do."

Delaine noticed again how straight the animal's back was. "Good to see the two of you again. Like I said the other day, I haven't seen many donkeys up north. Or Mexican people."

"I guess."

"I understand that Mr. Luna was Mexican, or Spanish, at least."

The boy shrugged. "I don't know the difference."

"Sometimes people say Spanish when they don't want to say Mexican."

"Mr. Luna wasn't very dark."

"Not all Mexicans are. You'll see some who are as light as you or me."

"When they found the dead man over in Willett, they called him a Mexican. I just assumed he was darker."

"They found a dead man?"

"That's right."

"When was that?"

"Three or four weeks ago."

"That wasn't the sheepherder, was it?"

"No, they found him out on the range in his sheep wagon. This one they found in town, or by the tracks, and they said he was a Mexican."

"Too bad for him. For both of them. The sheep-herder's name was McGill, or something like that, wasn't it?"

"Yeah. He was white. Had a white beard."

"Did you see the body?"

"No. I just knew who he was."

Delaine glanced toward town. "I'd better move along. Good to see you. I hope some work comes your way."

"Thanks. So do I."

———

In Harrow, it took Delaine all of a minute to find out that he had no mail. He rode south out of town, crossed the tracks, and rode east to pick up his circle.

He had imagined that his route would take him near Willett and then around north again near Kersey, the next town west of Harrow. He pictured the rail-road cutting across the bottom of a big circle.

The sun was almost straight overhead when he

reached Willett. The town did not look much different from before as he approached it from the west, except that he saw the back side of the schoolhouse on the hill. Places that had been closed on that Sunday, such as the feed and grain business, the livery stable, and the coal business, had their doors open. A couple of horses were tied in front of the general store and the post office.

Delaine noticed the name of the saloon, The Elkhorn, which he did not remember from before. As he recalled, "Elkhorn" was one of the three names of the railroad that ran across the view of anyone standing in the doorway and admiring the sagebrush scenery, as one man seemed to be doing. He wore an apron and no hat, and Delaine recognized the mustache, spectacles, and high balding forehead of the bartender who had been on duty the day of the fracas. The man turned away and went inside, closing the door.

Delaine did not take the gesture as an unfriendly one. No horses were tied in front, and the bartender might have seen him as a potential customer. Delaine thought of the bartender as a potential source of information, so he tied his horse and went in.

The layout was the same, except that the temporary table was gone. A single patron stood at the bar, a man about forty years old wearing grey work clothes and a dark hat with a low crown and a short brim. He gave a closed-mouth smile and returned to rotate his glass of beer.

Delaine took a place at the bar near the other customer and ordered a beer. The bartender did not show an indication of recognizing Delaine. He poured the beer, cleared the foam with his narrow stick, and set the glass on the bar. "Fifteen cents. Pay now."

Delaine put a dime and a nickel on the bar and recalled the man's name. *Dill.* He glanced upward and saw a single beam of an elk antler lying on a shelf above the bar mirror. It was shiny, as if it had been varnished. From the burr at the end that attached to the skull, Delaine guessed that someone had found it as a shed antler, pale and weathered.

The man on his right said, "Travelin'?"

The man must have seen the bag and bedroll on the horse. Delaine said, "I've been out overnight, looking for cattle. I ride for an outfit north of Harrow. The Six Mile."

"Oh, yeah."

"I stopped in for one at noontime." Delaine took a drink.

"That's what I do. One at noon. I work at the feed and grain. My name's Hal."

"Mine's Jess."

"Good to know you. What's the country look like?"

"Not bad. Thin in spots but good in others."

"That's good. We can always use a little more moisture. Rain or a late snow. It's not too late for that. I've seen it snow on the twenty-fifth of May."

"So have I."

"People talk about it snowin' on the Fourth of July, but that's in the mountains. Would be nice to have it here. Kill the grasshoppers."

Delaine nodded.

"You know how people are, though. They say they don't like it when things are too easy. They want to stay tough."

"I've heard that, too."

"I don't know how much they mean it. You get a hailstorm that ruins the wheat crop. There's nothin' funny about that."

"Not at all."

"Or a late winter storm when there's a lot of new calves on the ground."

"That, too."

"Somethin' like that can catch a fella that's sleepin' out for a night or two. I imagine you know how to be careful."

"I try."

"Still, men who know the country get caught in a blizzard."

"I've heard of it more than once." Delaine saw an opening. "Is that what happened to the fellow they found dead in town here?"

"Oh, him. Nah, the weather was clear. They don't know what he died of. It may have been exposure. He had dark skin, but it had an almost blue shade to it."

"Is that right? Where was he from?"

"No one knows. He didn't have anything on him. Just a common man, average height and weight. He looked like a working man, but he was dressed in a blue suit, not a very expensive one. Didn't have a hat or a traveling bag or anything."

"Huh. So no one knew who he was?"

"Just someone who died and was buried. They think he might have dropped off a freight train here. There's no record of anyone like him buying a ticket on the passenger train. The sheriff's office sent out notices on the wire, but that doesn't do anything unless someone else is looking."

"That's too bad."

"It sure is. But you know, people die every day." The man tipped up his glass.

"Buy you another one?"

"Nah. This is all I have at this time of day. But thanks. Good talkin' to you."

"And the same to you." Delaine turned to his beer. He did not need to drink more than one, either, and he had not come in to drink, anyway. He had dropped in to see if he could learn something, and now he needed to decide what to do with his knowledge. He took a drink.

He had an unexpected feeling. He thought he should feel lighter, or on the verge of liberation, with the prospect of fulfilling his purpose of finding Robert Sandoval, but he felt as if he was not done. His sense of obligation, what felt like a mission, had expanded. He had a suspicion that Sandoval's death and Luna's might be related, and he thought he had been on the right track in not telling people his business.

He stared at his beer with the slow, tiny bubbles rising. He was convinced that he knew where Robert Sandoval was but that he should not tip his hand yet. It was in the family's interest to know more, and if he disclosed his purpose now, the wrong party, whoever that was, could take warning, and he himself could become a target.

He decided to keep his knowledge to himself for a little while longer. He needed to finish the task he was on, which was riding the circuit. Nothing was going to change regarding the circumstances of Robert Sandoval or José Luna. He would return to the ranch, and from there it would be a short while until the end of the week. He could decide then.

He drank more than half of the remaining beer.

"Ready for another one?" said the bartender.

"No, thanks. I'm on the job."

———

RAWLINSON LISTENED with interest as Delaine gave his report.

"I made a general circuit, as you said, meandering here and there, and not going in a direct route for very long. I would estimate that I saw a hundred cows with the Six Mile brand. I didn't keep a tally because I saw only a sample. Most had calves, ranging from a few days old to three or four months. Like before, I saw yearling heifers and steers as well as good-sized bull calves that haven't been cut or branded. And I saw horses, mostly in the northwest. I didn't see anything to raise suspicion, but someone who knows the range and knows your cattle might have a better sense of whether the count is reasonable coming out of the winter."

"Like I said before, we'll have a clearer idea when we round up and brand. I've just been uneasy with the talk I've heard. Max and Jerry say that's just the way Melworth always talks, but I've heard it from others as well." Rawlinson looked at his fingernails and lowered his hand. "Thanks for the report. I'm glad you went. It's good enough for the time being, and you can go back to helpin' the boys tomorrow." Rawlinson drummed his fingers. "One thing occurs to me. I imagine you didn't go far into that range of hills to the west that run north and become a piney ridge."

"No, I didn't. It was beyond the general range you suggested."

"That's all right. You might see more of that area

when we go out to bring in the horses, which won't be too long from now."

"Everything in its own good time. I won't mind sleeping in a bed tonight. I put in some long hours in the saddle. And even when you sleep well under the stars, you're on guard as well."

"I know what you mean. Don't be shy if you want to turn in early."

Delaine yawned. I think it's catchin' up on me."

———

THE FENCE REPAIR had progressed around to the north side of the big pasture when Delaine went out in the wagon with the other two men. As usual, they kept the wagon and horses on the outside of the fence. As Hall explained, the horses could graze on public land for a while longer and save the fenced pasture.

The weather was warm and dry, and the immediate area had sparse grass patches of bare dirt, but the rangeland as it stretched away was green. At noontime, Brundage did not take extra care to clear an area when he scraped out a small hole for a cook fire. With the remnants of an old cedar post, he got a blaze going, with a narrow column of black smoke rising.

"Just a little squaw fire," he said. He took a couple of rocks from the wagon bed, round and low and smooth, the size of small bread loaves, which he used to chock the wagon wheels on slanted ground, and he set them close enough in the fire to hold the pot. With a wooden spoon, he stirred the beans. After a while, he lifted the pot with the crowbar, hooking the bail handle with the claw, and he set the pot on a bare spot of ground. Pieces of pork rind bubbled on the surface as steam rose. He picked up a few chips and scraps of cedar and threw them onto the coals.

The three men served themselves and sat down to eat. Brundage and Hall each sat against a wagon wheel, and Delaine sat cross-legged in the open.

Delaine was dipping a cold biscuit into his beans when Hall said, "I wonder what they want."

Delaine turned his head and saw three riders approaching. Even at a distance, he recognized the dark hat and hunched posture of Jim Rudy. Melworth rode in the middle, and Vick rode on the other side.

Hall said, "No one has to get up. Maybe they won't stay long."

Delaine shifted in his seat to watch the riders approach. Rudy was riding the large bay, Melworth was riding a dark-brown horse, and Vick was riding a sorrel with a white star and no other markings.

The three rode right up to the edge of the little day camp, and the horses shuffled around until they came to a complete stop. Low clouds of dust drifted across the area where the three workmen sat.

Hall set his plate aside but remained seated. "What can I do for you today?" he asked.

Melworth draped his reins around the saddle horn and sat up straight. "We saw smoke, so we came over to see what the fire was."

"Just a little cook fire to heat some grub. It's just about burned out now."

"I don't like someone havin' a fire out in the open on the range."

"It's just a little fire, and the grass is green."

"Well, I look into every one of 'em. You never know when someone's heatin' up a cinch ring or a runnin' iron."

"You can see we're not up to anything like that."

Melworth did not answer for a moment. He rolled a cigarette, and as before, he looked across it as he licked the seam, as if to see who was watching him.

Delaine took stock of the three men and realized that Sorensen was not among them again.

Melworth blew away smoke and said, "What's the crowbar for?" He motioned with his chin toward it where it lay near the fire.

Brundage answered in his pitched, nasal tone. "Been usin' it for a pothook. Most of the time, I use it to stretch wire or pull steeples."

Rudy backed his horse up, rode behind the other two men, nudged the horse between the wagon and the fence, and looked down into the wagon. With each step, the horse raised puffs of dust.

"Lookin' for somethin'?" said Brundage.

"Everyone's looking for something," said Melworth. "How about you fellas?"

"Just breaks in the wire."

Melworth shifted his horse so that he looked straight down at Delaine. His face had its usual hard cast, and his mustache looked like a paintbrush that been glued on. "How about this one? He was out snoopin' around on our range."

Delaine said, "Leo Rawlinson sent me out to get an idea of where his cattle were scattered."

"All over. What does he expect?"

"I don't know what he thinks."

Rudy brought his horse around, raising more dust, and stopped next to Melworth as before. He leaned forward with his forearms on the swells of his saddle, and he stared at Delaine as he spoke in his deep voice. "You know, it's common courtesy not to ride past someone when you see 'em out on the range."

"If I rode past you, it was because I didn't see you. I don't know when or where it might have been."

"Day before yesterday, in the late afternoon."

"I have an idea of where I was at that time, but I don't remember seeing anyone."

"Like I say, common courtesy. But maybe you don't know much about that."

Delaine flared up. "I know it's common courtesy not to ride into someone's camp, especially at mealtime, and look down on 'em, and ride around and kick up dust. People with manners get down off their horses at the edge of camp."

"Well, you're a smart one, aren't you?" Still leaning forward, Rudy rose in his left stirrup, held the saddle horn, swung his right leg over, and landed on the ground. "That's no way to talk to Mr. Melworth," he said.

"I was talking to you."

"He rode in with us. So you're saying he doesn't have common courtesy."

Delaine had more than enough. "If the shoe fits, wear it."

"You *are* smart." Rudy handed his reins to his boss, took off his gunbelt, buckled it and hung it on the saddle horn, and set his hat on top. Leaning forward, and with his spurs clinking, he turned toward Delaine. A receding hairline in front showed a lighter patch of skin than his face, and his large eyes with the shadows beneath them gave him an aura of mortality, as if he had been touched by the grim reaper. "Get on your feet," he said.

Delaine's resentment had gone down, and his

instinct for self-preservation was taking over. He set his plate aside, laid his hat next to it, and pushed himself to his feet.

Melworth backed up his horse, and the dull bay moved with him.

Vick had a squirmy smile as he kept an eye on the two men who were seated.

Rudy was hunched forward with his big fists at chest level. "C'mon," he said. "Let's see how smart you are now."

Delaine stood with his fists up. He did not see any reason to walk into a punch, so he waited. He knew Rudy had a long step and a long reach, and he wanted to fare better than Milligan did.

Rudy made his first move, and his fist grazed off the side of Delaine's head. Delaine moved back, and Rudy's left fist bounced off his forehead. The right came again, but Delaine threw up his forearm to block it. Rudy pushed away.

Delaine shifted backward and tried to regain his step so that he wouldn't be flat-footed. He knew he needed to keep moving and try to deflect whatever came his way. Rudy did not lead with either fist. His pattern seemed to be to punch with his right and then follow with a left and a right.

Here it came. Delaine knocked the first punch off target. The second skidded off the top of his head, and the third smacked him in the ear. He felt the jolt and saw little points like stars. He stayed on his feet, moved back, and bounced to his right.

Rudy's next punch was a roundhouse that swished the air in front of Delaine's nose and eyes. Delaine knocked away the left fist that followed, and he moved in with a left jab on Rudy's cheekbone.

Rudy blinked, as if he was surprised to be hit back. The two men were now too close for either of them to land a good blow, so Delaine stepped away, drew back with his right, and stopped Rudy with a punch between the cheekbone and the jaw.

Spittle flew, and Rudy surged forward with a wild right swing that caught Delaine on the shoulder and knocked him off balance. Delaine's feet went out from under him, and he landed on his hip and elbow.

Rudy stood back, touching the spot where Delaine's last punch had struck. Delaine thought he might be able to hit him again if he could get on his feet without being rushed. He pushed himself into position.

"That's enough for today," said Melworth. "He ought to have the idea by now."

"I'd like to give him some more," said Rudy, but he stood still, feeling his jaw.

"I said it's enough." Melworth tipped his head up as he smoked his cigarette and looked things over.

Delaine rose to his feet. He was pretty sure that Melworth wanted to quit when he was ahead, when his side had the appearance of winning.

Rudy said, "I just want him to understand—"

"Everyone wants something," said Melworth. "People in jail want to get out."

"I didn't like the way he talked to me."

Melworth stubbed his cigarette butt on his saddle horn and brushed away the remnants. "Neither did I, but it was just talk. Put on your stuff, and let's go."

Rudy put his hat on his head and buckled on his belt and holster. The boss handed him his reins, and his spurs clinked as he led his horse away to mount up.

Melworth looked down at the two men seated.

"Back to why we came here. It was because we saw smoke. Where there's smoke, there's fire. People need to be careful."

Dust rose as the three men turned their horses and rode away.

Brundage said, "He thinks he's the boss of everything, doesn't he? He goes out of his way to start trouble."

Hall said, "Where there's smoke, there's fire. Sometimes you wonder."

Delaine gazed at the men riding away. He agreed with what Hall said about Melworth. He also wondered about Rudy. He did not think the man remembered him from The Elkhorn, and unless he had some sixth sense about things that had not yet happened, he did not have much of a reason to pick a fight with either Milligan or Delaine. A grudge against the world in general might be sufficient.

6

———

Rawlinson shook his head as he heard Hall and Brundage tell of the altercation. Delaine kept to himself. The boss said, "It sounds more like Jim Rudy than Barton Melworth in that story. I don't think it means that we're at war with that outfit."

Hall said, "I don't think so, either. Rudy's always been a hothead. But Melworth's always picking at something."

Brundage looked up from curling his horsehair watch chain with his finger. "An' he shows how much he doesn't know. He thought someone would use a two-foot crowbar for a runnin' iron."

"It was a question," Hall said. "An insinuation if anything."

Brundage's eyes narrowed, and his face tensed. "He comes in like he's the big boss, sayin' he doesn't like this and doesn't like that, but everyone knows he lets Rudy run the ranch. And he let him pick that fight."

"That might be his way," said Hall. "Some people

thrive on having the lower levels bickering with each other. It doesn't seem to me that he cares very much about others."

Brundage doubled his fist. "I'd like to punch that cookie-duster of a mustache he's got."

Hall waved his hand. "Maybe he wants you to feel that way. And then he'll let you settle it with Rudy."

Rawlinson palmed his pipe and took a puff. "I don't disagree with either of you, but we want to stay out of trouble if we can. As soon as you boys finish with the fence work, you need to go out and bring in the horses. You know where that's going to take you, and you've got a good chance of running across one or more of them. If you finish the fence work tomorrow, you may go out as soon as tomorrow afternoon. If not, Friday morning. We're not in a hurry about anything, so let's be calm." He smiled at Delaine. "So did you hit him good at least once, Jess?"

"I got in one good one and another that was not too bad."

"Maybe he'll think twice before he tries it again. On the other hand, maybe he won't. He's not a very big thinker."

———

Delaine was riding by himself, looking for horses, when movement caught his eye. A buggy was moving across the rangeland. It looked like the same buggy that the man of leisure and his female companion had been riding in, but Delaine did not see a flash of light color. His spirits went down. After many days of not having so much as a glimpse at a woman, even a sulky one would be nice to see.

Delaine rode the horse through the grass and sage and waited by the trail. No one would say he was neglecting common courtesy. The buggy moved one way and another, following the trail, and the horse obstructed his view of the occupants. The trail straightened, and the moving object became larger. Cunningham was not driving. He was sitting where Miss Capps had sat, and the man driving bore a resemblance to the Slender Reed.

The driver was wearing a dull brown shirt and a short-brimmed hat of a similar color. Cunningham was wearing a tan duster and his brown homburg hat, and although he and the driver were not a matched pair, they had an air of compatibility as the vehicle came to a stop and settled.

Reed spoke out in his affable tone. "The people you see."

Delaine smiled. "Good afternoon."

"And the same to you," said Cunningham. "It seems we've met."

"I was fixing fence over that way with a couple of other hands, last week, when you dropped by."

"Oh, yes. And it appears that you know Mr. Reed."

"I do. I stayed under his roof for a short while before I came out here."

"Checkin' cows today?"

"On my way to look for horses, but not much different. The hired man on horseback."

"Ah, yes." Cunningham took off his deerskin gloves, allowing the blue stone and gold ring to glint in the sunshine, and drew out his cigarette case. He selected a cigarette, lit it, shook out the match, and dropped it the floorboard. "I've hired Mr. Reed to show me a little of the country, as I think I might like to invest in some land."

Reed smiled.

"He tells me he used to ride the range in his salad days and still knows something of the country."

Reed tucked his chin. "That was before I spent all my wealth on wine, women, and song."

Delaine sensed the difference between the two, and he thought Reed was trying to rise a level with his use of clever language while Cunningham was making a point of remaining silent.

Reed said, "By the way, I think there's a letter for you at the post office. If I'd known I was going to see you, I would have brought it along."

Delaine tried not to show his displeasure. He knew that people in the country delivered mail to one another, but he thought Reed was a bit presumptuous. "Thanks all the same," he said. "And thanks for letting me know."

"Glad to."

Delaine directed his attention toward Cunningham. "I hope you enjoy your tour and see something of interest. There's plenty to appreciate out here, in spite of the dust and the wind."

"Oh, I know," said Cunningham. He drew on his cigarette and flicked his ash at his feet. "What part do you like best?"

Delaine pondered for a second. "I don't know of any one thing. I can think of things I don't care for, like the cactus and the rattlesnakes, but as for what I like best, I might say it's the general quality of being away from towns and people and noise."

"That's it," said Cunningham. "You folks out here

know the secret of getting along without anyone giving you guff."

Delaine gave a short laugh. "Some people know more than others." He thought of Melworth's ready supply of generalities, and he said, "I tend to know about things. I leave the wisdom and ideas to others."

"That might be wisdom in itself," said Cunningham. "But we don't want to keep you from your work. What do you say, Reed?"

The driver nodded. "We came to see the country." To Delaine, he said, "Good seein' you again. Don't be afraid to drop in and say hello when you're in town."

"I won't."

Reed shook the reins, and the buggy rolled away. Cunningham raised a hand in farewell, and dust rose from the wheels.

———

TIME DRAGGED until Rawlinson let the boys go to town on Saturday afternoon. He gave them a parting word not to get into trouble, as they had more horses to hunt, come Monday morning.

Delaine tried not to show his impatience as he rode his own horse and sauntered along with the other two into town. Once there, he took leave of them. He had already told them that Reed had said he had a letter waiting, and from the direction they headed, he thought Brundage might want to have Teale write another letter to Hilda.

At the post office, Delaine tied his horse and went straight to the window without pausing to look at any of the posters on the wall. He gave the clerk his name and waited a minute in return until he heard the clerk's footsteps and had the letter in his hand.

Outside, with his back to the building, he opened the envelope and took out the letter. It was written in a woman's hand, and it was not very long. He had seen Rachel's initials on the envelope, but he rushed to the bottom of the letter to see her signed name and to be sure. Then he went back to the beginning and read with attention.

JESS—

I am writing to you from The Brookfield Hotel. There are some things I thought I should tell you in person, so I have come to this town. I know you are working in the country, so I will bide my time and hope you receive this letter before long.
Sincerely,
Rachel

HE RAISED his eyes and saw the hotel straight across the street. His heartbeat had picked up, and his mouth was dry. He made himself stop and think. He had to be discreet, but he had to go into the hotel and ask for her. If Reed or Cunningham or anyone else saw him, he couldn't help it.

He led his horse across the street and tied it in front of the hotel. Shade was starting to reach out. He went up the single step, across the porch, through the door, and across the lobby to the desk.

A middle-aged man with trimmed red hair, a full, flushed face, and a corduroy vest buttoned across his ample midsection gave him a calm appraisal.

"Yes, sir."

"I would like to visit with a person who I think is staying here."

"Name?"

Delaine lowered his voice and drew out the syllables. "Rachel Valera."

"You'll have to wait here."

"Of course."

Delaine stepped away from the desk and noticed the fireplace, which had been swept clean and had a supply of split firewood on the irons, ready to be lit. A newspaper lay on a low table between two chairs. He glanced at the stairway, then made himself stare out the window. After several minutes, soft footsteps made him flinch, and he turned to see Rachel walking toward him.

As soon as he met her dark eyes, his tenseness relaxed. His nerves were soothed by the sight of her bronze complexion and dark hair, loose at her shoulders. She wore a dark-blue dress, buttoned to the neck, with full sleeves. She held her hand out to touch his.

"How do you do?" he said.

"I'm fine. And you?"

"All right. I'm sorry it took me so long to get my mail. Hoe long have you been here?"

"Since Wednesday."

"I'm sorry. I knew I was taking too long, but I was stuck at work."

"It's all right. Shall we go out for a walk?"

"Of course."

"Just a minute." She turned away, moved to the desk, and gave the hotel man her key. "I'll be back in a little while," she said. He muttered something in a cordial tone.

Outside, she said, "He's very nice, Mr. Sullivan, but everyone has ears."

"We can go this way," said Delaine.

They walked south about a hundred yards to the edge of town. The railroad tracks were another hundred yards ahead, and the distinct sounds of town on a Saturday afternoon were behind them.

"I thought I should come in person," she said. "I did not want to write anything in a letter that might fall into the wrong hands."

Delaine thought of the Slender Reed and said, "It could happen."

Rachel took a full breath, relaxed, and began. "I have seen a letter that Mr. Luna wrote to Robert Sandoval. Robert left it behind, I think for the same reason of being careful. After he had been gone for so long, and we had no definite news from you, Mrs. Sandoval and her son looked through his things and found the letter. Then they showed it to me." She paused for a breath. "In it, Mr. Luna wrote about a box he had, a metal box, with information in it."

"What kind of information?"

"Business things. Mortgages and will-pay letters, promissory notes, for money that Mr. Luna had lent to another party. He did not name the person in the letter, but we can be sure the name is on the papers. Mr. Luna wrote that he thought the person was borrowing the money to pay someone else to keep quiet."

"Blackmail?"

"It seems like it. Mr. Luna thought there might be something dangerous about it, so he let Mr. Sandoval know, in case of—well, you know. In case something happened."

"Which may have. So, where is the metal box? In the bank?"

"No. Mr. Luna had money in the bank, but it was, or still is, in Douglas. The box was in his house."

"Hidden?"

"According to his letter, it is in the wall, behind a painting of The Last Supper."

Delaine felt the breath go out of him. "I've seen that painting. It's a heavy thing, made out of plaster of Paris. Luna would have had to take it down and put it up by himself. They say he was kind of soft, but he must have been able to do it."

"So what do you think?" said Rachel. "Who should we tell?"

Delaine took in a breath as he felt a pang of worry. "I think we need to go slow. Let me tell you first what I've found out."

"Oh, tell me."

"Well, first off, I stayed one night at The Blue Iris. It's being managed by a fellow named Reed, who acts like a simpleton. He said no one showed up to see about the inheritance, so a friend of Mr. Luna's, one Mr. Melworth, has taken over the business aspect. He's a cattleman. He has Reed running the place and trying to get it back into business. I've met Melworth a couple of times, and I don't care for him. My guess is that he's pocketing what little money there is. He even sold Mr. Luna's donkey for five dollars. And there are some valuables—a pair of gold-rimmed glasses and a turquoise-and-silver ring that are supposed to be set aside for someone to claim, but if the bank is in Douglas, I would bet that none of those things have gone that far."

"Do you think Mr. Melworth is the one who was borrowing the money?"

"I think there might be a good chance, but there's a way to be sure."

"Look in the box."

"That's right."

Rachel gave a thoughtful look. "I wonder if Robert Sandoval got that far."

Delaine had to take a deep breath. "I doubt it. I think I may have found out something about Robert Sandoval."

"What?"

"No one seems to have known of him here. I haven't asked any direct questions, because I had a sense from the beginning that I had better not show my hand, but I've asked roundabout questions about Mr. Luna, as anyone would. People say that no heir or relative ever showed up."

Rachel's countenance sank.

"But they found a man who matches his description in the next town before this one, coming the way you and I each did. Willett. They found his body, and they think he may have gotten off a freight train there. The person I talked to said 'dropped off,' so they might even think he fell off a train. There is no record of him buying a ticket."

"Oh, *Dios mío.*"

"You'd think that's as far as he made it, but I think he may have come this far and was taken back there to be found."

Rachel took in a quick breath. "Why do you think that?"

"Well, you remember that Mrs. Sandoval said he

was wearing his everyday clothes and a hat and had a blue suit in his valise."

"Yes, I remember that."

"He came in the stage, and that's why there's no record of him traveling on the train. But they didn't find a suitcase with him. or a hat. So I think he came to this town, changed his clothes in order to present himself for business, didn't get far at all in that regard, and was taken back to the other town to be dumped off."

"Oh, my God. How brutal."

"If that is what happened, someone had a great deal to protect."

"Then what do you think we should do?"

"First off, keep quiet. This thing is twice as big as we thought it was, and dead serious. If either of us says anything to the wrong person, we could be next."

"Is there any law here?"

"There's a town marshal, but he's just here to protect the peace. As one fellow told me, he's like a night watchman. The sheriff's office is in Douglas, and there's a deputy that comes by. If we wanted to talk to him sooner, we'd have to know how to get in touch with him without attracting attention like we would by sending a telegram. The post office and telegraph office are together, and I don't know how confidential that man is. For right now, I don't see anything urgent. Nobody seems to be concerned about either death."

"I'd like to see the lodging house," she said.

"It's called The Blue Iris, but you already know that. Nothing is very far in this town." He pointed north. "If you go back this way, past the hotel, it's on the second cross street to the left. You can't miss it because it's painted a light-blue color."

"Then I guess I should go back to the hotel and go to the lodging house when there's not much going on, but still in the daylight."

"That sounds like a good idea. But be careful. Like I said, the fellow might not be as simple as he lets on."

"And what are you going to do?"

"I think I might go back to Willett, maybe tomorrow, and see if there's anything else I can learn."

"And how do I get in touch with you, other than leave a letter here at the post office?"

"I think I have an idea. I'll find out and let you know."

She let out a sigh. "Oh, my. After all this time, and we see each other for only a few minutes."

"Kiss me quick, and we'll make up for it later."

After the kiss, she said, "Can you walk me back to the hotel?"

"Oh, yes. But I don't think we should be seen together any more than we have to until things change. In the meantime, don't get the wrong idea. I'm very glad to see you."

"So am I," she said. "I wish things weren't so dangerous."

———

DELAINE RODE his own horse again on Sunday and arrived in Willett in the early afternoon. The feed and grain business, the livery stable, and the coal business all had their doors closed, but The Elkhorn was operating as usual, with a couple of horses tied up in front. He tied his horse and went in. A couple of fellows who looked like range riders were scowling over their glasses of beer, and his conversationalist from a few days earlier, Hal, had a bland smile on his face as he stood with a forearm resting on the bar. He was dressed as before in work clothes and a dark hat.

"We meet again," he said.

"Good afternoon." Delaine called for a beer and set a quarter on the bar. "You're not working today, are you?"

"No, I'm not. But I don't have anywhere to go, so I came in here for one or two. I don't like to stay longer. I have to work tomorrow."

"That's good judgment."

"Could be worse. The girl who turned me down would say it's not good judgement to come into these places at all, but she's stuck swattin' flies in a dingy little house in Indiana, with four kids, and a husband in jail for having sticky fingers in the store where he worked. So it's not bad here. No one nagging in my ear." Hal took a drink. "How 'bout yourself?"

"Not much different from the last time I saw you." Delaine's beer came, and he took a drink. "But I couldn't help thinking about that fella you told me about that they found by the railroad tracks."

"Oh, him. Yeah, that was too bad."

"No one saw fit to look into it any deeper?"

Hal shrugged. "Hard to know what to look into. And no one has come to claim him or look for him. There's men that drift all over the face of this big country. A dead traveling laborer just doesn't hold much interest." Hal's face brightened. "On the other hand, if someone was interested in missing persons, there are some that are worth something. Rewards."

"I suppose so."

"There's a case of a boy from Billings, Montana, that's been kidnapped. Whoever has him has asked for a ransom, and his father, who's a grain broker in Billings, has put up a reward. A thousand dollars."

"Is that right?"

"Yep. Not my idea of how to make a fortune."

"Mine, either.But I've known of people who are interested in that as a line of work." Delaine took a drink.

"So have I. They want the reward. Meanwhile, the crooks are holding stolen jewels, stolen racehorses, stolen people. I've heard that in order to get the best of people like that, blackmailers or thieves or whatever, you have to be able to think like them. You hear of someone who works his way into a gang, lives like them, pulls some stunts with them, and then helps turn 'em in. If he's on the outside, he still has to know how they think."

"That's too deep for me," said Delaine.

"Me, too. And I wouldn't want any of it to rub off. You get into one of those gangs, and you eat possum belly and chew tobacco while you wait to blow up the train tracks, and next thing you know, it's part of what you are. Gets in your blood."

"Some of the bigger cattle outfits hire an agent to work his way into the crew and find out if anyone is doing something crooked. It can be dangerous."

"Rustlers," said Hal. "They're the plague of the country."

One of the surly range riders spoke up. "Be careful how you throw that word around, pal. Someone might take it wrong."

"We were just talkin'," said Hal. "We got off track from talking about that boy who's got the posters up."

"Talkin' is what gets people in trouble."

Hal shrugged. He tossed off the last of his beer and said, "That's good enough for me today."

Delaine said, "Good to see you again."

"You bet."

Delaine finished his beer a few minutes later and went out to stand in the sunlight. The businesses were all in a row, on one side of the street, facing the railroad. The town was not the kind of place that would interest someone like Robert Sandoval. Other travelers, like Milligan, might stop into a number of places to see what he could hear. He might have been on the job, in his own way, the day he sampled the lamb fries.

Delaine thought he should have learned more for the trouble of coming back here twice. He untied his horse and decided to ride the length of the little town before heading back.

Beneath the overhang in front of the post office, a poster was tacked on the wall. Delaine rode close and saw the printed word "Reward" in large capital letters. The figure of $1000 appeared in large type beneath it. He stopped and leaned forward in the saddle to see the details. The blurry photograph of a blond-haired boy had his name beneath it and then a description—ten years old, four feet six inches tall, eighty pounds. He was missing from Billings, Montana, since April 14. Delaine counted back. A little more than two weeks ago. He raised his eyes to read the name with more attention. In capital letters, smaller than the word "Reward" and the amount of money, was the name William Harris Banks.

———

DELAINE RETURNED to Harrow in late afternoon. He had not eaten since morning, so he had an occasion to go to the café. As he went inside, his upper body tightened at the sight of Barton Melworth sitting by himself at a table, clean-shaven in his cream-colored cattleman's hat. At least the boss did not have his henchmen with him. Delaine took a table on the opposite side of the café and paid no attention to the man at the other table. Melworth, in turn, ignored him and had a displeased expression on his face. He had pushed his plate aside and sat with his head tipped as he looked through a newspaper.

Teale came out of the kitchen with a coffeepot and picked up a crockery mug from the counter. As he poured coffee at Delaine's table, he said, "I think you know that we have reduced fare on Sunday afternoon. Reduced in what we can offer, that is, as well as in price."

"What do we have, ham and potatoes?"

"That's right.

"I'll have it."

"It won't be long." Teale went back to the kitchen.

A few minutes later, he appeared with a plate of food. It was not warm when Delaine held his open hand over it, but it appeared to be edible.

"This looks all right," he said.

Melworth coughed, scraped his chair, and stood up. He set two coins on the table, and without looking around or saying anything, he walked to the door with the newspaper under his arm.

Teale cleared the other table as Delaine sampled his meal. It was tepid but not bad.

Teale came out of the kitchen and said, "Is it all right?"

"As good as before," said Delaine. "Do you always work Sundays?"

"Yes. I have Saturdays off. Not an ideal arrangement, but it helps out the others. It might make more difference if I lived in a larger town."

"We get time off when the work's not pressing. For things like roundup and haying season, there's no such thing as a holiday."

"Like working on a dairy," said Teale. "Or a chicken farm, which I'm glad to say I haven't had to do."

"Me, too. That's one thing about farm work. If you live where you work, the boss might come and get you even on a day off."

Teale said, "In a bigger town, it's easier to get away from your work. Some businesses close up one day a week, and that's it. I worked in a flower shop. When I had a day off, no one came after me."

"A flower shop. I imagine that could be interesting."

"It was. I'll say one thing. You learn to be discreet."

"I suppose so. I've often wondered about people who work in telegraph offices."

"Or the post office. In the town where I grew up, they said the postmistress ruined her eyes trying to read mail through the envelopes. But, yes, someone in the telegraph office knows everything that goes out or comes in."

Delaine said, "So if a person in this town has a desperate love affair, does he have to go to the next town to send a telegram?"

"He might want to, unless the person he's sending it to is in this town as well."

Delaine laughed. "That would be defeating the

purpose. And I gather that at least someone in the post office here lets people know who-all has mail."

"It can help. Unless someone wants to be discreet."

Delaine lowered his voice. "I've got a friend who's staying at the hotel. Not a desperate love affair. But if one of us wanted to send a note to the other, I don't know how we would do it. I don't know how curious or gossipy the hotel owner is."

"I think it depends on who you are. Your friend wouldn't happen to be a person with a Spanish name, would she?"

Delaine felt a small pang of worry. "Do you know her?"

"Not in person. I know of her. A friend of mine works at the hotel—cleaning rooms, sometimes doing laundry. I believe that she and your friend are on speaking terms."

"I see."

"So if you had a letter, or your friend had a letter, and you wanted to have it conveyed without going through the front desk, it could be done through Elmira. That's my friend's name."

Delaine nodded. "So if I gave you a letter, it could get to her. But if she gave your friend a letter, it could get out of there, but how would it get to me at the Six Mile?"

"I know a boy," said Tele. "Maybe you know him. Name of Dan. He does work of that nature, carrying messages and other things."

"Will that donkey take him out to the Six Mile and back?"

"I don't know. But I don't think he would worry that much about going on foot."

"I'd have to tip him well."

Teale shrugged. "It's all a matter of what it's worth."

"It's better than having the postal clerk tell the Slender Reed that I have a letter waiting for me, which has already happened."

Teale laughed. "So you know him. Yes, he's a good one."

"All right," said Delaine. "Can we leave it that way, that if she has a message to send me, it will get to me? That's the part we're concerned about right now."

Teale nodded.

"Then I'll have to find some way to let her know."

"Elmira can tell her. So we have the communication flowing from the start."

"That's very nice. I suppose I should offer you something for the trouble."

Teale raised his hand. "No reason to cross my palm with silver. If you happen to think of me when you're at the apothecary's, that would be all right."

Delaine recalled the token that Brundage had bought in the saloon. "The apothecary's," he said. "I know where that is."

7

Brundage rode in front, leading the pack of horses. Hall rode along the flank, and Delaine took up the drag. The eleven horses they had gathered stayed in a bunch, two and three wide, loping as if they all had a single thought and that was to go with the rest. They had not all been that way earlier in the day, playing hide-and-seek in the pines and cedars along the ridge. But now they were together. They knew each other and the horses the three men rode, and they could not but know that they were headed for the home corral. As punchers were fond of saying, horses were horses. They liked to run free and play hard to get, but they liked to comply and please. And they liked oats and hay, which, Delaine imagined, they associated with the direction in which they were headed.

Brundage led the group for about four miles, southeast across public range and deeded land. Rawlinson stood by the gate, nodding as if he was counting, as the horses thundered. Delaine drew rein as the herd milled, throwing up dust and nickering. He rode the horse to the gate, which Rawlinson had closed behind him and now opened for him to pass through.

"Eleven," said the boss. "More than half in just one day. Add them to the ones you boys brought in the other day, and that leaves only half a dozen. But they'll be the hardest to find and to bring in."

"I expect so," said Delaine. He had a picture of bringing them in one at a time on the end of a rope.

Hall came to the gate, and Rawlinson let him through. Brundage followed a minute later.

"There's a little red horse that's got a bad foot," he said. "Other than that, they all look good

"Glad to see 'em," said the boss. "I'll look 'em over a little more when they've settled down some. Did you have any trouble?"

"Nothing to speak of," said Hall. "We didn't see anyone else, and the horses seemed to get the idea."

Brundage and Delaine were sitting outside the bunkhouse, waiting for the call to supper, when a stranger rode into the ranch yard. He sat easy in the saddle as the horse walked up to within five yards of the seated men, and he stopped it. He was a young fellow, in his middle to late twenties.

"Is this the Six Mile Ranch?" he asked.

"It is," said Brundage, who sat with one leg hiked up and his right hand closed over his folded pocketknife. He had been cleaning his fingernails.

"I'm wonderin' if you're puttin' on any help."

Brundage's voice rose in its nasal tone. "Can't speak to that. You'll have to ask the boss."

Rawlinson's voice came from the open door

nearby. "That would be me. I'm not puttin' anyone on right now, but you're welcome to stay the night."

"I appreciate that."

"Max will show you where to put your horse."

"Thanks." The young man swung down.

Delaine imagined he had stayed in the saddle in case he had to move along. He seemed well-mannered as he took off his hat.

"My name's Joel Wyman, sir."

He was blond-haired and blue-eyed, not quite a pretty boy but a type that Delaine recognized as one that the girls would like. And he had a smile such as Delaine had seen before, with people who seemed to have learned that their smile worked well for them.

Brundage stood up, put away his knife, and brushed his vest with his hand. "This way."

———

THE VISITOR, Joel Wyman, found out soon enough that Delaine was the newest man at the ranch. When it came time to wash dishes, Wyman offered to take Brundage's place. Brundage did not object. He took a place down the table a ways, rolled a cigarette, and lit it. He drew out his watch with the horsehair chain, opened and closed it, and put it away. Hall had gone out back, and Rawlinson was perusing the almanac.

Wyman said, "You know how it is, tryin' to find work."

"Oh, yeah," said Delaine.

"Seems like there's always some kind of work, but to find a good job that lasts, that's not so easy."

"No, it's not."

"Some work, you barely make enough to get by.

With others, what money you have gets eaten up between one job and the next."

"That seems to be the way."

"And then there's work, you don't know if it's on the square."

"I think I've known of one or two of those."

"You don't like to have to take a job just because you're up against it."

Delaine did not know if the young man was trying to make an impression of having wide experience or if he was interested in someone else's point of view. Delaine answered him straight. "In my experience, it's better to take a job that doesn't pay very much than a job that might be questionable."

"Oh, yeah," said Wyman. "No doubt." After a few seconds, he said, "What kind of work have you been doing here?"

Delaine thought the young man was just making conversation, but he went along. "Fixing fence, looking for cattle, bringing in horses."

"I saw you had quite a few in the corral."

Brundage spoke up. "We'll be workin' with 'em pretty soon. Get 'em back into their better habits."

Wyman spoke to Delaine again. "Then there's other work. I think it's on the up-and-up." After a pause he said, "Collecting a reward. I don't know if any of you have seen posters or heard about this boy from Billings, but they're offering a thousand dollars for anyone who finds him. That would be a good way to put together a stake and be able to look for a good situation, not have to take a job cleaning sludge and dead pigeons out of water tanks."

"I've seen a poster," said Delaine.

"It could be a good way to make a thousand dollars."

Delaine cringed. The young man was likable, but he reminded Delaine of others he had known, and of himself at one time—a young person who should be looking for a chance to go straight but might be an opportunist on the lookout to make a good sum with one big job. "It might not be easy," he said. "I'm sure there are others looking for him, and I'm sure whoever has him doesn't want to be found."

"I think you're right," said Wyman.

Hall came in from outside as the last of the dishes were being put away. "Thanks for washing the dishes," he said. "Max likes to do it because it gets his hands clean."

"That's a benefit," said Wyman. "Washing dishes is a good thing to know how to do. Kitchen work might not pay very well, but you don't go hungry. And it's inside work, warm in the winter."

Brundage said, "Better than havin' to sing for your supper."

"Oh, I can do that, too."

"Is that right?" said Brundage. "That's something we don't get much of, out here. Are you any good at it?"

Wyman smiled. "I don't think I'm the one to say."

"Give us a song," said Hall. "We can decide."

"Aw, I don't know. I get bashful."

Brundage said, "No one here to worry about. We've heard a little of everything, from the roundup camps to the whorehouses."

Wyman laughed. "Then I might not be the worst you've heard."

"Sounds like we're going to hear a song," said Hall.

"I guess I could."

"Go ahead and give it your best. Nobody here but us mice."

"All right." Wyman stood at the end of the table with his back to the kitchen. "I'll sing one that I don't think you've heard before. I didn't make it up. I borrowed it from the fella who did. Name of Bill Deaner. It's called 'Beneath the Elms,' and it goes like this." He held his hands together at his waist, and he sang in a smooth, clear voice.

> *The elms stand in shadows, the branches all*
> > *bare,*
> *She walks up the lane with the breeze in her*
> > *hair,*
> *Her face clear in moonlight, her troubles remote,*
> *Her hands in the pockets of a dark woolen*
> > *coat.*
>
> *I stand by my horse in the moonlight so thin*
> *As the branches above shift and creak in the*
> > *wind.*
> *I hold my breath still as I tend to the sound*
> *Of her tread on the leaves and the hard winter*
> > *ground.*
>
> *The time that we share seems like no time*
> > *at all.*
> *As she turns in the moonlight I feel my hopes*
> > *fall.*
> *'Neath the branches so stark and the moon on*
> > *the wane*
> *Her coat like a shadow as she walks down the*
> > *lane.*

The years have gone by but they haven't erased
Those short times we shared in our moonlit
    embrace,
When love seemed so real and so sure to prevail
That life would turn into a broad sunny trail.

I know in this life I won't see her again,
So I travel in mem'ry to a thin-shadowed lane
Where she walks 'neath the elms with her coat
    gathered tight,
Her face raised to mine on a clear winter night.

A round of applause sounded in the bunkhouse. Hall said, "That was good."

Wyman shrugged. "Just a song I happen to know. But don't ask me to do another one. That's the only one I've practiced enough."

"I don't believe that," said Hall. "You've got a very practiced voice, and most people start out with well-known songs and have a bunch of them, but we'll let you go."

"Thanks," said Wyman. He lowered his head as if in modesty, but he didn't seem to mind the attention.

———

AFTER A DAY of brushing and combing horses and riding them in the round pen, the men were eating supper when a knock sounded on the bunkhouse door.

"I'll answer it," said Delaine, and he rose from his seat. He wondered if Joel Wyman had returned, and he doubted it. He opened the door and let the lamplight shine on an individual who was shorter than he expected. As he adjusted, he recognized Dan, the boy from town.

"You're Mr. Delaine, aren't you?"

"Yes, I am."

"I have a message by way of Mr. Teale." The boy raised an envelope for Delaine to take.

"Thanks. Let me read it." Delaine broke the seal, took out a folded sheet of paper, opened it, and read.

J—

I have gone to stay at the lodging house. If you can get away this evening, you can find me at the café from nine until they close at ten. We can go from there to talk. If you cannot be there tonight, I will go there again tomorrow.

Sincerely,

R

Delaine folded the letter and put it in the envelope. "Wait here for a minute," he said. "How did you get here?"

"I came on foot."

"Let me think. I'll be back in a minute."

Delaine returned to the table and spoke to his boss. "There's a boy here who brought me a message that someone wants to see me in town. Someone I know. I'm sure I can be back later tonight and not have this interfere with work tomorrow."

Rawlinson raised his eyebrows. "I suppose it should be all right. Take one of the ranch horses. It'll be easier than going out to the pasture and catching yours."

"Thanks."

"Sit down and eat the rest of your meal."

Delaine did not like to wolf down his food while

the boy waited, but it would be an offense to expect someone to throw out what he didn't eat. He sat down to finish his bowl of stew.

Hall said, "I guess we'll have to eat that pie ourselves."

Delaine raised his eyes. "When did you make a pie?"

"I didn't. Just wanted to make you worry for a minute."

———

DELAINE PICKED a sturdy horse that would carry the kid on back without wearing out, and the two of them rode into town as evening turned into night. Fifty yards short of the café, Delaine let the boy slide down and gave him a quarter.

"You don't have to pay me that much," said the boy.

"It's a long walk. At least you didn't have to hoof it both ways."

"Thanks."

"Thanks to you."

Delaine tied up at the café. He waved from outside the window, and he caught Rachel's attention. She got up, settled with the night waiter, who was someone other than Teale, and came outside.

"I'm glad you could make it," she said. "Did you have any trouble?"

"Not to speak of. It was a little awkward asking permission from the boss, but I told him it wouldn't keep me from working in the morning."

"It shouldn't."

"Shall we walk this way?" he said, pointing in the

direction of the general store and post office, which were closed.

They walked south in the direction of the railroad tracks, and they were by themselves in the night within a couple of minutes.

"So you've gotten into the castle," he said.

"That's a way of saying it. Mr. Reed isn't quite like the Duke or King in a story, but he seems to have a sense of his own importance."

"I stayed there for one night."

"It might be different for a woman."

Her tone made him laugh. "I don't doubt it."

"He had another woman hired, but there weren't any other guests, and no work for her to be paid for. When I told him I was looking for work, he dismissed her and told me I could have a room without charge, and we would 'even up' when there were rooms to clean. And he said he might be serving meals in the future, so there would be kitchen work as well."

"He sounds very accommodating."

"He is. He sits around drinking whiskey and making forward comments. I don't think the other woman was very receptive."

Delaine felt a stir of jealousy. "I hope you aren't."

She smiled in the moonlight. "Don't worry. I'm just polite, that's all."

"The other woman—that's not the one who works at the hotel, is it?"

"Elmira? No. she worked there before, when Mr. Luna was there. But she went to work at the hotel, which is where I met her, of course. Since then, Mr. Reed arranged with this other woman to work, but there was just about nothing for her to do, and I don't think she minded being let go."

"So you've seen the painting."

"Yes. I've seen the heavy screws that hold it to the wall, and I've found the screwdriver in the kitchen."

"Very good. Has an idea occurred to you about how we might try to get a look behind it?"

"I think I can let him get drunk enough to fall asleep, but I'll have to see if he does. Then I can let you know, and we can see if it works again."

"In other words, I wait for another message like the one you sent this evening."

"I think so. If my plan doesn't work, we'll see what we can try next."

"I hope he's not too worried about where you are tonight."

"Oh, if he becomes a little…disconsolate, he might be easier to deal with."

"That's quite a word for a small town like this."

"The big words are more common in Spanish, so it came to me in a light moment."

He laughed. It was silly to think there was anything to be jealous about, but he appreciated the assurance. "What about me?" he asked.

"What about you?"

"You're not going to brush me off, are you?"

She touched his chest with her fingertips. "You're the one who was so serious in broad daylight. We don't have that problem now. Just the moon and stars."

———

DELAINE PICKED his way along the base of the pine ridge, looking into inlets. Some of the crevices led into grassy areas large enough to be called canyons. Twice he spooked deer. He was looking for horses. Deer favored shadowed canyons and hillsides on warm afternoons, and in cooler weather they frequented places where the sun reflected off surfaces like bluffs or rocks. Ranch horses would drift into canyons, but they often stayed out in the open and were given to bolt and run, maybe circle back. Some would stay out ahead all day long, while others would run back and forth. They seemed to be fatalists, knowing at some point when the game was up.

The horse Delaine was riding was new to him, one of the eleven they had brought in. The animal was steady and attentive, but Delaine believed in the principle of not trusting any horse one hundred percent. The most obedient horse could leave a rider in a pile of rocks ten miles from the ranch, which was how far out he estimated himself to be at the moment.

He rode into a side canyon where grass grew around earthen boulders, but he found no animals. On the way out, he paused, as was his habit, before riding into full view.

Less than half a mile away, two riders were moving north. The horses were on a fast walk, going somewhere. The larger rider was on a light-colored horse with a dark mane and tail, one of many shades that fell under the general description of a grey horse. The man's dark hat and rounded shoulders made him easy to recognize, and the sleeves of a light-blue shirt contrasted with his dark vest.

The other rider, in a brown hat and vest, was slender and not tall. He was riding a reddish horse that from a distance looked mottled and might be a roan.

Delaine waited for several minutes until the men on horseback were specks in the north. He was sure that he was on public land, and he was not doing anything furtive to make him feel guilty. He was hunting horses, and he hoped to have one on the end of his rope before long, but in the meanwhile, he did not need a confrontation with Vick and Rudy.

———

THE SUN HAD CROSSED over the high point of the sky when Delaine saw a pair of horses grazing in a shallow draw. He rode up close enough to see the 6M brand and took down his rope. The horses, a sorrel and a dark brown, took off on a trot. When he picked up after them, they began to lope. Up on a level area, they kept going, then veered to the right. Delaine leaned into his ride and tried to cut them off, and they turned the other way. He slowed, and they did the same. He stopped. They slowed, turned, and stopped. They watched as he walked his horse forward. When he was within fifty yards, they took off at a trot again. He stood in his stirrups and let his horse trot fast. He thought that if he went into a lope, the other horses would do the same. They did anyway, so he spurred his horse, caught up with the two fugitives on their left, swung his loop twice, and made his throw at the sorrel.

The horse turned to the right, which Delaine had expected, and he had thrown ahead in that direction. The loop settled over the horse's head, and the animal slowed. Delaine was pleased. The sorrel was the kind of horse that would stop in the corral if a person on foot tossed the loose end of a lead rope over its withers.

Delaine turned his horse around, and the sorrel followed. The dark horse fell in alongside the sorrel, and the three of them headed for the ranch.

DELAINE WAS PUTTING his saddle away after a day of working in the round corral when a small rider on a soot-colored horse came riding into the ranch yard. The person wore a cloth cap and bounced in the saddle as the horse came to a stop.

"Mr. Delaine," came the voice.

Delaine stopped in the middle of the yard with the saddle and blanket in his hands. For once, Dan was not looking up at him. Delaine gave him and the horse a looking over and said, "Where'd you get the trans-portation?"

"Mr. Teale borrowed it for me."

"That was good of him."

"I have another letter for you." The boy reached into his shirt, took out a curved envelope, and reached down to hand it to Delaine.

"Let me put my saddle in the barn. Slide down and rest your haunches."

Delaine returned to the spot where the boy stood by the horse, and he took the letter. He opened the envelop and took out a folded paper that had very little writing on it.

J—

I think we might be able to look at something this evening, Thursday. Same time as before. If you wait outside the house, I will look for you.

R

"Thanks for coming out," said Delaine. "You don't need to wait for me to go back, do you?"

"No, sir."

"Then take this." Delaine took out a quarter and handed it to the boy.

"I didn't have to walk this time, and I don't think Mr. Teale had to pay for the horse."

"It's still a full trip for you. Don't be shy."

"All right. Thanks."

"I'll be along a little later. I need to wash my face, eat a bite, and clear things with my boss. I don't think you need a written answer."

"No one asked for one."

"Good enough. Take care going back. You should still have good light."

"Thanks." The boy led the horse to the corral, stopped it, held the reins and saddle horn as he climbed up onto a plank, and jumped into the saddle. The horse stood still, then grunted as the boy nudged with his heels and pulled the horse's head with the right rein. The horse's hooves struck the hard ground as the animal took off on a jolting walk.

DELAINE WAITED outside the lodging house in the dark. He didn't like to be lurking, but no dogs had barked, and no one was out walking.

The front door opened, and Rachel walked out onto the porch. She made the sound that Mexican people used to get someone's attention. "*Ch, ch.*"

Delaine whistled a short note. She came down the steps, and he met her.

"Have you been waiting long?" she whispered.

"Ten minutes or so. Just enough to get the jitters. Is he passed out pretty good?"

"I think so. He started early. I think he had a hangover from last night and didn't want to say anything. He started right in when I asked him if he wanted me to pour him a drink."

"What do you have to do to get him to drink that much?"

"Don't worry. Nothing like those girls in those places do."

"I don't know anything about that."

"Neither do I, but I know that they rub up against a man and let him touch them. In some parts of town you see it on the street or through the open door of a barroom."

"I may have seen something like that."

"And you know what beasts men become."

He recalled hearing the word *embrutecerse* in a discourse against alcohol. "I do. That's why I never have more than two drinks."

"Never?"

A noise sounded inside, and Delaine quit joking. "What was that?"

"He snores."

"That's not so bad. Do you think we can get started?"

"I think so." Rachel went up the steps and through the open door almost without a sound.

Delaine followed, making his footsteps as soft as he could. The front room was in dim light, and the Slender Reed was slumped in the chair he had sat in when Delaine had filled his glass. He made a blubbering sound with his lips as he breathed out. The colors of The Last Supper were not very vivid in the subdued light, but the object had its prominent place in the room.

Rachel whispered, "Wait here." She went to the

kitchen and came back with a wooden-handled screwdriver.

Delaine took it and went to work. He moved the empty chair aside, then backed out the two bottom screws and put them in his vest pocket. He whispered, "If you can hold it against the wall, I'll take out the other two."

The piece was about two and a half feet tall and about four wide, with a thickness varying from an inch in the middle to an inch and a half on the border. When he had the two top screws out, he and Rachel lowered the heavy object to the floor and leaned it against the wall.

In the middle of the area that the painting had covered, a grey metal box stood on its end in a recess where the lath and plaster had been cut away. It was a typical metal box such as people used for keeping gold coins, heirloom watches, bonds, and other important documents. The handle was facing him, so Delaine took the box from the wall.

In a low voice, Rachel said, "Let's go to the kitchen where we can have better light."

Delaine set the box on a raised work table with a thousand knife marks in it. Rachel placed a lantern on the same table and turned up the wick.

"Here goes." Delaine opened the latch and lifted the lid on its hinge. Several folded documents occupied almost the whole area in the box, which was about four inches deep. "Do you want me to look at them?" he asked.

"Go ahead. I think you'll see their meaning quicker than I will."

He unfolded the first document and saw what it was. "This is a promissory note for a thousand dollars, lent by José Luna to Barton Melworth, with a section of land—that is, six hundred and forty acres—for security." He set it aside and picked up the next one. "This one's the same, but the location of the land is different. So he was lending him money for a thousand dollars a section. That's a high price for land, but he wasn't buying it outright, just taking it for security." Delaine went through two more, set them on the new stack, and came to a different kind of document. "This one's an actual mortgage, with the deed attached. The dates become earlier as we go down the stack. This is for a thousand dollars as well. That seems to be the regular amount that Melworth needed, about every two months."

"That's five thousand so far."

"Right." He set the mortgage on top of the promissory notes and took out the next mortgage. "This is the same. Again, a different parcel."

"That's six."

Delaine went through three more and came to a different one for two thousand dollars. It was a promissory note, and the collateral was given as fifty head of cattle of the lender's choice. After showing it to Rachel, he said, "These go back more than two years. I don't know why Luna would go from a mortgage to a promissory note unless Melworth didn't have a clear title to these later properties. Still, this is a lot of money, and you can see that he was getting in deeper and deeper. He had to keep his debt secret because he had to keep secret whoever he was paying off and why." Delaine stopped and listened to a stirring in the other room.

Rachel went to the doorway and came back. "He's still asleep."

Delaine put the papers back into the box in their original order, with the most recent note on top. "I wouldn't be surprised if Melworth did in Luna, or had him done in, in order to get back these papers and to keep everything quiet. He must have had reason to believe that Luna had the papers on hand, and he must have been pretty desperate."

Rachel said, "I would have thought to look behind the painting, but maybe that's because I think more like Mr. Luna. The old stories from Mexico are full of *entierros*, money buried beneath the floor or in the thick adobe walls."

"It seems easy now, but maybe it's like Columbus and the egg."

"What is that?"

"A famous story we read about in school. After Columbus went back to Spain, they had a banquet for him, and one of the dignitaries said, 'This is very good, but don't you think that if you hadn't discovered the New World, someone else would have?' Columbus sent for an egg from the kitchen, and he challenged everyone at the table to stand it on its end. Nobody could. When it came back around to him, he crushed the end and stood it up. Then he said, 'Once the deed is done, everyone knows how to do it.'"

"That's a good story. I hadn't heard it."

"Maybe it's made up, but I think it's well known. But I'd better stop talking and get back to business."

"What do you think we should do with the papers?"

"Same as before. Put them back in the wall and wait for the deputy to come back to town. They're not ours, and I wouldn't want to be accused of having stolen property on my hands, although I wouldn't consider it stealing."

"What if someone finds them and takes them?"

"They haven't yet. That painting weighs more than fifty pounds. Luna must have had a system for raising and lowering it, like boards to prop it onto. It might not occur to someone that he could have moved it himself. But that doesn't mean no one will think of it. But the box shouldn't be here for very long. You're here, so if someone does find it, you should know as soon as it happens."

"I'm afraid someone will find it."

"So am I, but I have a hunch that Mr. Melworth is more desperate about other things. That last note was dated more than three months ago. I would guess that he is looking for a way to make his next payment. I'm sure he has already searched this place, and I'm sure he'd like to find those things, but I think he's looking for money right now."

"Unless he has found it."

Delaine felt as if he was stopped in his tracks. "Money. That could be, but it seems to me that he's in a state of agitation. Let's put these things away and hope for the best."

Rachel had worry on her face. "I can't keep them. And I understand why you don't want to have them in your possession."

"They're not mine, and it would be the kiss of death if someone found them on me on my way home. And where would I hide them—under my bunk?"

"Is there someone else you could leave them with —someone of confidence, as we say in Spanish?"

"Someone discreet. Maybe I can think of someone."

"Is there something I can do?"

He considered the question. "If you can, see if you can find out when the deputy is going to be in town. In the meantime, I think I have an idea of where to leave the box."

"Good. Let's put this painting up and be done with it."

In five minutes, they had The Last Supper on the wall again and the chair in place. Reed had blubbered and snored but had not opened his eyes.

Delaine said, "I've got a jacket tied onto the back of my saddle. I can wrap the box in that."

Outside in the dark, she stood by his horse as he tied the bundle in place.

"I'm glad you're taking it," she said. "I was very worried, knowing that it was in the wall."

"I feel like the boy who stole the fox and had it eat his insides."

"I remember that story," she said. "He was Greek."

"Yes, Spartan. It was part of the code not to let out a peep."

"Now you're nervous. I can tell."

"Just like you were. I need to leave this thing somewhere for safe keeping."

"Can you tell me where?"

"Only for a kiss." After a long minute, they drew apart. "I need to be going," he said.

"Are you going to tell me where?"

"To Mr. Teale's. I think he should be home at this time."

8

———————

Delaine's nerves were on edge as he ducked into the Diamond Horseshoe Saloon to buy a pint of whiskey. When he returned to his horse, all was normal. He swung his leg high and over, and he rode to the back street where Teale lived.

He guessed the time to be about ten-thirty. He held the bundle with one arm as he knocked on the door at the bottom of the stairs.

Teale opened it. "Oh, it's you. What's new?" His eyes shifted. "What's that?"

"It's not a gift." Delaine set the bundle on the couch and took the pint bottle from inside his shirt. "This is a gift."

"How thoughtful of you. Thanks." Teale gave a dubious look at the jacket covering the unknown object. "Are these related?"

"The whiskey is an expression of good will." Delaine lifted the jacket to reveal the metal box. "This is a request, which you don't have to go along with if you don't want to."

Teale lifted the bottle a couple of inches. "I happened to be out of this substance, so I appreciate it. Would you like a drink?"

"I haven't had one for a few days. I could use one now."

Teale poured a couple of ounces into each of two glasses and handed one to Delaine. "Let's sit down."

Delaine sat on the couch next to the box, and Teale sat on the chair by his desk. He rolled a cigarette with his little machine and lit it. The light in the room was not bright, and with the low ceiling, Delaine had a sense of sitting in a basement-level apartment. He took a drink and felt the whiskey spread its warmth.

Teale had a whimsical expression on his face as he took a second drag and exhaled. "Are we going to play what's in the box?"

"We could," said Delaine. "But we don't have to. It's something that I'd like to leave with you for safe keeping, if you don't mind."

"Depends on what it is."

"It's not money, and it's not stolen property. You don't have to look inside if you don't want to. They're just a stack of documents."

"No doubloons, then, or gems with radiant powers, or some mummified object with a curse?"

"None of that."

"Then I don't need to look inside. I'm not one to read someone else's mail, or journal or diary. I suppose that if they were confessions of crimes, I should have a scruple."

"Not quite that, either," said Delaine.

"Then I won't worry about it. You can leave it here. I'll find some place where the servants won't get into it."

"Do you have servants?"

"Does it look like it?"

Delaine glanced around. "Not really."

"Then think no more of it. We'll talk about something else. Your friend is all right, I hope."

"Rachel? Yes, she's fine. She's gone to stay at The Blue Iris."

"I know that, of course."

"Yes. She's a good worker. If Reed had any business, he'd find her very valuable." Delaine took another sip of whiskey and felt as if it was calming him.

"Luna did all right with it, but he had his own way. I don't know where Reed's real talents lie."

"Neither do I. I stayed there one night and had a drink with him as you and I are doing, but you don't get to know someone all that well in one visit."

"Or even three or four. You and I have talked more than that, but I don't know if you're a fugitive being sought for trying to overthrow the government."

"Do I have it written all over me?" Delaine glanced at the box.

"No. People who come to the panoramic West to forge a new identity don't bring a box of damning evidence along."

"Back to Luna," said Delaine. "It seems to me that there's something of a mystery about how he died. Reed said that he may have died of gout or apoplexy. I believe he said that was what other people thought."

Teale tipped his head and raised his eyebrows. "I've heard that as well."

"You seem skeptical. I myself was wondering how likely it was."

"Call it my morbid curiosity. But I was one of a

couple of others who helped the barber move the body to the back room of his shop. We've got a county coroner, but if there's not great cause or a specific request, and the person dies here in town and not out in the country, the barber does the job of town coroner as well as undertaker. The county coroner doesn't have to come all this way, and the town pays the barber a little for it."

"Like the constable."

"The town marshal might make a little more. He has regular duties, not just on occasions."

"I shouldn't have interrupted."

"It's all right." Teale took a sip of whiskey. "Anyway, as I was saying, I helped move the body. I think of gout and apoplexy as things that give a person a red face and make them swell up. Luna was soft and pudgy, but he didn't look…inflated. He didn't go out very much in the sun, and he was pale, a very light-brown, almost a yellow tone. And when we moved the body, I noticed what seemed to me, at least, to be a kind of blue pallor, like the effect of some kind of poison or drug."

"Did you say anything?"

"No. I didn't want to get poisoned myself. I waited to see what the barber would say, and he didn't say anything until the next day, when he said the cause of death might be gout or apoplexy. But they're two different things. Apoplexy is a stroke, and gout is a chronic condition, sometimes aggravated by rich living, as with English country squires. It seemed to me that the barber might be repeating what someone else told him, just as Reed and others have repeated it since then. I didn't have a personal interest in the case, so I thought I would wait to see if anyone did. You and I have a level of confidence, so I don't mind telling you that I'd like to see someone bring light to this little shady area." Teale took another sip. "Is Rachel related to Mr. Luna?"

"No."

"Well maybe something will happen. I expected a male relative anyway."

Delaine drank from his glass. "It's getting late, and I still have to ride back to the ranch."

"Yes, and I have to work tomorrow as well. Doesn't hurt to have a dram, though."

"I hope not."

Teale smiled. "And I appreciate the gesture."

"I appreciate your taking care of this little thing." Delaine motioned with his head toward the metal box.

"Don't mention it. I'll put it somewhere safe and not think about it."

———

RATHER THAN RIDE back the same way he came, Delaine rode around the block and came out onto the main street south of the main businesses. As he rode past the hotel, he saw that someone was sitting in the lobby, which was still lit. The person was reading a newspaper. Delaine did not recognize the full head of blondish-brown hair, but as the man turned his head, Delaine saw a brush-like mustache, and from there he noticed a cream-colored hat sitting on a low table next to the man's chair.

The scene struck Delaine as being unreal and out of place, with a detachment between the lit lobby and the dark street, but there was no question that the man was Barton Melworth. He did not seem to be waiting for anybody or keeping an eye out for anybody, just reading the newspaper. Delaine imagined that the hotel must be a convenient place for someone to read the paper for free at a time when not many people were around.

Delaine rode onward, and in a few minutes the lights of town, few that they were, were well behind him.

———

DELAINE'S EYES were tired as he rode out of the ranch the next morning. That was the way it was at sunrise when he hadn't had a full night's sleep. He was used to it from several years of working on roundup. He did not know if he would still be working at the Six Mile come roundup time, but now was not the time to worry about that. The case of Luna and Sandoval was in town, and he would get back to it as soon as he could. For the present, he was out looking for horses again.

He rode north and west again, to the area of pines and cedars and a ridge that seemed to be a divide between one grassland and another. The scenes registered with him as good places for deer when the grass was dry and the leaves were changing with autumn. Everything was green now, but not as fresh as when he started out on this journey. All the carpet flowers were gone until next year. It was possible to have another snow, but it was also possible to have a hailstorm or a drought.

As the sun rose in the sky and warmed the day, he began to perspire. He stopped to take off his jacket and tied it onto the back of his saddle. He was at the base of the ridge, where the shapes of him and his horse would be absorbed by the trees and rocks and earth. He stood by the horse for a moment to let the silence fill in as he gazed at the landscape.

A hawk landed in the branches of a dead pine tree some twenty yards away. The tree was not very tall, maybe eight feet. Trees lived and died and fell and decomposed in this country. This one was at a moment when it was still useful to a bird.

The hawk opened its beak and let out a *scree*-ing sound. Delaine held still. The hawk made the sound again and again. It moved its head one way and another and did not show an awareness of the man and the horse. The fierce-looking bird continued to call, for a total of a dozen times. Delaine did not move until the bird flew away.

Delaine waited another minute, then mounted up and rode on. There was no predicting where horses would be, but Rawlinson had told him to look in the breaks and canyons, so he did.

He came to an area a little farther north than he had ridden before, a country of breaks with bowl-shaped canyons and the kind of deep draws that men from Texas called headers. He found a trail, one that was more traveled than he might have expected this far out. He did not see any cattle tracks, but he remained alert to the possibility that someone out here might be moving cattle after all.

He followed the trail for a short while until he became aware of not being able to see very far ahead or behind. If this trail was traveled, he might run into someone he would rather avoid, and he might have someone undesirable come up behind him.

He followed a draw to his left that did not have

much of a trail. The day was warming, but the grass was green, and he was not down between canyon walls where the sun reflected off rocks.

Keeping in mind the direction where the trail had been leading, he tried to follow the breaks in a parallel direction so that he could go up and look over from time to time. He was sure the trail led to something, and he would like to have a look at what it was.

Each time he went up the side of a ridge, he dismounted and led the horse. It was in a horse to give a burst of effort to go up a hill, and Delaine did not want to pop over a ridge and attract someone's attention. As a result, he expended quite a bit of energy climbing hills on foot in his riding boots, but his caution allowed him to rise up and peer over in slow motion.

His reward came in a flash, a glimpse. He ducked down by reflex, then rose again to let his eyesight clear the ridge.

The layout in the small canyon below looked like a line camp, with a shack, a horse corral, and a couple of pens large enough to hold several head of cattle or horses. The larger pens were empty, with grass growing around the edges. A horse stood in the corral, and a saddled horse was tied at the rail in front of the shack. What he saw agreed with the amount of wear he had seen on the trail. No one had moved bunches of stock in and out.

The horse at the rail caught his attention. It was not shiny under the late morning sun. It was a large bay such as the one he had seen Jim Rudy ride.

He shifted his attention to the corral. The horse there was a sorrel, not unlike the one Sorensen had ridden. Delaine recalled that he had not seen Sorensen for a while, and he wondered whether the man had been working out here. Rudy might have brought him some groceries.

Delaine settled onto his knees and let the camp go out of sight. It was an interesting scene, but it did not have anything sinister about it, and he did not know how much business he had spying on it. On the other hand, he assumed it was Melworth's line camp, and Melworth was caught up in one dead man's affairs and perhaps in another's, so there shouldn't be much harm in confirming whose horse was tied up in front.

Still on his knees, Delaine rose, watched for half a minute, and sank back. He continued the routine for several minutes until the door of the shack opened. Delaine's pulse jumped as Jim Rudy came out and lumbered toward his horse. The man in the dark hat did not look around as he untied the reins, checked his cinch, and stepped aboard. He reined the bay horse around and rode away.

Delaine settled back and let out a long breath. He did not know for sure if Sorensen was out here or on what business, but he knew enough for the time being. He would give Rudy a half-hour's head start, and he would go back to hunting horses—but not without making sure he knew the way back in here.

DELAINE FOUND a single dun horse with the 6M brand and put a rope on it. He headed across open country toward the ranch, which he estimated to be about seven miles away. The dun knew the ranch horse that Delaine was riding and did not give much trouble, just balking once in a while.

Halfway to the ranch, Delaine saw a rider coming his way. He had no reason to avoid another person, so he slowed on the trail. The other rider was a large man, and when he had come within a quarter of a mile, Delaine recognized him as the man named Milligan. He rode a large, heavy-built horse the color of a palomino but without the lighter-colored mane and tail, what some men called a "yella horse."

The two riders slowed and came to a stop about ten feet apart.

"We've met before," said Milligan.

"That's right. My name's Delaine."

Milligan's narrowed eyes in his full face seemed to squint as he looked over the dun on Delaine's rope. "Looks like you're at work."

"I am. I work for a ranch over this way."

"So am I. Just different work." Milligan raised his reins and shook them.

"Good luck to you," said Delaine.

"Same to you."

When Delaine looked back a few minutes later, he had to search to find the man on the yellow horse. He had made a turn and was riding southwest. Delaine shrugged. He assumed the man knew where he was going. If he didn't, he would find out.

Before long, Delaine heard hoofbeats pounding behind him. it sounded like more than one horse. He turned to see two riders bearing down on him, so he led the dun horse off the trail.

Jim Rudy was riding a grey horse like the one Delaine had seen him ride out on the range, and Vick was on the sorrel with a white star on its forehead. The two riders thundered by without a word or a shout.

So much for common courtesy. Now that he

thought of it, Milligan might have gone the other way to avoid meeting them. Maybe Rudy and Vick thought it was their turn to snub someone.

———

DELAINE RINSED and hung the two dishpans on the wall and took his seat again at the table. Brundage had rolled and lit a cigarette, and Rawlinson was smoking his pipe, so tobacco smoke mixed with the aroma of fried salt pork. Hall was reading a newspaper article about a jackrabbit drive in Idaho in which an army of men and boys had formed a long net with woven wire, drawn it close, and clubbed more than a thousand jackrabbits.

Brundage gave a thoughtful expression. "Doesn't say what they did with all the dead ones. Jackrabbit isn't all that good to eat."

Rawlinson said, "My nephews in Michigan go out and shoot cottontail rabbits to sell at a mink farm. They'll shoot a pony cart full and sell the load for a dollar."

"I wonder if they have any mink farms in Idaho." Brundage took out his watch and looked at it.

"I don't know," said Rawlinson. "Depends on where it is. It might get too hot in the summer. That's a problem with rabbit farms. Domestic rabbits. They die in the heat."

"Never thought about rabbit farms."

"They raise 'em for the meat and pelts both. Mink are smaller, and they raise them just for the pelts. Much more valuable, of course. Those mink are mean little things. Need to keep 'em in good strong cages."

Hall said, "I've known people who raised rabbits

on a small scale. They're docile animals. Doesn't take much to keep them penned in."

The talk went silent, and Rawlinson spoke to Delaine. "Did you see anything worth mentioning where you went today?"

"I saw more of that pine ridge than I had seen before. Went into the breaks. I saw what looked like a line camp, with a shack and corrals, but no cattle in there, and no signs of anything being driven in or out. A few horse tracks, and I even saw two horses there. It looked like Jim Rudy leaving on one of them."

"Broken Horn," said Brundage.

Delaine gave him a questioning look.

"They call that area Broken Horn. There's a Broken Horn Spring and a Broken Horn Canyon. And there's a few good spots in there for grazin'."

"Looks like good deer country to me."

"It is." Brundage took a pull on his cigarette and raised his head in an attitude of authority.

Rawlinson said, "Melworth controls most of that area. That's his line camp. He's got deeded property. That's his way. He's got deeded property here and there, kind of like a checkerboard, and that allows him to control property in between. You want to be careful where you go. Don't go on anything that's posted or fenced. You already know how touchy some of his men can be."

"Two of them rode right past me quite a bit later in the day. One of them was Rudy, on a different horse. Looked like they were on their way to town and didn't want to be late for the show."

"Some show in Harrow," said Brundage.

Hall set down the newspaper. "Do you like the burlesque shows you see in larger towns?"

"They're all the same," said Brundage. His voice went up as he sang, "Pay two bits to see two tits."

"Be careful about buying the whole cow," said Rawlinson.

"Buyin'? I think those are for rent. Back home when I was growin' up, they had a sayin' about girls that were easy. 'Why buy the cow when you can get the milk for free?' But none of it's free."

"That's right," said Rawlinson. "There's lots of old bachelors in this country, and it's not because they're all old and ugly and don't think a ranch is a place for a woman. Some of 'em have been stung."

"Some of 'em are just that way."

"Well, yes," said Rawlinson. "Some of 'em don't care for women. Don't count me in that bunch, or the bunch that's been stung. I'm just careful. Maybe some day things will change, and I won't eat in the bunkhouse any more, and I'll have boys that want to go out and shoot rabbits, but I'm not in a hurry."

"Every man should have a chance," said Brundage.

No one spoke. Hall picked up the newspaper and said, "Ready for another story?"

———

WHEN THE THREE hired hands reached the edge of town on Saturday afternoon, Delaine asked the other two if they were going to see Mr. Teale. Hall deferred to Brundage, who said he would wait.

"I might drop in to see him myself," said Delaine.

Brundage gave a light toss of the head as if he was about to ask a question and decided not to.

Hall said, "We'll stop in for the mail at the post

office, and if you want, you can meet us later at the Diamond Horseshoe."

"Sounds all right to me." Delaine separated from the other two and took the cross street.

He turned again on the street that ran parallel to the main drag, and he went on to the building where Teale lived. He had thought of bringing another bottle of whiskey, but he did not want to overdo anything or make Teale feel as if was being bribed.

Teale answered the door and let him in. Light from a single lamp showed thin smoke hanging along the low ceiling, and the smell of cigarette was noticeable. As Delaine walked into the room, he saw a woman sitting on the couch. She looked up over her shoulder and smiled.

She appeared to be about the same age as Teale, worn with a few wrinkles. She had greying brown hair pinned at the sides, light-blue eyes with creases at the corners, and an amiable expression. She sat forward in her seat but did not rise as Teale said, "This is Mrs. Beck. Also known as Elmira."

Delaine took off his hat and gave her his hand. "Jess Delaine. A pleasure to meet you."

"And the same to you."

"Have a seat," said Teale.

The woman moved to the far end of the couch, and Delaine settled down on the near end. He saw a glass of beer and an ashtray and cigarette on the low table. Another glass and lit cigarette sat on the desk.

Teale motioned downward with his hand. "We've got a bucket of beer. Would you like a glass?"

Delaine recognized the covered pail as the type that came from taverns. He imagined the beer was fresh, but it did not appeal to him at the moment. "No, thanks. I don't care for anything right now."

Teale gave a faint smile as he sat in his chair and took up his cigarette. "Elmira knows you by name."

Delaine smiled at her.

She said, "And I know Rachel, of course. A very nice lady."

"She is, indeed," said Delaine. He moved to include Teale as he said, "Anything new?"

"Not in that quarter," said Teale.

"In some other?"

"Just town gossip." Teale waved at the smoke rising from the ashtray and reached for his glass. "I don't know if you know of this fellow named Cunningham who's been staying in town."

"I've met him a couple of times when he's been out looking at the countryside. He let on that he might be interested in buying some property."

"'Let on' might be all there is to it."

"Oh?"

"He seems to have run out of money." Teale glanced at Elmira, as if for confirmation. "He owes for his room, his lady friend's room, and all of their meals. Now that I think of it, I believe Max Brundage and I talked about them the first time you came here."

"I believe you did."

"Yes. And I can't say that the woman was treated very well, as it terms out. The hotel owner told her that her rent was past due, and she packed up and left. She pawned some jewelry in order to raise the travel money. She left on the train."

"And what about him?"

Teale shrugged. "He's trying to keep up a good front. Smiling. He says he's waiting for his ship to come in. Still smoking tailor-made cigarettes, but it's not clear how long he can live on credit."

Delaine grimaced. "I'm glad I'm not in a situation like that."

"So am I. And the hotel owner, Sullivan, is kind of stuck. If he puts him out in the street, he stands to lose everything, but if he keeps him on a while longer, he might or might not get something for his trouble."

"Too bad for him."

"Yes. As I read once, when a man who throws money around goes to the devil, he takes others down with him."

Delaine swallowed. A glass of beer might not be bad, but he didn't want to stay that long.

"Anything else today?" asked Teale.

"You must have been reading my mind. I already understood there were no messages for me, but I was wondering if I might send one to The Blue Iris."

Teale glanced at Elmira. "I think it can be arranged. How soon do you need it to be sent?"

"Not until evening, I guess."

"That should be all right. I'll take this bucket back when we're finished with it, and one of us can deliver the note. Do you have it written?"

"Not yet. I wanted to see if I could get it sent."

Teale stood up. "Here's pen and ink and paper. Go ahead and write what you need."

Delaine took a seat at the desk. He opened the ink bottle, dipped the pen, and wrote.

R–

I am in town and could see you at the same time and place as last time. I'll wait outside.

J

He folded the paper and handed it to Teale. "Do we need an envelope?"

"I don't think so." Teale lit a candle on a candle holder sitting on the desk and sealed the note with a few drops of hot wax. "None of that Wilkinson stuff," he said.

"Who's he?"

"The man who informed on Aaron Burr." When Delaine did not show understanding, he said, "A former conspirator in the secession plot."

"Oh."

Teale lowered his eyelid in a slow wink as he put out the candle with his finger.

———

Delaine took his time as he walked his horse to the Diamond Horseshoe Saloon. He told himself to make the drinks last and not have more than a couple. He was just killing time until after dark.

A few patrons were standing along the bar as usual on a Saturday. Brundage and Hall were seated at a table with the same three punchers as before, so Delaine made his way to the bar to order a drink for himself. As he approached, a man turned away from the bar. He had his hat set back on his head, and his blond hair and blue eyes were familiar. Delaine searched for the name and came up with it. *Wyman.*

"Ho," said the young man, stopping. "I know you." His face was flushed, either from a day in the sun or a while at the bar. He held his hand forward.

Delaine shook. "On your way?"

"Yeah. I've had enough. I've got things to go check on."

"I won't keep you, then."

"We'll have a drink next time." Wyman gave his winning smile, nodded his head, and walked away.

As Delaine waited for the bartender, he noticed the steer head, the buffalo head, and the antelope head, all staring ahead with dull glass eyes. Above the mirror, the raccoon and the prairie chicken appeared dusty and motionless.

Delaine ordered his drink and took it to the table to join his friends. It was not a bad way to pass the time. Maybe someone would sing a few songs.

———

DELAINE HAD BEEN WAITING outside The Blue Iris for about ten minutes when Rachel came out. She walked past him, away from the direction of the main street, and he followed.

When he caught up, she spoke in a low voice. "Let's walk out here to the edge where we can talk."

Darkness had gathered, and a quarter moon hung in the sky. The air was dry, with the scent of dust and sage. The plain landscape stretched to the west in the dim moonlight.

"It's good to hear from you again," she said. "I was wondering when we would do something about what we know."

He heaved a breath. "I get tied up at the ranch, and I don't want to quit and come to town and have to wait. I also keep thinking that something related is going to come up, out there by Melworth's. Do you know when the deputy is supposed to come to town?"

"He's supposed to be here on Monday," she said.

"That's good. I'll see when I can get to town, and then we'll sound him out."

"We?"

"I suppose I will. We'll see how it goes."

"And the papers are safe in the meanwhile."

"I'm sure they are. Mr. Teale didn't say a thing about them. By the way, I met Elmira. Very pleasant."

"Yes. The type of person who seems like you've known her a long time. Someone who can be trusted, I think."

"I believe both of them are. Teale likes to use the word 'discreet.'"

"It's a good word, don't you think?"

He put his arm around her waist. "Yes, it's a very good word."

9

HALL HAD DROPPED A CROCKERY COFFEE MUG AND WAS sweeping up the pieces. He said, "I'm sorry I did that, Leo."

"Don't worry. I've broken one or two myself. That's why we have tin cups and plates for the chuck wagon. And they don't weigh as much."

Hall said, "It's not the first one I've broken. Several years back, when I was still at home, I dropped a crockery mug that had belonged to my grandfather. It broke clean into two pieces, and it had a double wall. Interesting to see. But I sure felt bad about breaking it." He set another cup on the table and poured himself coffee.

Rawlinson said, "I know there's still a couple of horses out there, but I'd like to put in another good day at working with the horses we've brought in. Then, when you go out to look for the others, you can keep your eyes open for anything irregular."

"Which reminds me," said Brundage. "I did see a dead cow on Thursday, over on this side, between the

Six Mile's deeded land and Melworth's, on public land. It was a Hereford, been dead for a while. Might have died in the winter but might have died from somethin' else. It was layin' on its left side, and I couldn't see a brand."

"No telling," said Rawlinson. "There's a lot of different things can kill a cow. Thanks for letting me know."

Brundage gave a small shrug and a tip of the head.

Hall said, "I'll be ready to go as soon as I drink my coffee."

Monday, Delaine thought. This was the day the deputy was supposed to be in town. He would like to put in a good day of work and then see about a way to go to town.

———

DELAINE WAS BRUSHING his second horse of the day when a rider he did not know came galloping into the yard. The man was lean with a sunburned hook nose and a mustache that looked like two strands of manila rope. As he came to a stop, his horse bunched under him and the dust caught up. He said, "Where's Leo?"

Delaine pointed with his brush. "He's in the round pen, riding a horse."

Hall came around the back of a horse he was working with. "What is it, Carl?"

The man spoke between quick breaths. "There's a dead man out there. About a mile north. Not far from your fenced pasture."

"I'll tell Leo. Somebody needs to go to town. I don't know if the deputy's there. If he isn't, someone needs to send word on the wire."

"I can't go. I need to go back and tell George."

"I'll tell Leo and see if he wants to send someone. I suppose one or more of us should go out and keep watch on the body."

"I don't know," said Carl. "But I need to go back and tell George. He's said all along that somethin' was goin' to happen."

"Go ahead," said Hall.

Delaine continued brushing the horse, a shiny bay. He put on the double blanket, hefted the saddle, and settled it into place. He went around to the other side to be sure everything was clear, then came back and drew the cinch. He ran the latigo through the ring three times and poked the spoke through a hole. After buckling the rear cinch, he went for the bridle. The horse took the bit, and the headstall went on without any trouble. Delaine was leading the bay away from the rail when Hall and Rawlinson came walking from the round corral. Rawlinson was leading the brown horse he had taken to ride.

Delaine waited for them to come to a stop on the hard-packed earth of the ranch yard. He wondered if he should offer to go for the deputy, but he could see displeasure on the boss's face, so he waited for him to speak.

"I'm sending Max to town. He should come back with someone—if not the deputy, maybe Galen, the marshal. If they don't bring a wagon, I suppose I should offer one. Meanwhile, I think you and Jerry should go out there, find the body, and stay with it." He heaved out a short breath. "Always somethin'."

Hall said, "No idea who it is, of course. We'll see. I would think that if it was from someone out here, Carl would have known."

"You'll find out," said Rawlinson. "Whoever it is, nothing is going to change that."

Delaine waited for Hall to get his horse ready, and the two of them rode out with the sun at their backs.

"I won't ask you if you have a hunch who it is," said Hall.

"I don't," Delaine answered. "If I did and I was right, I think I would feel guilty. If I did and I was wrong, I think I would still feel bad."

"I'd like to say I hope it's someone we don't know, but I think it's better not to hope anything. Like Leo said, it's already happened."

Delaine kept an eye out for birds floating in the sky, but he did not see any. Maybe the cool morning was keeping the scent down. On warm fall afternoons, he had known magpies to settle on a deer in the time it took him to fetch his horse.

The land rose and dipped in gentle swells, and a faint breeze from the east drifted across. Delaine was sure they had come more than a mile, and he wondered how much they were going to have to ride around, when Hall said, "Over there."

A small patch of white showed in the grass. The two riders approached at a walk, the horse hooves thudding on the prairie sod. More of a human form became visible.

A man in a brown herringbone jacket and wool pants lay face-up with his left arm flung out. He had wavy brown hair and a light-brown mustache, and the rosy complexion had faded from his face. A red spot about six inches around appeared on his white shirt.

"Cunningham," said Delaine.

"It sure is."

Delaine did not see a hat or gloves or any personal

items lying around. "Looks like someone just dumped him here. Or took him here and shot him."

"It's better not to move him or try to guess."

"Oh, no. Leave him as he is." Delaine nudged the bay a couple of steps closer. "He's not wearing the ring that he seemed to show off. A gold ring with a blue stone."

"I remember seeing it."

———

DELAINE AND HALL sat in the shade of their horses for more than two hours, not saying much. The sun was nearing its high point when a figure came riding over a rise in the south. Delaine and Hall stood up and waited.

The rider was too big to be Brundage and too wide to be Rawlinson. He was on a large brown horse that kept slowing and had to be urged on.

"Looks like Engel," said Hall.

"I don't know him."

The horse slowed for the last twenty yards and came to a stop on its own. The rider rose in the saddle, swung his leg, and lowered himself to the ground. With reins in hand, he turned to face the two ranch hands.

Delaine guessed him to be Rawlinson's age or a little older, between forty-five and fifty, as he had a bristly mustache that was beginning to grey and a midsection that was beginning to hang over his belt. He wore a six-gun on his hip and a badge on his leather vest. He had a perturbed expression on his face as he took off his riding gloves. He peered at the body and came back to Delaine and Hall.

"Do you know who he is?"

"A man named Cunningham," said Hall. "He's been staying in town at the hotel."

The deputy shook his head. "Don't know him."

Delaine said, "He came out this way a couple of times. When he talked to me, he said he was looking at property."

The deputy leveled his grey eyes. "I don't know you."

"Jess Delaine. I work here at the Six Mile."

"Deputy Engel, Converse County Sheriff's Office." The deputy gazed at the countryside. He said, "We aren't too far from Barton Melworth's ranch, are we?"

Delaine's pulse ticked. He had already considered that Cunningham was the unnamed blackmailer, but he had the sense that he had to be cautious with this deputy.

Hall said, "No, we aren't. His headquarters are north and east of here, maybe two miles."

"That's good," said the deputy, still looking outward. "He's someone I can talk to. He might be able to tell me something about people who come and go out here."

"I didn't know how well you knew him," said Hall.

"I've known him for a while, like I've known others. Stay on friendly terms." The deputy brought his line of vision back, as if it was a practice of his to bear down on witnesses. "Does either of you have any idea of why someone would want to do harm to this man you call Cunningham?"

"I don't," said Hall.

Delaine admitted to himself that he did not know anything for sure, and he thought that if he blurted out his suspicions, the deputy might repeat them to Melworth. "Neither do I," he said.

"That's the way things often are," said the deputy. "But sooner or later, someone knows something."

Delaine said, "One thing we noticed is that this man is missing a ring we had seen him wear. Sort of a flashy thing, gold with a dark-blue stone."

"That's something I'll keep in mind." Engel walked to the body, squatted, and studied it without touching it. He stood up, walked around, and, leading his horse all the while, returned to the spot where Delaine and Hall waited. "Looks like someone's been in and out of here on horses. I saw what looked like a spray of blood on the grass. When we load him into the wagon, we'll see if he bled here. My hunch is that someone took him out here on horseback and shot him. Or shot him and took him out here on a horse. Either way is easier than a wagon, and I don't see any wheel tracks."

"Do you have a wagon coming?" Hall asked.

"Your boss told Max to hook one up. I expect him to be here in a while."

———

WHILE THE THREE ranch hands loaded the body, which had gone stiff, the deputy stayed at the site and studied the ground. When he joined them at the wagon, he said, "Looks like he bled here."

"Any idea when?" Hall asked.

"I'll let the coroner determine that. We'll have the county coroner come in for this. But my guess would be sometime in the night or early morning."

"Too bad," said Hall.

"They all are," said the deputy. "I've seen a lot of

it." He turned to Delaine and said, "What did you say your name is?"

"Jess Delaine."

"I know a man in Douglas named Delaney."

"They're two different names."

"Uh-huh. Did this fellow Cunningham come out here by himself? How did he get here?"

"The first time I saw him, the three of us were fixing fence. He was driving a buggy and had a younger woman along with him. I understand that she has since left town. The second time, he was in the same buggy, which I assume he rented in town, and it was being driven by a man named Steven Reed."

"I know him."

"Cunningham said that Reed knew the country and was showing him around."

"I'll talk to Reed." The deputy turned to Brundage. "Ready to go?"

"Should be. I'll go with you as far as the ranch. I've already been to town once today, and Leo says these two can take the wagon in and back." Brundage's nostrils moved, and his chest went up and down.

"What else?" said the deputy.

Brundage said, "That woman who was with him. I think she was just in it for the money. But when that was all gone, she left."

"I'll find out about her, too."

———

HALL DROVE the wagon around in back of the barbershop. News had spread since Brundage's visit much earlier, so it did not take long for men to gather and watch as Hall and Delaine moved the body onto a table inside. The small crowd followed, and Sullivan, the hotel proprietor, kept himself in front. His red hair was neat and in place, but his face was flushed.

He said to the deputy, "This is too bad. And not just because he owed me a great deal of money. He was a visitor here in town, but he was here for over a month, so this is something that happened to someone from here."

"How much did he owe you?"

Sullivan cleared his throat. "I don't have a precise figure, but it was quite a bit. There was a room for him, and one for his lady friend, and all their meals, and their drinks. Also his cigarettes, and chocolates. Things we keep on hand for the convenience of guests." Sullivan's corduroy vest swelled as he took in a breath.

"When did she leave?"

"Last Friday."

"How did she leave?"

"On the train. She pawned some jewelry with Ambler so she could pay the fare."

"Where's he? I'd like to talk to him."

A man Delaine did not recognize came forward. He was of medium height, slender, in a dark suit, white shirt, and bow tie. He had dark hair parted in the middle and held in place with pomade. His dark eyes had furtive movement, and his stringy mustache twitched. "I'm Bill Ambler," he said.

The deputy peered at him. "What was the woman's name?"

"Evangeline Capps."

"Did she pawn some jewelry with you?"

"She came to my watch and jewelry shop. It's not a pawnshop *per se*, but she asked me if I could lend her some money if she left me some jewelry for collateral. So I lent her fifty dollars."

"Did she say she would be back?"

"They all do. You never know until they show up. I told her I would give her six months."

"But you're not a pawn shop."

"Not in any official way, but if someone needs help, and has something to offer as security, I sometimes see my way to it."

"I can imagine. How about Mr. Cunningham? Did he pawn anything with you?"

"It wouldn't have been a pawn, but, no, he didn't approach me. To tell you the truth, I thought he might, but he didn't come around, and then this happened."

"Then he didn't pawn a blue ring he was known to wear."

"No. But I think I know the ring you mean. I noticed it. I thought it might have been cobalt."

"Did he come into your shop?"

"He came in with Miss Capps. They looked at merchandise, but he didn't buy anything."

"I see. Thanks for telling me what you know. The sooner I can get information, when it's fresh, the better."

"I'm glad to help." Ambler made a partial bow and moved backward.

The deputy returned his attention to the hotel owner. "What else can you tell me, Fred?"

"I think this man had one dose of bad luck after another. He said his money was being tied up, which anyone could say, but I could see that he had had money and now had some turn of luck. Then his lady friend left him. She might not have been an angel in personality or conduct, but it was still a loss, and it must have hit him hard. Then this."

The barber had put a sheet over the body, but Delaine could feel its presence and the effects on others.

The deputy said, "What was this woman like—young and attractive?"

Sullivan answered. "Yes. Not a fashionable lady or what you would call a lady of society, but attractive, and quite a bit younger than he was."

"Did she have any other men come and see her?"

"Not that I know of. I think she was quite on her own when she left. She was done with him, from what she said to me, so I don't think there was anything for anyone to be jealous about, and as far as I could tell, he was all out of money. So I don't know why someone would want to do something to him."

"Thanks, Fred. It seems to me that you knew him at least as well as anyone else in town did, and there might even be things you don't want to say in front of other people, so there's a good chance I'll talk to you again."

"Very well. I'm glad to help, like anyone else. I just have to say again that this is too bad, and I'm sorry to see it."

"I'm sure we all feel that way."

The deputy's answer was so routine that Delaine wondered how many people did feel a sincere sadness for the man under the sheet.

Delaine and Hall walked out to the wagon in the alley.

Hall said, "As long as we're in town, we might as well stop in at the Diamond Horseshoe for a quiet drink. By the time we get back to the ranch, it'll be too late to do any work, anyway."

"No argument from me," said Delaine.

Hall drove the wagon around to the main street and parked it in front of the saloon. Inside, patrons were talking in groups of two and three, and the tone was not as casual as Delaine would have expected on a Monday afternoon. A man in a modest suit, who looked as if he might be a businessman, was talking to Galen, the town marshal. In passing, Delaine heard the man in the suit say, "He was from Rockford, Illinois."

Hall and Delaine each ordered a whiskey. Hall said, "You can feel it in the air. I was glad to get out of that room in back of the barber shop."

"So was I."

Delaine felt a hand clamp down on his right shoulder, and he turned to see the smiling face of the Slender Reed.

"Quite a little stir," said Reed. "I heard that a couple of Rawlinson's men brought the body in. Did you find it?"

"No, someone else did. We stood watch until the deputy came, and then the boss had us help with the wagon."

"Terrible thing," said Reed. "You know, I knew him."

"I remember seeing the two of you together."

"It was just a couple of days ago, maybe three, that I heard he was broke and his little woman was leaving him. Then this. Everything came down on him at once. You wouldn't have had an idea of any of it the day I went on a drive with him. He paid me for the day, and he paid for the buggy."

Delaine glanced away and saw Galen still in a conversation with the man in the suit, but the marshal's attention was diverted.

A large form came through the doorway, blocking the light and letting it show again before the man closed the door behind him. Delaine recognized the man as he came into the lamplight.

"Do you know him?" Reed asked.

"I've met him."

Milligan nodded as he moved up to the bar and ordered a beer. When the drink came, he took the glass, left a coin on the bar, and moved in Delaine's direction. "Afternoon," he said. He raised his chin and took a slow look around the barroom, and the lamplight fell on his sallow complexion.

"Good afternoon," Delaine answered. He noticed an expression on Reed's face as if he was waiting to be introduced. Delaine said, "Your name's Milligan, isn't it?"

"Yeah. We've met a couple of times."

"I remember. I just wanted to make sure before I introduced you. This man is Steven Reed. He manages a business here in town."

Reed tucked his chin and smiled. He shifted his drink to his left hand and held his right forward. Milligan shook.

Reed said, "I've got a rooming house. Better rates than the hotel. I've seen you in town more than once, so I thought I'd mention it."

"I'll remember it."

"Do you work hereabouts?"

"I work around," said Milligan.

"Oh. If you don't mind my askin', what's your line of work?"

Milligan took a drink from his glass of beer. "I help find people."

"Bounty hunter?"

"Not quite. I more often look for people who have gone missing. Most of the time, the family has offered a reward."

"Oh, I see. Runaways, kidnappings, or just disappearances?"

Milligan shrugged one shoulder. "Depends on the case. Sometimes the family doesn't know. They just know their loved one is missing."

As on an earlier occasion, Delaine noticed an unexpected high pitch to Milligan's voice and something like a sarcastic edge.

Reed said, "Then you're like the undertaker. You make money off of other people's misfortunes."

Delaine was impressed one more time with Reed's readiness to cross personal boundaries. But Milligan had his response.

"I don't take advantage of people, if that's what you mean. They've already decided how much they want to offer, and sometimes I can help them find what they've lost. On top of that, sometimes there's a party responsible, and if I happen to help cause them to be caught and punished, I'm doing a service to society."

"Well said. I hadn't thought about the point that they make the offer to begin with."

"Sure. Take for example the case of this kid from Billings, Montana. If that kid's father didn't have a thousand dollars, he wouldn't offer it. From what I understand, he's got a lot more, but that doesn't matter. Not to me."

Reed said, "I think I've heard of that case. Do you

think it has anything to do with the man they found dead out on the range?"

"What man?" said Milligan.

"Fellow named Cunningham. Stayed at the hotel."

Milligan shook his head.

"They found him shot dead. I doubt that he had anything to do with a kidnapping. It just occurred to me."

"What did he do?"

"Not much. He hung around the hotel for about a month like he was on vacation. Smoked tailor-made cigarettes, drank white wine, and played kootchie-koo with a young woman who up and left when he ran out of money."

"Doesn't sound like a kidnapper to me. Hard to hide a kid like that in a hotel. And he doesn't sound like a detective. They don't have any money to begin with, and they can't afford to sit around like that and do nothing."

"Are you a detective?"

"I don't call myself one."

"Ha-ha. It's like they say. Do you call a man a dairy man if he squeezes just one little tit?"

"I grew up in Wisconsin. They've got a lot of dairies there. Ship huge amounts of milk to Milwaukee and Chicago. I'll just say, I've squeezed a few tits."

"I bet you have. Well, I'm going to move along. Good meeting you." Reed smiled at Delaine and Hall. "Good seeing you again."

Milligan spoke to Delaine. "I just stopped in for one. Seems like things are busy."

"This death has people talking."

"That'll do it." Milligan drank about half his glass and hitched his gun belt, which had the holster riding on his hip and seemed to help hold up his trousers. He squared his shoulders and looked all around the room with his eyes that seemed to have a permanent squint. He drank the rest of the beer, set the glass on the bar, and said, "So long."

"See you later," said Delaine. He saw that Reed had moved on and was engaged in conversation with two other men. It occurred to him that he could drop in on Rachel without having to send a message.

He turned to Hall, who did not seem impatient and who had suggested going to the saloon to begin with. "I hope you don't mind if I step out for a few minutes. I shouldn't be long."

"Go ahead," said Hall. "I'm not in a hurry."

Delaine tossed down his drink and walked out into the light. The sun was slipping in the late afternoon. He made his way to The Blue Iris and knocked on the door.

Surprise showed on Rachel's face as she drew the door back. "What are you doing here? I heard something happened, but I didn't hear much."

"Can I come in?"

"Of course. Reed's gone downtown to hear all the gossip. What is it?"

Delaine took off his hat as he stepped inside. In the dim light, he was glad to see The Last Supper still in place. Meeting Rachel's eyes, he said, "A man's been killed. Another rider found him out on the range near the ranch where I work, and the deputy came out. Our boss had me and another man bring the body in. We went to the saloon to have a drink, and Reed stopped to talk to us. When he went on to talk to some other men, I thought I could drop by here without any complications."

"I'm glad you did. Who is the man who was killed?"

Delaine realized he was still catching his breath after the fast walk. "A man named Cunningham. He had been staying at the hotel for about a month, like a man of leisure. He had a young woman for company. I saw the two of them out in the country on a buggy ride, and later I saw him and Reed in the same outfit. He said he was thinking of buying property. Then it seems that he ran out of money. He owed for his bill at the hotel, and his lady friend left him. Not long after that, he turned up dead. Someone shot him and left him out there."

"Oh, that's terrible." Rachel paused as if in thought. "You say the deputy came out. Did you talk to him?"

"About the dead man, yes. About this other matter, no." He waved his hand at the room. "I think this man Cunningham, who died, might have been the one who was blackmailing Melworth. I have no idea why, but it seems to fit. Meanwhile, the deputy is one of those who don't like to be told things they don't ask for, or that is to say, other people's suggestions. So I held my tongue, and when he said he knew Melworth and was on friendly terms and would go talk to him, I decided to wait to say something. I thought that if I told him what I knew, not to mention what I suspected on the basis of it, he would either ask Melworth about it or just tell him. Spill the beans."

"Oh, no."

"So I kept it to myself. When he asked us if either of us knew why someone would want to do harm to Cunningham, I said no, because in truth, I don't know. I just suspect."

Rachel had a downcast expression.

"I was careful about what I said to Reed as well, because he works for Melworth."

"How did the deputy happen to mention him?"

"We were out on the range between the ranch where I work and Melworth's. The deputy knew where we were, and he mentioned it that way."

"What do you think we should do, then?"

Delaine took a breath. "I think I'd like to find out more about Cunningham. I'd like the deputy to have time to talk to Melworth before I share my theory. He also might find out that someone killed Cunningham for a whole different reason. I don't expect it, but I have to keep my mind open. I can't just look for evidence to fit my theory, and I think there's more to be known about Cunningham. Well, of course there is. What I mean is I hope I can find out whether he has anything to do with our case. Then, if I my hunch is true, I have something more definite to present to the deputy. At that point, we could bring forward the box of papers. I just don't want Melworth to know where they are."

"Do you think the deputy would 'spill the beans'?"

"I don't know. Some of these cattlemen are cronies of the county sheriff, and I don't know anything about these people around here, but the deputy speaks as if he and Melworth were friends. I think we can wait to see what develops in the next couple of days."

"You say you want to learn more about the man who died. How do you think you can do that?"

"With the most discreet person I've met in this town."

"Mr. Teale."

"Yes. I think I might drop in on him at the café to

see if he's too busy for a word or two. My partner from the ranch is waiting for me at the saloon, so I had better not be gone for long." Delaine glanced at the door. "You never know when Reed will come back, thought he seemed to be coasting in easy water when I left."

"Always in a hurry, and putting things off."

"I don't think this situation is going to last all that long. Afterwards, we'll have all the time in the world."

She met his eyes. "One more minute now won't make a difference."

He moved close. "No, it won't."

———

DELAINE FOUND Teale in the company of Elmira. They were the only two in the café, sitting at a table drinking coffee.

"Well, it's you," said Teale. "Sit down. Would you like some coffee?"

"No, thanks. I can't be long."

Teale's calm eyes moved over him. "What's up?"

"I'm sure you've heard of what happened. The man who was found dead."

"Of course. Everyone's either at the barber shop or at the saloon, talking about it. I heard that one of you ranch hands found him."

"A fellow who works with another outfit did. It was close to the Six Mile, so Hall and I stood by and then brought the body in."

"Did you know the man?"

"I did. I'd met him a couple of times." Delaine kept his voice low. "What I'd like to know is how I might be able to find out a little more about him."

Teale's eyebrows went up. He glanced at Elmira and came back to Delaine. "Hoping to remain discreet, but is this related in any way to an item of confidence that passed between you and me in the recent past?"

"I don't know, but I think it might. I was about to say that if I knew more, I would know more. I'm getting ahead of my words."

"That's all right. I think I know what you mean. So you want to learn more about the deceased."

"Anything I can add to what I've heard. Of course, there's a lot to be known about him, but I don't have the liberty to go to Rockford, Illinois."

"Neither do I. Nor is Rockford, Illinois, going to come here. Though something similar may have happened." Teale glanced at Elmira.

Delaine shook his head. "I don't follow you."

Teale said to Elmira, "Do you think you could tell him anything?"

"Maybe something." Creases showed at the corners of Elmira's eyes as she gave Delaine a closed-mouth smile. She summoned a breath. "There was a person who came to see him twice at the hotel. She was a horrid-looking woman, and it was clear that she wanted money. She knew where he was staying, but she didn't dare go in through the front door, so she came around to the back. She asked me to help her, and I felt sorry for her. I arranged for her to talk to him once on each occasion."

"Do you think this woman was some kind of a former…"

"Paramour?" said Teale.

"That's a word," said Delaine.

"I don't think so," said Elmira. "It didn't seem like

it. I had the impression that they had been into something together and she thought she still had something coming."

"Do you know where she was from?"

"I would guess she was from some place in his past. At this point, she said she was staying in Ashton. She came and went on the train. She may still be there."

Ashton. That was the next town to the east of Glenrose. From Harrow, it was Willett, Glenrose, Ashton. Delaine said, "Do you think she went back there to stay a little longer and then come back here to try again?"

"Like I say, it was just a feeling, but it didn't seem as if she was going away without the thought of coming back, because I don't think she got the money she wanted, if any."

Delaine nodded as he took in the information. "Thanks for telling me what you could." To both of them, he said, "I'm sorry to be in a hurry, but I've got my partner from the ranch waiting for me."

"It's all right," said Teale.

Delaine spoke to Elmira. "Do you think you'll tell this to the deputy?"

"If he asks. Otherwise, I'll wait."

"Thanks again, to both of you." As he rose from the chair and began to walk to the door, he placed Ashton in his mind again.

He stopped and wheeled. Still keeping his voice low, he said, "What was her name?"

"Beatrice," said Elmira. "I never learned more than her first name. Beatrice."

"Thanks."

She gave her pleasant smile. "Don't mention it."

10

Night had fallen by the time Hall and Delaine returned to the ranch. Rawlinson was like many bosses who assigned work in the morning, so Delaine made his request in the evening rather than aggravate him the next morning.

"Sir, I'd like to ask for a couple of days off to attend to personal business. I hope it's not too much trouble."

Rawlinson did not answer for several long seconds. "I suppose so. Things aren't pressing yet, but they will be. I lost almost a full day with all three of you yesterday. If someone's got to take off, now's the time to do it. I can't have it during roundup. If you can't be here for that whole month, let me know ahead of time so I can find someone who can. When you hired on, I said I'd pay you for every day you worked. Yesterday was a work day. I sent you to town. You boys stopped in to have a drink, and I don't mind that. If I had had to deliver a dead man, I would have wanted a drink, too.

But if you're going to take two days now, it'll be without pay."

"I assumed that."

"And if you can't be here all the way through roundup and branding, tell me straight out so I can find someone else."

"Yes, sir. Thank you."

———

DELAINE RODE HIS OWN HORSE. The distance from Harrow to Ashton was twenty-five miles or a little more. If he cut across country from the ranch and picked up the man trail somewhere around Willett, he would save time and distance, but he thought he should leave word with Rachel.

He left the ranch early, but the day was underway when he reached town, and he thought he would catch Teale at a busy time. As he approached The Shamrock Café, he saw Dan with his donkey tied up in front of the general store. He assumed the boy was waiting for errands, so he rode up to him. The donkey's ears went up and forward. Delaine dismounted so he could speak in a low voice.

"Good morning, Dan. On the lookout for work?"

"Yes, sir."

"You know who I mean when I refer to the woman who is staying at The Blue Iris?"

"The one that people say might be a relative of Mr. Luna's."

"Why do they say that?"

"I don't know. Maybe because they're both Spanish. Or Mexican."

"Well, she's not his relative. I didn't know him, but I know her, and I'd like you to take a message to her."

"Written?"

"I think it would e easier if you just asked her if she could get away to talk for a few minutes. If you could ask her without someone else hearing, that would help. I'll go up the street and wait on the other side of the hotel, so I'll be closer when you have an answer."

"I'll do it." The boy left the donkey tied and took off at a fast walk.

Delaine waited a couple of minutes and followed on foot, leading his horse. He walked past the hotel, where he had seen Cunningham and Miss Capps sitting on the porch and Melworth sitting in the lobby. He wondered if Melworth had been there to watch for Cunningham, to intimidate him, to ask for a reprieve, or for some other reason. He wondered if, as others wondered in the case of Rachel and Mr. Luna, whether Melworth knew Cunningham. He may have just been reading the newspaper.

Delaine walked onward, passing the saloon and reaching the next block. The watch and jewelry shop was closed, as was the business that served as drug store, tobacco stand, and newsstand. Dan came back to the main street and met him near the corner.

The boy said, "She can see you. She said she'd wait out front."

"Thanks." Delaine handed the boy a dime.

"Thank you."

Delaine proceeded to the cross street, turned left, and saw Rachel standing in front of the guest house. The sun was shining on her bright blue dress and dark hair. She raised her hand in a wave, and she walked forward to meet him. They strolled west toward the edge of town.

"I didn't expect to see you again so soon," she said.

"I've decided to go on a trip. Is Reed on the lookout this morning?"

"He's still in his room, snoring. This is your horse, isn't it?"

"Yes. I asked for two days off so I can go to Ashton. That's twenty-five miles east of here."

They came to a stop, and her eyes met his. "Is there something new?"

"There might be. I found out from Elmira that there was a woman who came around a couple of times to see this fellow Cunningham. She seemed to be trying to get money out of him. She was staying in Ashton."

"And you're going to talk to her?"

"I hope to. She might be able to tell me whether there's any connection between him and Melworth. That's something I'd like to know before I go any further with the deputy."

"What kind of a woman is she?"

"Elmira described her as horrid-looking, so I'm prepared for something…unpleasant."

"Well, if you feel that you have to go—"

"This fellow Cunningham's death has been weighing on me. I don't know if it's related, but I feel that I need to find out. On one hand, I feel more drawn in than I agreed to. I could get out if I wanted —that is, get out of the whole thing. Or I could let this part go. But it seems that I have to do this, to know what I'm dealing with. I'm just an average fellow with no special means, but I agreed to do something, and I believe I can do some good. I just need to know where I am before I hand things over to the deputy."

She put her hand on his arm. "If you feel that way, you should give it a try, as long as you don't bring the danger onto yourself."

"I hope not to."

"I see that you're wearing a gun."

"Just a precaution. I don't wear it when I'm fixing fence and working with horses, and I tend to forget about it. I've got a rifle, too, but I've left it in the bunkhouse all this time. As for the pistol, I put it in my saddlebag when I ride out checking cattle or looking for horses, but if it's going to do me any good—that is, if I need it—I should have it on me. It's pretty normal for traveling."

"I know. I just hope you don't have to use it."

"So do I."

The sun was in her face, and her features were strained. "Two days?"

"That's what I plan. One day to go there, one day to return. I'll try to let you know something when I get back, but it may not be that same day."

"Won't you come back through town here?"

"It's shorter if I cut across country, but I'll try to make it a point to come this way."

"You don't have to."

"Maybe I'll want to." He moved the horse sideways to make a minimal barrier between them and the town, and he took her in his arms for a moment.

———

DELAINE RODE into Ashton in mid-afternoon. He recalled being there once before, almost fourteen years earlier, and seeing the town strung out on the road running north and south. The town did not have a direct crossroads. The trail from the west came in on the south side of town, and the trail going east led away from the main drag a few blocks to the north.

Delaine turned to the left, taking note of the general store on the east side of the street. Almost a block north, still on the right, he came to an establishment called The Drover. Thinking that it might be a good place to acquire information, he tied up and went in.

The saloon was airy and well lit, with steer heads and branding irons on the wall. The bartender was a red-haired man of about forty with a pale scalp showing through his thinning hair, bags under his eyes, and a beard trimmed to a narrow strap.

Delaine asked for a beer, and the bartender served it.

"Pay when you're done," he said.

Delaine took a drink. "I was in this town several years ago. It doesn't seem to have changed much."

"It hasn't." The bartender smiled. "Still a scarcity of women."

"That seems to be a widespread condition."

"Here and elsewhere. Going north? South?"

"I'm thinking of going west tomorrow. I've traveled enough for today. Where do folks stay?"

The bartender pointed to the north. "There's a place up here on the left, called The Drake Hotel. It's clean and not too expensive. Farther up, past the turnoff to the right but still on the left side of the street, there's a place called The Royal Hotel. It's a little less expensive, if you know what I mean. People stay there by the week and the month, but you can get a room for one night."

"That's good to know. Any place I should stay away from?"

"You mean to spend the night?"

"Either that, or to spend the evening and look at things."

"I don't know if you mean that you want to go to a place where you shouldn't, or if you want to make sure you don't go there, but it's all the same to me. There's a place called The Kismet. It's on a cross street between The Drake and The Royal, lookin' south. There might be women there. I don't go, so I don't know for sure. But there might be people bumming drinks or others looking to separate a fool from his money."

"Thanks for the warning. I'll heed it. By the way, can I buy a pint of whiskey here?"

"To take with you? Sure. Better to drink it in your room than to go to a place like that."

———

DELAINE LAY on his bed in The Drake Hotel, staring at the ceiling. After putting his horse in a stable and eating in a café across the wide street from the hotel, he was waiting for dark. Places like The Kismet might have hangers-on from the morning onward, but he thought his best chance would be when the creatures of the night began to gather.

When dark was showing outside the window of his room, he put on his hat and jacket, felt for the pint in the left pocket, and went out.

The Kismet was a dingy place. Unlike The Drover,

it did not have a high ceiling, so the tobacco smoke and lantern fumes hovered. The lighting was dim. The bar ran along the right side of the establishment, with card tables on the left and an aisle that ran straight to an exit in the middle of the back wall.

Delaine stood at the bar and ordered a beer. He saw a couple of women who had made up their faces and trussed up their bodies to look attractive, and he saw half a dozen men who ignored them, but he did not see anyone unsavory enough to be called horrid. Beatrice might not come to this place, but he had a hunch that someone who knew her might spend time here.

Delaine drank one glass of beer and ordered another. A few more patrons drifted in, but no one looked like the dregs. They had money to buy drinks. No one approached him to make conversation, bum a drink, or offer services. The customers drank, smoked cigarettes, rolled dice, played cards, swore, and laughed, but no one did anything out of hand or sinister.

Delaine signaled to the bartender, a man of about fifty with a hard face and a full head of dark hair, not to take away his glass. He walked to the back exit without staring at anybody, and he found a pissoir in a roofed passageway between the barroom and the separate low building behind it. These would be the rooms where men went with the women who worked in the night.

A woman who looked like a maid came out of the hallway that led back with rooms on each side. She was wearing an apron and carrying a bucket and a mop. She was about forty-five with straight dull hair, no makeup, and a slumped figure. She ignored Delaine and went into a room that must have been a supply room, for she came out with a two-gallon galvanized bucket and a rolled towel. He assumed she would put water in the bucket and take it to a room.

"Excuse me," he said. "I wonder if you could help me."

"No speakin' English." She looked at him for a second. She had dark eyes and a light-shaded complexion.

"*¿Habla español?*" he asked.

"*Sí.*"

He continued in Spanish. "I am looking for a woman named Beatrice. *Beatriz.* I think she is an unfortunate woman who is staying in this town. It is possible that I can help her."

The woman said, "She does not work here. If you want to talk to a woman here, you have to talk to her in the saloon and then come back here with her." The woman spoke all in Spanish, except for the word "saloon," which fit well into a Spanish sentence.

"I do not want to go to the room with a woman," said Delaine. "I want to find a woman in this town who is named Beatrice, or *Beatriz.* I want to talk to her, nothing more."

The woman looked him up and down. "You do not look like a friend of hers."

"To tell the truth, I do not know her. But I think she knows people I know, and I think I can help her."

"You are not family?"

"No. I could lie and say I am. But I am not. I think I may know someone that she knows, but I have to ask her to be sure."

"You have to go to the Royal." In Spanish, the word sounded like *Royale* in English.

"The hotel?"

"Yes. It is just a hotel. None of this, there."

"I am not looking for any of this tonight," Delaine said with a smile. "But here is this for you." He gave her a quarter.

Still in Spanish, she said, "Thanks to you, sir. Very good of you."

Delaine finished his beer and went out the front door. The pint was still riding well in his left coat pocket. He found the main street and The Royal Hotel, which he had ridden past earlier in the day. Now on foot, he went inside as if it was a regular destination.

A clerk with a thin neck and sparse mustache, who might have passed for a brother of Bill Ambler, the man with the watch and jewelry store in Harrow, had his feet on the desk and was reading a newspaper. He swung around and stood up, and with the newspaper still in his hands, he asked Delaine how he might help him.

"I'm looking for a woman named Beatrice. I was told she might be staying here."

The clerk folded his newspaper as he spoke. "I don't know what business you're on."

"No actual business. I think she might know someone I know, and I might be able to help her out."

The clerk glanced over Delaine's person and showed no response. "You can knock on the door and see if she's there. It's room ten, down the hall on your right." The clerk pointed at a hallway that led straight back into the building.

"Thanks."

"Not at all."

Delaine interpreted from his demeanor that the

clerk assumed that nothing illicit was going to take place; he might even hope that Delaine could help Beatrice pay her rent.

As he turned and walked down the unlit hallway, his eyes adjusted to the faint light. The first number he saw on his left was a three. Four was on the right, five was on his left, and so on until he came to ten, the second-to-last door before a person would step out the back door and into the alley.

He knocked on the door. The creaking of a bed was followed by footsteps and the turn of a latch, and the door opened. The features of a woman appeared in the subdued light. She had straight brown hair streaked with grey, muddy-brown eyes, and a splotchy face. A limp, dark-blue dress fell over a body that sagged but did not bulge in the middle. Her left hand held the door by the knob, and her right hand settled on the doorframe.

Her mouth moved. "What do you want?"

"I was hoping to find a woman named Beatrice."

"What for?"

"I would like to know more about a man named Edward Cunningham."

Her eyes relaxed and drifted over him, as if she might be looking for a badge. He had left his pistol and holster at his room, and he hoped he did not look intimidating.

"Where do you know him from?" she asked.

"I met him a couple of times in Harrow. The lady who works at the hotel told me about you and said you were staying here in Ashton."

"She's all right." The woman's chest went up and down as she took a breath. "You're not with the law?"

"No, ma'am. I'm a cowpuncher." He took off his hat.

She flicked another glance and said, "I guess you can come in." She stood aside and opened the door.

He stepped into a narrow room with a wall close by on his left and an iron bedstead along the wall at his right. Ahead on the left, a dresser stood with an oval mirror on a swivel frame. A single chair sat in front of a curtained window, and a nightstand sat between the chair and the bed. The only light came from a lamp on the nightstand.

"Go ahead and sit down," she said. She closed the door and sat on the bed.

He took a seat with his back to the curtains, and as his eyes adjusted to the light, he could see her well enough. She had a rough complexion with broken veins on her upper cheeks below her eyes, then brownish spots in the hollows between her cheekbones and her jaws. He saw spots on the backs of her hands as she put them together on her lap.

"There's a lawyer in this town named Cunningham," she said. "No relation."

"I didn't know that."

"So what do you want to know?" She seemed to be holding herself upright with a tenseness, and he noticed a roughness to her voice.

"I don't know what there is to know. That is, my question is more of a general one. By the way, do you care for any of this?" He took the pint bottle from his coat pocket and set it on the nightstand.

Her eyes followed the bottle with its amber contents. She said, "There are a couple of glasses on the dresser. I think you can reach them easier than I can."

He stood up and saw the glasses next to a glazed pitcher with daisies painted on it. One glass was right-side-up, and the other was upside-down with a faint coating of dust. He set the one that looked as if it had been in use close to her, and he set the other near him. He uncapped the bottle, poured each of them a couple of ounces, and handed her glass to her.

"Thanks." She cleared her throat and took a sip. She stared ahead, and her body lost a little of its tenseness. She said, "There was a time when a man giving me a drink might want to take advantage of me, but I don't think a young fellow like you would want to touch an old thing like me."

He wondered if more than fifteen years separated them, but the gulf was great. "Don't worry about that," he said.

"You're here on business of some kind. Does he owe you money?"

"Cunningham? No, I'm sorry to be the one to tell you, if you haven't heard it yet, that Mr. Cunningham is dead."

"No! What happened to him?"

"He was killed. Shot."

Her voice rasped. "The son of a bitch. I knew he would so something like that. The son of a bitch." She breathed with her mouth open, and he saw her uneven teeth, some of them decayed.

"I think I might know who you mean. Don't feel that you have to name names if you'd rather not."

"Name names! You don't know the half of it." She took a drink. "I know them both from way back, and they're both as crooked as a dog's leg. But Tick Mason is by far the worse of the two."

"Tick Mason?"

The woman opened her nostrils and lips as she said, in a contemptuous tone, "Melworth."

"The cattleman."

"Yes, the cattle man. the one who never earned what he has got, and had to pay off someone who threatened to tell on him."

"Cunningham."

"You call him that. I've got no great love for him, either, but he was not as bad. Tick Mason is a dirty son of a bitch." She turned her dull eyes on Delaine. "What part of their case are you interested in?"

"Only the part about where the money was going and why. My own interest is in a man named José Luna and a family member who would have been his beneficiary."

"I heard of Luna. He was the goose with the golden egg. I don't know if he ran out of money, too, or whether he just tightened up and didn't want to lend any more."

Delaine said, "That's yet to be determined. What I was most interested in knowing was whether Cunningham was squeezing Melworth for money."

"I should say he was."

"Then that would give Melworth a reason to have Cunningham done in."

"No doubt about that. The reason, anyway. And as far as whether he would do it, or have it done, which is more likely, I have no doubt there, either. Tick Mason never cared about anyone but himself." She drank from her glass.

"Anything you can tell me of your own free will might help."

"It's all one long, miserable story. From my view." The woman stared ahead, past Delaine.

"Like I say, I'll listen to any part of it you care to tell."

A breath went out of her, and she seemed to sink where she sat.

He noticed that her drink was almost gone. "Would you like a little more?"

She took in a breath and rose a little. "I could use it," she said. She handed him her glass.

He poured as much as before and gave the glass to her again.

"Thanks." She held the glass near her mouth, lowered it, and raised it again. She took a sip. Staring ahead, she said, "This goes back more than fifteen years." She seemed to need to start again. "I was never a pretty girl, just a plain working girl. I was a little over thirty years old and didn't know if I would ever get married. I was working for a well-to-do family in Chicago, taking care of their little boy. That was when I met Tick Mason. He took an interest in me, or pretended to, and bought me little things like flowers and candy and cheap jewelry. He was just sweet-talking me, but I didn't know it. While he was at it, he reeled me in all the way and took advantage of me— more for his purposes than anything else. I was sure later, but at the time, he had me pulled in so close I couldn't see much."

She set her lips together, swallowed, and took another sip.

Delaine waited.

"He introduced me to a friend of his, Tom Raymond, the one you know as Edward Cunningham. They knew each other in Rockford, Illinois, which is northwest of Chicago, just another town, nothing special in itself."

"I've heard of it."

"And there was a third friend, who went by the name of Bill Smith, but I didn't ever know what his real name was."

Delaine nodded.

"So after I had known Tick Mason for a few months, I found out that these three men were scheming to kidnap the boy I was in charge of and to hold him for ransom. Tick had me under control and used me to find out how to get into the house in the dead of night, where the boy slept, where the parents slept, and all of that. He promised me that no harm would come to the boy, who was named Charley, and I was already so taken in that I went along with it."

She took a deep breath, fortified herself with a drink, and went on.

"And so they did it. They took the boy and hid out in St. Louis, and through a complicated system of messages through Peoria and Springfield, they collected some of the ransom. But the private detectives and the police tracked them down. The bad part was that the boy had died and they had disposed of the body somewhere. The man who called himself Bill Smith was killed in the arrest. Tom Raymond was arrested, and Tick Mason got away. He took the part of the ransom they had collected, about ten thousand dollars, with him."

"And Tom Raymond went to jail?"

"He did. For more than ten years. They could never convict him for the full crime, because they never found the boy or the money, but they got him for extortion, the part where he sent some of the messages. They were able to prove that. They tried to get him to talk, but he wouldn't."

"And Tick Mason came out here, changed his name, and bought some land and cattle."

"That's right. He never cared about what happened to anyone else—not Charley, or Bill, or Tom, or me. He had no conscience, no sense of how anyone else suffered. Complete disregard."

"He seems to have hired a foreman with some of the same qualities."

"I've heard of him. I think Tom may have been more worried about him than he was of Tick. Because he had it over on Tick. He never squealed on him. He sat out his sentence, got out a little early on good time, and went to look for Tick. He thought he deserved his share. He found Tick and began to bleed him for money, and he went back to St. Louis and lived it up pretty well. But then either Tick ran out of money or decided he'd paid enough, and he cut Tom off."

"Quit paying him."

"Right. So Tom went to where he was living, to make the threat a little more immediate. After all, they could still take Tick in if they knew where he was."

"Whew." Delaine drank from his glass. "So how did you end up out here?"

She drew herself up with a breath. "It took me a while to find Tom after he got out. I never had found Tick. But I found out where Tom had gone to, which was St. Louis, what he had changed his name to, and where he had gone to after he left St. Louis. I understood that he had been spending his money almost as fast as he could get it, and he had a little hussy to help him."

"So he was almost broke when he was staying in Harrow, letting on that he was looking for property to buy."

"That's what it seems like. Gloating as he was hoping to take more. But I still felt like I deserved something. My life had gone to pieces. I had hit bottom. The guilt was as bad as a prison sentence, and I was never able to do anything more than get by. I knew Tick would never give me a dime, but I thought that if I could get something through Tom, I deserved it. So I tracked him down. To Harrow. The first time I saw him, he gave me a few dollars and told me I had to keep my mouth shut. The second time, he said everything was dried up and he didn't know when he would have money again. So I came back here, thinking I would try one more time before I went back to Illinois and started over, though to be truthful, I don't know what I'd do next."

"I'm sorry life has been rough for you."

"I brought it on myself. I didn't know better, but still, I let him take me in the way he did."

"You may have done some good by telling me what you have. I don't know how much I can do, but I hope someone can do something."

She let out a tired breath. "Sometimes I wonder if anyone can or will. If Tom was shot, I have no doubt as to who was behind it." She brought her eyes to bear on Delaine. "What can *you* do?"

"I don't know for sure. I have to watch my step."

"I'd say you should."

He took a drink from his glass. He felt sorry for the woman sitting on the bed with her sagging posture, bloodshot face, and bad teeth. "Is there anything I can do for you today?" he asked.

She raised her eyebrows and looked at the floor. "I wouldn't ask for anything."

"And I wouldn't want to do anything that didn't

seem right. But if you're having trouble with some-thing like your room rent—"

"I wouldn't take money from a man who came to my room. It wouldn't look right, even though I don't think that clerk would think we had done anything."

"What if I leave him something on my way out? Not as a tip, but to put on your bill."

She did not look straight at him as she gave a partial shrug. "If you wanted to. I don't think it would hurt. I can't pretend that I don't need the help."

He drank the rest of the whiskey in his glass and pointed at the bottle. "I'll leave this here."

"Thanks."

"And just so I can speak in proper terms with the clerk, do you mind telling me your last name?"

Her chest went up and down, and her eyes met his for a couple of seconds. "Lennox. Beatrice Lennox."

He stood up with his hat in his hand. "Very good, Miss Lennox. We may meet again. Either way, thank you for your cooperation and your courtesy."

"The same to you." She stood up and took a step toward the door. "I don't think I heard your name."

"I'm sorry," he said. "It's Jess Delaine."

"Very well, Mr. Delaine." She went to the door and opened it. "Goodbye."

"Goodbye to you. Thanks again." The door closed behind him as he walked down the hall.

The clerk stood up as Delaine walked into the reception area. Delaine handed him a five-dollar gold piece. "I'd like to contribute this toward Miss Lennox's room rent."

The clerk stared at the coin in his hand and gave Delaine an uncertain look. "Are you a family member of some kind?"

"Just someone who wants to help."

———

DELAINE ARRIVED in Harrow in the afternoon. He did not think he was fooling very many people at this point, so he rode to The Blue Iris himself, dismounted, and called out, "Yoo-hoo!"

Rachel came to the door, raised her hand in greeting, and made her way down the steps and across the small yard. "Did you have a safe trip?"

"Yes, I did. Shall we walk?"

"We don't have to if we don't talk loud. Reed's out."

"Good. I decided to come by on my own. I figured that by now, enough people had seen us together."

"He mentioned it. I let on without telling a direct lie, that I had met you since I came here."

Delaine shrugged. "Sometimes it's tiresome to keep up a pretense, and I hope we can resolve things before too long. But as I told the person in Ashton, I have to watch my step."

"Oh. You were able to find her."

"Yes, and in case you need to know for some reason, her name is Beatrice Lennox and she's been staying at a place called The Royal Hotel, which is a little more modest than its name." He paused for a couple of seconds. "She matched the description Elmira gave me. She looks like she's had a hard time of it."

Rachel nodded. "And did she tell you anything useful?"

Delaine kept his voice low. "She confirmed what I thought, that a certain party was blackmailing another.

It was for a crime they both took part in. I'll tell you the whole story when we have a little more liberty." He looked to each side. "I wanted to check in with you to give you a short version and to let you know I made it back all right."

"I'm glad you did. Thank you." Her eyes met his, and she smiled.

Still holding his reins, he gave her his left hand. "I hope this is good enough for the moment."

Her touch was assuring as she said, "It is."

"It's good to see you," he said. "I could even say refreshing, after meeting with that woman. She's not disagreeable as a person, just dreadful in her appearance and depressed in spirit."

"That sounds like enough."

"It was." He smiled. "It helps me appreciate your presence."

"Good."

———

DELAINE STILL HAD plenty to think through as he rode on the trail north out of town. He came to the area where the land began to open up, and he figured he was about a mile from the turnoff to the ranch. The sun was slipping into late afternoon, and the scattered cedar trees were casting dark shadows.

Two riders appeared on the trail ahead, coming his way. There was no avoiding them even if he wanted to, as the dry creek bed ran along the right side of the road and a grassy hill rose on his left.

His spirits continued to sink as he confirmed that the two riders were Vick and Rudy. Vick was riding the sorrel with a white star, while Rudy was riding the bay with dark, dull colors. They rode straight toward Delaine and met him with one on each side and not enough room for him to go through. They stopped and blocked his passage.

"You again," said Rudy, in his deep voice. "Why don't you stay home?"

"Why don't you? I have as much right to be on this trail as you do."

"Sure, you do."

Vick, on Delaine's left, laid his hand on the brown horse's bit. At the same time, Rudy swung his right arm around, past the head of Delaine's horse, and caught Delaine across the face. Vick held the brown horse while Rudy spurred ahead, dragging Delaine backward.

Delaine shook his feet from the stirrups to keep from being stretched, and he felt himself being dragged back across the horse's haunches, then slipping down and landing on the ground with Rudy on top of him.

Delaine scrambled to his feet, and Rudy came at him, spurs jingling. Rudy's hat had fallen away, and he had his head lowered, with his shadowy, sullen eyes looking for an opening.

His right hand came up and around, and Delaine blocked it. Rudy stepped forward with a left that hit Delaine on the jaw and jolted his head. Delaine stepped back, felt himself rubbing up against his horse, and stopped to regain his footing.

Rudy hit him two more times, and he fell with horse hooves shuffling near his head. He rolled over and came up onto his hands and knees.

"Look at you," said Rudy. "Like a dog. Pah. You know what you should do?"

"No."

Rudy had his big left fist doubled and was pointing with his right index finger. "The best thing you could do is give up snooping, pack up, and go somewhere else."

Delaine was pretty sure Rudy was referring to his looking into things on the range as he searched for cattle and horses. He did not think Rudy knew he had seen the line camp, and he was quite sure he did not know about Delaine's trip to Ashton. "I might do that," said Delaine. "But not today."

"You can't do it soon enough." Rudy leaned to one side and picked up his hat. Vick had let Delaine's horse go and had taken Rudy's horse by the reins, and he brought it around. Rudy took the reins, set them in place, and stabbed his foot in the stirrup. He pulled himself aboard, spit off to one side, and spurred his horse toward town. Vick followed.

Delaine reviewed what he thought he knew. He did not think Rudy had anything new on him unless it was his acquaintance with Rachel. Delaine had no way of knowing how much Reed told Melworth. For a moment, Delaine felt superior for what he had learned in Ashton, but he admitted to himself he might be way behind in other areas.

He gazed toward town. If he had not come back that way, he would not have met up with Rudy and Vick. Not today, anyway. Still, he could always expect one more confrontation with Rudy.

11

Hall cooked bacon and hotcakes for breakfast, and some of the bacon came out crisper than normal. Smoke and the odor of almost-burned bacon hung in the air. Rawlinson set out two new coffee cups, tan crockery mugs. He said he had gone to town to order supplies for roundup and had picked up a couple of cups when he was in the general store.

Delaine felt as if he had been gone for a long time. "Did someone break another one?"

"No," said Rawlinson. "But someone might."

When the men had finished eating and were drinking coffee, Rawlinson said, "There's still a couple of horses out there that we need to find and bring in. Max knows what they look like."

"A grey horse and a red one."

"Now that I've got all three of you again, I'd like you to go out and find these two if you can. That's one thing that I feel we're behind on."

The three hired men nodded. Brundage smoked

his cigarette with an expression of great thought and looked at his watch.

"And of course," said the boss, "keep an eye out for anything you might see about the Six Mile cattle."

———

DELAINE RODE the sorrel with a blaze and three white socks. He rode to the left of Brundage, while Hall rode on the other side. They headed north and west out of the ranch, and Delaine assumed they were going to the area where they had made their gather more than a week earlier.

The morning was cool, and grey clouds in the west suggested that the day might stay that way. Delaine was wondering how frisky the loose horses might be when he and his fellow riders topped a rise with a dip or bowl ahead of them. A dark horse stood by itself, not grazing. Delaine did not expect to see a horse so soon. At the same time that his mind was registering a horse, he saw that it had a saddle and bridle with the reins trailing.

He glanced at Brundage, who was peering straight ahead. Delaine said, "Looks like a ranch hand's horse, out early. Wonder if someone got thrown."

The lay of the land was such that the lower part of the bowl came into view as they rode forward and downslope. The riderless horse was halfway up the other side. The hooves of the three Six Mile horses swished and thudded as the bottom of the depression rose in view. In an oblong area where the grass was sparse, a man lay face down. He had blond hair and wore a tan vest and a light-colored shirt. A dark hat with a round brim sat on the ground a couple of yards away, with its crown up.

Closer, Delaine saw an ominous stain in the middle of the man's vest.

"Leo isn't going to like this," said Brundage. "Another work day gone to hell."

The horses slowed to a walk. Delaine had a premonition of who the man was. When the horses stopped about five yards away and the three riders looked down, Brundage spoke.

"Looks like the fella who spent the night a while back. The one who sang the song."

"Wyman," said Delaine. "Joel Wyman." He recalled the borrowed song about borrowed love.

Brundage said, "Jerry, it's your turn to go deliver the news."

Hall said, "Let me see first what there is to report."

"It's a man shot in the back," said Brundage. "Down in a hole where it looks like he was goin' to build a brandin' fire."

A small pile of dry sagebrush branches sat near a bare spot of dirt about twelve feet away from the dead man's outstretched hand. Closer to him, an iron rod lay on the ground. It was a familiar-looking object to Delaine, about five-eighths of an inch thick and sixteen inches long, with a rounded tip.

"That's a runnin' iron if I ever seen one." Brundage took in a long sniffing breath.

"It's a perfect layout," said Delaine.

"Almost too perfect," said Hall.

Delaine nodded. "That's what I was thinking."

"Well, I'll go. You two can stand watch."

Brundage shook his head. "Leo isn't going to like this."

WHEN DEPUTY ENGEL arrived on the scene in late morning, the clouds had cleared away and the deputy was beginning to perspire. He said Hall was on the way with the ranch wagon. Delaine wondered why the deputy had not hired a buckboard in town, but he knew it was not his place to ask.

The deputy had Brundage hold his reins while he walked around the scene and squatted here and there. Delaine and Brundage had brought in Wyman's horse, and Delaine had been holding its reins.

"And this is his horse?" said the deputy.

Brundage answered. "It's the one we found here, and I believe it's the one he had when he spent the night at the ranch."

"And how long ago was that?"

Brundage looked at Delaine. "Maybe a week and a half ago."

"Then he's been around here."

Delaine said, "I saw him once in town in the meanwhile."

"Any idea of where he was working, or if he was?"

"No. I believe he said he had things to check on. When he stayed at the ranch, he said he was looking for work."

The deputy frowned. "If he wasn't working at a particular place, then he could be out here doing what it looks like."

Delaine hesitated to express his opinion, but he went ahead. "As we were saying earlier, it seems almost too perfect. Like it was set up."

The deputy stretched to one side and scratched the back of his waist. "That's what your partner Hall said.

But until I know better, I've got to consider it as being, as a possibility, a case of someone getting caught when he was about to change a brand."

Delaine said, "But there was no calf tied up, and his coiled rope was on his saddle."

"I know."

———

DELAINE AND BRUNDAGE went to town with the body, after hearing Rawlinson's complaint that he couldn't get anything done. The boss seemed to take pride in making his civic contribution. All the time that they waited for the wagon, loaded the body, and headed back, Delaine wanted to ask the deputy if he had talked to Melworth. At last, when they came to the edge of town and the deputy was riding close, Delaine spoke.

"Did you get a chance to ask Melworth about the other man who was found out there—Cunningham?"

"Not yet. And now things are complicated. I've got two separate cases to work on. This second one seems more pertinent to Barton, but I can almost predict what he'll say. What every cattleman says. There's always someone out lookin' to steal their cattle."

They delivered the body to the same place as before. A smaller crowd had gathered. Delaine wondered whether the novelty had worn off or whether Cunningham's death was more interesting news than Wyman's.

Delaine and Brundage were folding the canvas tarpaulin they had used for covering the body when a distraught woman's voice pierced the air.

"Where is he? Where is he?"

The deputy came out of the back room of the barbershop and blinked his eyes.

A disheveled young woman spotted him and headed straight for him. "Where is he?"

The deputy held up his hand. "Where is who?"

"Joel. Joel Wyman." The woman had shoulder-length curly blonde hair that streamed out from her head. She wore a loose shawl and a flowing dress, both of a dark grey. She was slender, with a drawn face and watery eyes.

The deputy pointed with his thumb over his shoulder. "We've got him in here."

The woman went to push her way past. "I have to see him."

The deputy held his arm out to block her. "I think you'd better wait until he's been made more presentable."

She drew back with an expression of dread on her face. "I heard you found him dead. Is that true?"

The deputy closed and opened his eyes as he made a slow nod. "Yes, ma'am. He was found that way, out on the rangeland."

"Well, how did it come about?"

"I can't tell you with perfect knowledge, but it appears that he was shot in the back."

"Why? What for? Who did it?"

The deputy seemed accustomed to slowing things down. "I'm not goin' to jump to conclusions, but the deceased appeared to have the materials nearby to alter a brand."

"Alter a brand?"

"On livestock. Or he may have been preparing to brand an unbranded calf."

The young woman exploded. "Joel wouldn't do

something like that. But that's the way it is in this country. People jump to conclusions."

"I just said I'm not goin' to. I'm just sayin' what it looked like, and three other men saw the same thing."

"That's the way it is. A young man has a hard time getting by, and they just want to make it harder." She heaved a breath, then spoke again at her fast pace. "He told me he was trying to get a stake together, but it was hard because he didn't want to do anything wrong. We were going to get out of here."

"You and Joel Wyman?"

"Yes, and don't look at me that way. Me and Joel Wyman. We were going to get out of this lousy place."

"Were you related in some way?"

"We met. Well after my husband died."

"And you had plans."

"He was going to help me get out. We were going to go somewhere better. I hate it here, and he knew it."

"Better than here—this town, or this part of the country?"

Her face was filled with bitterness, and her voice slowed down. "This whole part of the country. I came out here to follow someone else's dream, and it killed him. Froze in a winter storm. I was a homesteader widow. I already hated the place. The loneliness of a land that stretched away in every direction, empty, with no trees, nothing but dry grass wherever I looked. I hated the wind. I hated the grasshoppers. I was afraid of the rattlesnakes and the coyotes." She sniffled and raised her head. "So I gave up. I was not as fortunate, or I didn't have what it took to stick with it, like some people who can prove up on a claim, sell it, and go on to something else. I just gave up. it was too much."

"Where have you been staying?"

"Here in town. In a flat over there on the back street." She pointed in the direction of Teale's lodging. "I came into town to see if I could make enough wages washing clothes to take me back home."

"Home," said the deputy. "Where is that?"

"Iowa. Joel was going to help me."

The deputy took a slow breath. "I'm sorry it's been so hard."

She stared at him with her bloodshot eyes. "Maybe you are. I don't know why you would care, if you did. At least I'm still alive. I can't say the same for Frank, the boy I married, or Joel, who was going to help me."

The deputy moved his head up and down in slow motion, as if he was waiting for her to talk herself out.

She caught her wind. "What are you going to do? About this?"

"I'm going to find out what I can."

"I hope you do more than just assume that things are what they look like."

Still unhurried, the deputy said, "I have to do things in my own way. Everyone wants to tell me what to do. But I've seen a lot more of this than any individual that comes into the case." The deputy looked her over. "By the way, what's your name?"

"Sienna. Sienna Wilson. Why do you care?"

"I might want to talk to you again about Joel Wyman."

———

As Brundage turned the wagon onto the main street, he said, "That woman's a real spitfire. I've got to say I feel sorry for the two men she outlived, not because of her but because they died, but I don't know if I would want to be the next one to take up her cause."

Delaine said, "It's hard to know what she's really like, based on that one meeting. We saw her at what I imagine was a bad moment for her. Very emotional."

"She might have a lot of moments like that. From what she said about hatin' everything in this country."

"It could be. I think I have a soft spot for women who suffer, even when I don't find them appealing in a personal way. I hope she goes on to something better."

"So do I." Brundage twisted his mouth to one side and the other. "You remember what Leo said about him not mindin' if someone has a drink after deliverin' a body?"

"I do."

"I don't think he would mind now. Do you?"

"I would hope not."

Brundage drove on and found a place to park the wagon near the saloon. As Delaine was climbing down on his side, he heard a voice.

"Mr. Delaine."

Dan was hurrying across the street from the direction of the barbershop. The donkey was nowhere in sight.

"What is it, Dan?"

The boy spoke in a low voice as Brundage lingered on the other side of the wagon. "You know the woman who was staying at The Blue Iris?"

"Of course I do."

"She told me to tell you, if I saw you, that she was staying at the hotel again."

"Thanks for letting me know." Delaine reached into his pocket.

The boy held up his hand. "She already paid me."

"Thanks."

"You bet." The boy headed back toward the barbershop, hub of the latest news.

Delaine met Brundage on the other side of the wagon. "I need to stop in at the hotel for a couple of minutes and talk to someone. If you don't mind, I'll catch up with you inside."

Brundage touched the lower part of his eyelid, near his cheekbone. "I'll keep an eye out for you."

Delaine went into the hotel, where the red-haired proprietor with a flushed complexion waited behind the reception desk. He had a knowing expression on his face as he raised his eyebrows.

"Yes, sir."

Delaine remembered the man's name. *Sullivan.* "I'd like to be able to speak to Rachel Valera," he said.

"You'll have to wait here."

"Of course."

Sullivan pulled his corduroy vest down from the bottom, brushed off his ample front, and turned away.

Delaine wandered away from the desk. A few minutes later, the sound of footsteps drew him around. The sight of Rachel in a bright blue dress sent a wave of happiness through him. He waited for her to come up to him where he stood with his back to the farthest corner of the lobby.

"I wondered if you would come to town," she said. "I heard there was another death."

"There was. And the deputy doesn't seem to want to go to the trouble of renting and driving a buckboard himself if he can get someone else to do the work."

"Did you get to talk to him?"

Delaine looked past her to see that no one was close by and listening. "Not much. Just like before. He hasn't talked to Melworth yet, and I don't want to give him something to take with him. So I think we have to wait." He met her eyes. "So you came back here."

She huffed out a breath. "I got tired of Reed. I wasn't doing any work except sweeping and dusting the front room and the kitchen, and it didn't seem as if anything new was going to happen there, so I told him I was going to move back here and look for work that paid. He said I could look for work from there, and I told him it wasn't the same. So here I am." After a few seconds she said, "Do you have an idea of what to do next?"

"I have one. I'd like for you to go with me to Ashton to see if we can get Beatrice Lennox to come here. We can get to the center of this thing and quit stalling around."

"Do you think she'll come?"

"I think we'd have a better chance if a woman persuaded her."

"Could be. When are you thinking of trying it?"

"Today's Thursday. I think we can to go Ashton and back on the train, all in one day, on Sunday. I've checked the schedule. I can take my horse to the next town west of here, catch the train there, and then take the train back to the same place. It will go past here both ways, and you and I won't have to be seen getting on and off together."

"That's an idea," she said, in a not-very-definite tone. "What if she comes back with us? Where would she stay?"

"I suppose she could stay here at the hotel if we wanted. It would cost us more. We could see if there's any room in the tenement house where Teale lives. Maybe you can ask about that, through Elmira."

Rachel's eyes widened and returned to normal. "I can ask. What about this man who just died? Do you think it has anything to do with this whole thing we're working on?"

"I have a feeling that it could be, but I don't know if that's just an easy idea. Two things happening close together doesn't mean they're related."

"I know."

He looked around, saw that no one was watching, and gave her a quick kiss. "You sound like the deputy."

"I'm not. I'm the girl you forget about for days at a time."

"I don't forget about you. If things work out, we'll go on a nice vacation together in a couple of days."

"Soot and cinders on the train."

"And all the lovely sagebrush flowing by."

She huffed a breath like before. "Whether it's that, or staying here, it's still better than being stuck at The Blue Iris."

———

DELAINE SAT on the right side of the car as the train headed east. All four of these towns—Kersey, Harrow, Willett, and Glenrose—were flag stops, and he did not think many people would be standing by. In towns where there was a train station, people came out to watch and to offer their services such as transportation and lodging. Harrow had only a ticket agent, who also operated the telegraph and the post office, and even he might not take the trouble to wait around.

Delaine was right. Rachel was standing by herself at the stop. The porter let himself down, put a box-like step in place, and stood by as Rachel climbed aboard.

Delaine had taken a seat where he could see that much, and his tension relaxed as she climbed the steps into the car. The porter followed with her bag. The train whistled and began to move.

Delaine moved over to the window to let Rachel sit on the bench beside him. They were the only two passengers in the coach.

"I left my horse in a stable in Kersey and had half an hour to spare," he said.

"I stood almost that long by the tracks."

"Well, we're on our way now."

"I hope it comes to something."

"So do I."

"You still haven't told me much about what the woman told you."

Delaine raised himself up to see that the porter had taken a seat at the front of the car. In a low voice, he said, "The story goes back more than fifteen years. This woman was working for a wealthy family in Chicago when she met M. His original name was different, and it also starts with an *M*. He sweet-talked her, to use her phrase, got into her good graces, and more. He introduced her to C and another fellow, and he manipulated her into being an accomplice from the inside so they could kidnap the son of this well-to-do family. They held him for ransom and collected something like ten thousand dollars, but the deal blew up. The boy died and disappeared, the third partner was killed, C was arrested, and M made off with the money. He came out here and re-established himself with a ranch and a new name. C put in his time in prison, and when he got out, he found M and took to blackmailing him. All this time, the woman's life has gone to ruin. She has been eaten up by guilt over what happened to the little boy. She found C and followed him here, thinking she deserved something for all of her suffering, but he had squandered almost everything by then. She was waiting in Ashton, thinking she would put the touch on him one more time, when I gave her the news that he was dead. She wants to get back to Illinois, but I don't think she has the means to do it or a way of getting by once she is there. Quite a sad case, but you could argue that she deserves it, and she admits she brought it on herself."

"And M, as you call him, has gotten away with all of it."

"So far."

"What if she doesn't come back with us?"

"Then it looks as if we went on a picnic, for anyone who knows we went together. We would be no worse off than before. We still have the mortgages and promissory notes, which show motive for Mr. Luna's death, but that is only circumstantial, as I think they say. And if all I have is this woman telling me that C was blackmailing M, that part is hearsay. So she could make a big difference if she came in person, and it could lead to someone holding him responsible for the original crime as well as what he might have done here."

Rachel looked straight ahead for a minute and returned her attention to Delaine. "Does she look as bad as Elmira said she did?"

"I think so."

"By the way, there is nothing available in the building where Mr. Teale lives."

"Thanks for finding out. We'll see how we fare."

———

THE TRAIN STOPPED at the small station in Ashton, on the north side of town. Delaine carried Rachel's small bag along the east side of the street, in the shade where there were buildings. They stopped at the café across the street from The Drake Hotel and went in.

After a late breakfast of ham and eggs and toast with rhubarb jam, they went out. Delaine took them across the street and north to The Royal Hotel.

The same clerk was on duty, seated at the desk and making notes in a ledger. He set his pen aside and looked up with his mouth closed but dropping. His eyes went to Rachel, and it occurred to Delaine that the clerk might expect him to ask for a room in the middle of the day.

"Yes, sir?"

Delaine met his eyes, which, if not insolent, were non-committal. "We would like to visit with Beatrice Lennox, if she's in."

"She might be. Let me see." The clerk walked down the hall, rapped on a door, spoke a few words, and came back. "Go ahead. It's room ten, down the hall on your right."

"Thanks." Delaine wondered if the clerk was being discreet in not recognizing that Delaine had been here before.

Rachel held his arm as they walked down the dim hallway. Delaine stopped at the same door as before and knocked.

The door opened, and the woman appeared. "It's you," she said.

"Yes, and I brought a friend with me. Rachel Valera." Delaine motioned with his hand. "Beatrice Lennox."

"What do you want?" said the woman.

"We'd like to talk for a few minutes."

The woman's eyes roved over the two of them, and she stepped aside. "I suppose so."

They went into the narrow room. Delaine took off his hat and remained standing. Rachel sat on the chair, and the other woman sat on the bed.

She had not changed in appearance. Her face was still a wreck, and her straight, dull hair did not look as if it had been washed in some time. She wore the same limp dress that fell over her sagging body.

"What do you want today?" she asked.

"We would like to ask you to come with us to Harrow."

"Oh, no."

"It would help a great deal."

"I can't do it. I only went there before to talk to Tom, and even then, I had to hide out."

"You can stay out of sight again. No one has to know who you are. You can stay with Rachel, or you can have a room of your own. We'll pay for your stay. Meals as well."

The woman's eyebrows drew together. "Why are you so willing to pay for everything?"

"The family of a relative of Mr. Luna gave us some money to find out what happened. Expense money. Your room and board for a couple of days won't be much."

"And train fare."

Delaine shrugged. "Still not much."

"I can't." The woman shook her head.

Rachel leaned forward and put her hand on the bed near the woman. "You can do some good," she said. "We want to clear up what happened to Mr. Luna and his nephew, and the sheriff's office would very much like to know why someone would have a reason to harm Mr. Cunningham."

"I don't trust Tick Mason."

Delaine said, "We'll keep you out of sight. If you want, we'll ask the deputy to put you under protection. I think the man you mentioned will be taken into custody so soon that he won't be able to do anything."

"This place is bad enough. That place is worse. I'll be stuck there."

"We'll buy you a ticket back."

"To be stuck here. I don't even want to be here."

Delaine took a deep breath. He had thought of this possibility, and he did not know how much it would cost them in the end, but he wanted to do everything he could to follow through. "I'll tell you what," he said. "We'll buy you a ticket back to Illinois. We'll pay any rent you have here, and when we're done in Harrow, we'll get you a ticket to Illinois. I don't like to make money the main consideration, but I can offer that."

"I don't know what I would do when I got back there."

Rachel leaned forward again and took the woman's spotted hand. "Look. I don't know everything you have been through, but I know you have been through great guilt and sadness because of what happened to the little boy."

"I deserved it. It was my fault."

"I can't tell you about that. But I lost a child of my own. A little girl. I do not think it was my fault, but I carry the sorrow and always some measure of guilt. I am sure it is only a portion of what you have felt. But this could be your chance to do something right. What was the little boy's name?"

The woman seemed to freeze, staring ahead with

her mouth partway open, until she said, "Charley. I loved him like—" Tears started in her eyes, and she broke down in a sob. She raised her head, sniffled, and said, "I'm sorry. I'm sorry for everything."

Rachel patted her hand. "Take a minute to think about it. You could do some good."

"I was never found out for my part in it. I could be now."

Delaine said, "All we need is for someone to tell the deputy that Melworth had a reason to do harm to Cunningham. There's enough here that they don't have to go back that far to lock him up. They'll want to keep him here. All they need is a good reason."

"Tom never told on him, and he, Tick, wouldn't tell on someone else. That's the way they are. Unless he knows someone told on him."

"We'll keep you out of sight, and I'll make sure the deputy knows how important it is to keep you anonymous."

"What if he goes to trial?"

"It will be for crimes here, and you'll be back in Illinois by then. I'm sure they'll have him for more than one thing here."

"That's the part I don't like. That Tick could get back at me."

"He doesn't have to know you were here."

"I don't know. I have to think."

Rachel patted her hand. "Take all the time you need."

Delaine felt a relief. He was afraid Rachel would try to play on the woman again and plead with her to do the right thing for Charley, but Rachel knew her own way.

After a long moment, the woman rose up a little

and said, "I'll do it. I'll stay there two days, and then I'll leave for Illinois, no matter what. If no one talks to me by then, or if no one wants to listen to me, I will have done my part."

"It's a deal," said Delaine. "We'll get a name for you."

"How about Mary Hamilton? It's a name I've gone by. And Beatrice Lennox isn't my name anyway."

———

NIGHT HAD DRAWN in dark by the time Delaine made his way back to Harrow from Kersey. He tied his horse in front of The Brookfield Hotel and went in. The clock behind the desk showed a little after ten.

Sullivan, the proprietor, put his hands on the counter, raised his eyebrows, and said, "Yes?"

Delaine said, "Does the deputy sheriff stay here when he's in town?"

The man's flushed face showed surprise. "Well, yes, he does."

"Would it be possible to talk to him now?"

"It might be, if he was here. But he isn't. He's gone back to the main office, and I don't expect him in town again for a couple of days."

Delaine felt as if everything went out of him at once—his breath, his energy, his hope. He picked himself up. "Did he learn anything new before he left?"

"Not that I know of." Sullivan gave Delaine a close look. "You're one of the men who helped bring in Cunningham, aren't you?"

"Yes, I am."

"What a terrible thing to happen. It has people worried."

"I believe the deputy said he was working on two cases. There was the one about the young fellow named Wyman as well."

"Oh, yes. Him. To be sure, he's interested in them both." Sullivan tipped his head side to side in a slight motion. "I don't know what else to tell you."

Delaine said, "Well, I wonder if I could see Rachel Valera if it's not too late."

"Oh. I suppose I could see. Wait here."

Delaine moved away from the desk. The proprietor came back within a few minutes, and Rachel was not far behind.

When she met Delaine, she said, "Let's go out where the air is fresh." They walked to the door without touching.

Outside, the town was quiet around them as they stopped on the porch. Their hands touched. Delaine said, "I trust that you got Miss Hamilton settled in her room."

"Yes, I did. Right next to mine."

"That's good."

"She still has about half of the bottle you bought for her."

"That's good, too." Delaine looked around. "I asked Mr. Sullivan for the deputy, and he said he went back to the sheriff's office and won't be here in town again for a couple of days."

"Oh, dear."

"I didn't get an idea of whether he would be here early or late in the day on Tuesday."

"So we just sit here."

"I think so. Sit tight. I need to go back to the ranch

and report for work. Sullivan said he didn't hear anything new from the deputy. I'll see if there's anything new out there, but I don't expect it."

"When will I hear from you again, then?"

"On Tuesday. I may not be able to get in here until late in the day, or evening, but I'll look for you as soon as I do."

"All right." She put her hands in his. "This seems to be taking forever."

"Longer than I ever expected. I just hope the deputy is cooperative."

"So do I." She tugged at his hands and relaxed. "I think I had better go in. I feel that I need to be there if Miss Hamilton needs something."

"First this," he said, and he drew her close.

———

DELAINE DRANK his coffee at the end of breakfast, waiting for the orders of the day.

Rawlinson said, "I feel caught up again with the horses you boys brought in on Friday. Max and Jerry, I'll let you work with those two, and then go on to what others you think need it." He turned to Delaine. "Jess, I think I'll have you go out and take a look at things again. Finding that dead man with the running iron didn't do me any good. It may have been set up and it may not have been, but I still have a feeling that something's not right out there. Call it a hunch or call it a suspicion, but I'm not wrong very often."

Delaine thought the boss was giving him these assignments even when he knew that Rudy had picked a fight over his riding out and looking things over. Delaine had not told anyone at the ranch about his more recent encounter with Vick and Rudy, but he was sure that Rawlinson understood that Melworth's men were hostile to Delaine's surveillance. Delaine suspected that the boss thought he was getting ready to move on and that he thought he might as well get as much of this kind of work out of Delaine as he could.

"I'll do it," he said. "Do you want me to ride out to the north and the west again?"

"Wherever you think you've got the best chance of seeing something."

"Good enough. I'll see what I can do."

———

DELAINE RODE A DULL, yellowish-brown horse from the ranch. He knew that stock detectives and running-iron men often rode dark horses, but that was for night work. The bay he had ridden a couple of times was dark but shiny, and it could attract attention from a distance.

He took his time and did not ride in a straight line, and by late morning he had arrived in the area of breaks and canyons where he wanted to look. He remembered the way he had taken in and out the day he had seen Rudy at the line shack. The name of the area went through his mind. *Broken Horn.*

Although he couldn't be sure about what happened to Wyman, it seemed as if everything crooked led back to Melworth. For all Delaine knew, Melworth's men could be moving cattle and using the line camp even if they didn't have livestock there.

Delaine paused to watch his back trail, then followed the passageways and came to the ridge he had looked over on his previous visit. He dismounted and made sure his pistol was riding on his hip. Trailing the horse behind him with the reins loose, he took his time to climb the slope. As he had learned to do in deer hunting, he paused to catch his breath and take off his hat before he crept the last few inches and peered over.

A grey horse was tied in front of the shack. Delaine sank back. It could be the grey horse he had seen Rudy riding before, once at a distance and once closer, but he was not sure. Delaine raised his line of sight again. He thought it was the same horse.

He rose and sank back a few times until he saw motion at the front door. He held still. A man came out of the cabin, said something over his shoulder, untied his reins and checked his cinch, and mounted up while the door closed. It was Rudy for sure, with his dark hat and hunched shoulders. He rode away without looking up and around, and Delaine let out a breath of relief.

The same sorrel horse was in the corral as before. Delaine assumed Sorensen was in the cabin, but he thought he would wait around to see for sure. He resumed his pattern of looking up over the edge every minute or two.

His pulse jumped when the door opened again. A person with a head of light-colored hair stepped out into the sunlight. Because of the angle from which he looked down, Delaine could not tell how tall the person was. He thought it might be Miss Capps. He was trying to make sense of that possibility when Sorensen came out of the shack. That made sense. Sorensen followed a few steps behind the light-haired person, who was shorter. Delaine thought it might be a boy. It was a boy, who went through the motions of undoing his pants and stood in the posture of taking a pee. A tingling sensation went through Delaine's scalp, and he felt as if the interior of his head was expanding. He understood what he saw, and he searched his memory for the black letters he had seen beneath a blurry photograph on a white poster. A boy's name. *William Harris Banks*.

12

———

Delaine had a hard time keeping his knowledge to himself as he sat through the evening meal at the Six Mile bunkhouse. He recalled phrases he had read in stories, such as "He was beside himself" and "He could not contain himself." He was sure the boy he had seen in Broken Horn Canyon was the missing boy from Billings, the object of great interest for people like Milligan and perhaps Joel Wyman. The knowledge welled up, like a pot of chokecherry jelly at a rolling boil. Delaine felt that if he did not say something, he would erupt.

At last he said, "I saw something today that I think I should tell the deputy about."

"Not about rustling?" said Rawlinson.

"No." Delaine had already given his report about seeing nothing out of order regarding livestock. "It's not about cattle, but it might be related to some of the other shady things going on."

"Oh."

"The deputy is supposed to be back in town tomorrow."

"Then I suppose you should go."

———

DELAINE SADDLED his own horse for the trip to town. The other men were working with their first horses of the day and did not pay him much attention when he brought his rifle and scabbard out of the bunkhouse and buckled the straps to his saddle. With his six-gun on his hip and the rifle under his left leg, he set out for town.

———

NOT MUCH ACTIVITY was stirring on the main street when he turned his horse in at the hotel. The man who ran the general store had set a barrel of brooms out on the sidewalk, and a saddled horse was tied in front of the café. He tied his horse and went into the hotel.

Sullivan was clear-eyed. His red hair was combed into place, and his pink face had the benefit of a fresh shave. "Good morning," he said.

"Good morning. I don't suppose the deputy is in yet."

Sullivan shook his head. "Nah. He stops at towns along the way. Sometimes he puts up at a ranch. Look for him in the middle of the morning, at the earliest."

"I guess I'll ask to see Rachel Valera, then."

"I'll see if she's available." The proprietor brushed his vest with a single stroke of his hand and set off down the hallway. A couple of minutes later, he returned to the reception area without a word.

Delaine waited and kept himself from staring at the hallway. After several minutes, he heard footsteps, and he turned to see Rachel approaching. She was wearing a grey dress and had her hair tied back.

"How are you?" he asked.

"All right. A little tired."

"Have you not slept well?"

"More or less. You know, doing nothing and always being a little on edge."

"And Miss Hamilton?"

"I haven't heard from her yet this morning. I was getting ready to have something brought to our rooms for breakfast."

"Maybe I should come back later."

"Let me see if she's up, and what she feels like. I'll come back to order something, and I can talk to you while I'm waiting for the food."

"I'll wait here." He watched her walk away. Sullivan might have watched her as well, as he now stood at the reception desk, turning over a sheet of paper. Delaine walked to the window and stared out at the street without seeing much.

Rachel came back with a concerned look on her face. "She doesn't answer her door. I'm going to ask the man to open it for me."

"Do you think I should go along?"

Rachel crossed her arms and tapped her left forearm. "I'm trying to remember what time it was when I saw her last night. I think it was about ten." Her dark eyes met Delaine's. "Yes, I think you could go with me."

She led the way to the reception desk, and Sullivan looked up as if he had not noticed anything.

Rachel said, "Miss Hamilton does not answer her

door. I've knocked and knocked, and I've called her name. I would like to ask you to open the door for us, to see if she is all right."

Sullivan glanced at Delaine. "Both of you?"

"Yes," said Rachel.

Sullivan reached below, out of sight, and made the motion of opening and closing a drawer. He raised his head and said, "Stay behind me."

He led the way down the hallway and stopped at a door with the number 19 on it. He knocked on the panel. "Miss Hamilton. Miss Hamilton." He knocked again. "Miss Hamilton. This is the front desk. Management. If you can't come to the door, I'm going to have to open it." He waited for about ten seconds and fitted a key into the keyhole. As the latch clacked, he turned the doorknob and pushed the door inward.

Dim light came in through a curtained window, and Sullivan's form blocked the view until he was a few steps into the room. Delaine and Rachel went around each side of him and stopped with him a couple of feet from the bed.

The shape of a woman in a shabby nightgown lay with the rumpled bedcovers thrown back. A pillow covered her face.

"This doesn't look good," said Sullivan. "I don't think we should touch anything. But just to be sure—" He leaned forward, touched the pillow, and drew back. "I'd rather not. But I think we should be sure of who it is and that she's, well—not alive." He raised his hand and lowered it. "I'd rather not. I don't feel good about it."

Delaine, on Sullivan's right, was closer to the pillow. "I'll do it if no one else wants to."

"If you don't mind."

Delaine did not want to, but he felt he was designated. He met Rachel's eyes as she gave a faint nod. He took a breath, focused on his task, and lifted the pillow.

The woman's muddy eyes were lifeless. Her bloodshot, spotted face had lost some of its hue but had retained its expression of pain. Her mouth was open, and the tips of her discolored teeth were showing. Below her chin, which looked weak and fragile, Delaine observed what he thought were bruises on her throat.

"I don't think there's a question," he said. He lowered the pillow and let it rest on her face.

"This is no good," said Sullivan. "We can send for Galen, but this should be the jurisdiction for the county. A questionable death at the very least. I think we should leave everything just the way it is, lock the door, and stay out."

"I don't mean to be blunt," said Delaine, "but it seems to me that someone else has been able to get in and out."

"It can be done. I can ask Galen to stand guard. I'll get him a chair, and he can sit in the hallway. I'll send out a wire to find out when the deputy will be here."

Delaine said, "I suppose I should wait in the lobby." To Rachel he said, "Did you want to have something to eat?"

She shook her head. "I don't think I could eat anything right now. I'll wait with you."

The two of them sat in silence in the lobby as the sunlight streamed in. After several minutes, Delaine said, "I feel as if it's my fault. I don't think she would ever have come if it wasn't for the money."

"The money?"

"Well, the means to get out. It was the one way to have her room rent paid in Ashton and have a ticket bought for her to go back to Illinois. It's as if I took advantage of her. It wasn't a bribe, but if she had had any money at all, she wouldn't have come here."

Rachel said, "That may be, but we wanted her to come here because it was the right thing to do. You told her you didn't want to make money the main consideration. I remember your words."

"I know I did. But our purpose was one thing, and I believe hers was another. This shouldn't have happened."

The sound of footsteps made them look up. Elmira was walking toward them with a sad but sympathetic expression on her face.

"I am very sorry to hear about this," she said.

Rachel spoke in a soft voice. "We feel as if it's our fault. She didn't want to come here, but we talked her into it."

"This happened because she knew something. She knew Mr. Cunningham, and he came to a bad end. I won't ask about your part in it, but I'll have to tell the deputy what I know."

"Of course," said Rachel. She exchanged a glance with Delaine. "And we'll tell him what we know."

Elmira said, "Someone knew she was staying here. Someone who saw her before. There's a rat who works in the kitchen. He talks to Reed and others, and maybe I don't need to say any more."

"The deputy should be told that," said Delaine. "I wouldn't be surprised if there's a regular chain there, link to link, even if the ones on this end don't know how serious it is."

"I think you're right. I just wanted to tell you how

sorry I am. I knew her, and she was not all bad. You could tell she had had a hard life." Elmira drew herself up. "I need to get back to work. I've let Edwin know, and he might come over when he has a chance."

"Thank you," said Delaine.

"Yes," said Rachel. "Thank you." She took Elmira's hands in hers for a second and let go.

Delaine and Rachel sat without talking for a while longer until Edwin Teale came into the lobby.

"I got away from work for a few minutes," he said. "I'm sorry to hear about what happened. The deputy should be here before long, I think."

"Thanks," said Delaine. "We feel as if we made a big mistake, or at least I do, but we thought this woman could be a great help."

"If she knew things about Cunningham, she would have been."

"She did." Delaine lowered his voice. "I think it may be time for me to hand over the box. I still have my worries about how much the deputy wants to listen. It's still in safe keeping, I assume."

"Oh, yes. Just say the word, and I'll get it for you."

"I appreciate it."

"Always willing to help. Is there anything else I can do at the moment?"

"Not that I can think of."

"Good enough. I'd better get back to work. Best wishes to you both."

"Thank you," said Rachel.

When Teale was gone, Delaine said, "You've met him?"

"Yes. When we were sending messages."

"Oh, yes."

A man in a black hat and suit came in and crossed

the lobby to talk to Sullivan. As he walked, his coattail flapped, and his gun and holster showed for a second.

"That's Galen," Delaine said. "The town marshal."

Rachel nodded.

Sullivan went with Galen down the hall. A few minutes later, Sullivan returned to the lobby and approached Delaine and Rachel where they sat. "The deputy should be here pretty soon," he said.

Time seemed to drag on. Delaine kept himself from looking at the clock every minute or two. A young man with blond hair, wearing a tan hat and jacket, came into the lobby and walked straight to the desk. He spoke in a low tone, and Sullivan led him down the hallway.

"I wonder who that is," Delaine said. "I don't think the coroner could have gotten here this soon."

He and Rachel lapsed into silence again. Sullivan made himself busy at the desk but did not stand still. Time went on.

Footsteps sounded, and the young man with blond hair stopped at the desk to exchange a few words with Sullivan, who pointed at Rachel and Delaine.

The man came their way. He was blue-eyed, clean-shaven, and slender. Delaine placed him at about thirty-five. When he stopped, he took off his hat and said, "How do you do? I'm Deputy Corle of the Converse County Sheriff's Office." He moved his jacket aside to show a badge pinned to his vest.

Delaine stood up and took off his hat. "I'm Jess Delaine, and this is Rachel Valera."

The deputy nodded. "Mr. Sullivan tells me that you two brought this woman, Mary Hamilton, to town on Sunday."

"That's right," said Delaine.

"Then I'm going to want to talk to each of you. But first, I need to talk to a couple of people who work here at the hotel. So if you can oblige me, Miss Valera, I'll ask you to wait in your room, and I'll ask you, Mr. Delaine, to wait out on the porch."

"Are you taking over the whole investigation in this town?" Delaine asked.

"Yes, I am. I'm picking up where Deputy Engel left off. I didn't expect this development, but I have to tend to it first. I'll get to each of you before long."

"I'll wait on the porch," said Delaine.

Rachel said, "And I will be in my room."

Deputy Corle smiled. "Thank you for your cooperation. Both of you."

Delaine went outside and sat in a chair. The sun had risen enough to cast the whole porch area in shade. Delaine's horse stood at the hitching rail with the rifle stock in view. A wagon creaked along to the south. Three horses were now tied in front of the café. Delaine took a long breath and resigned himself to a wait.

His eyes had closed, and a jumble of scenes had passed through his mind, when a voice brought him to.

"Mr. Delaine."

He sat up straight and opened his eyes wide. He looked around and down until he saw the boy Dan standing by the step.

"Mr. Delaine. Mr. Teale sent me to tell you something you might want to know."

"Come up here so you don't have to speak so loud, Dan."

The boy went up the step and into the shade of the porch. In a lowered voice, he said, "Mr. Teale said to tell you that a certain lady has come back to town to pay for her jewelry."

"Did you see her?"

"Yes, I did."

"Well, that's a very good thing to know, Dan. Take this." Delaine handed him a dime.

"Thank you."

"You're welcome. Was she alone?"

"No, she had a man with her."

"How did they get here?"

"They came on the train. I think they have to stay over so they can catch it again tomorrow."

"Where are they now?"

"They've gone to Ambler's. They were in the café for quite a while."

"Very good. Thanks."

"You bet."

Delaine was awake now. It had been a long time since breakfast, and he was hungry, but the deputy had told him to wait here.

He went back to reviewing the events from earlier in the day, from the day before, and the day before that. Today was Tuesday. They had found Wyman on Thursday. Time seemed to slow down and speed up. He imagined that time stretched on, one long day after another, out in Broken Horn Canyon.

A voice in the street brought him to attention. A woman with bright blonde hair, wearing a light tan jacket and dress, with a straw hat that had pale yellow flowers on one side, was walking along with a man who carried two valises. He wore a dark-brown suit, a white shirt, and a bow tie, topped off with a flat-crowned hat that some people called a gambler's hat.

They turned in from the street, went up the one

step, and paused in the shade of the porch. The man set the bags down and nodded at Delaine. He was about thirty, with brown eyes, brown hair, a clipped mustache, and a light complexion.

"Here," said Miss Capps. She opened the door and went in. The man picked up the bags, caught the door with his elbow, and followed her in.

Delaine returned to his own thoughts. The death of Beatrice Lennox, or Mary Hamilton, kept coming back to him. He was sure Melworth was behind it. She had even anticipated it, or at least feared it.

A sound from the street distracted him. A man was calling to his team of wagon horses.

Back to his train of thought, Delaine reminded himself not to make assumptions first and then try to make the facts fit. Any of a number of people could ease their way into a hotel room with simple locks such as The Brookfield had. Sullivan said it could be done; it might have been done before in this very place. The woman who died was not very strong and might not have put up much of a fight.

The door of the hotel opened, and Deputy Corle stepped out onto the porch. "I'm glad to see you're still here," he said.

"Just doing what I was told."

"I appreciate it. If you don't mind, I'd like you to come inside, where we can talk without interruptions from the street." The deputy glanced around and smiled. "It's pretty quiet now, but when something like this happens, you never know who might barge in."

Delaine imagined Melworth himself demanding with authority to know what happened. "Sure," he said. He rose and followed the deputy into the lobby.

"Let's sit over here." The deputy indicated the two

chairs near the fireplace, where Delaine and Rachel had sat earlier.

The deputy picked up one chair and carried it toward the farthest corner, and Delaine did the same with the other chair. When they were both seated with their hats off, the deputy said, "I'd like you to tell me what you know. That is, as it pertains to these recent deaths and how you happen to be involved."

Delaine had come to town to tell what he had seen in Broken Horn Canyon as well, but in the meanwhile, after the discovery of the woman's body, he thought he might save that information until he thought it would not distract anyone. So he set it aside in his mind and focused on the topic as the deputy had laid it out.

"I'll begin with how I was drawn into it," he said. "The family of a man related to José Luna, who had lived in this town and had died a while earlier, said that their family member, Robert Sandoval, had come here to see about his inheritance and to settle the affairs. He had been gone almost a month, and they had not heard from him, so they asked me to come and see what I could find out."

"I see. And where does this family live?"

"In Overton."

"Go ahead."

"I came here, and I had already decided not to state my business right away. I stayed at Mr. Luna's lodging house, a place called The Blue Iris. People talked about him, but nobody mentioned Sandoval. A couple of people even said they expected a relative to show up and no one had done so yet."

"Overton is not that far."

"It was a two-days' ride for me. I understood that

he came on the stagecoach. There's not a direct train route from there to here."

"True."

"After I had been here a while, and I had gotten a job with Leo Rawlinson at the Six Mile Ranch to give me a cover, I heard about a man who had been found dead in Willett. He was described as a Mexican man, so I went there. I learned that he had been found by the railroad tracks, as if he had jumped off or fallen off a train. He had no luggage or anything to identify him, so they sent out a notice of an unidentified man and buried him."

"I have a vague memory of that. It didn't seem connected with anything else. An itinerant laborer, I think he was called."

"The curious thing is that he was wearing a suit, a blue suit. His family told me he had a blue suit in his valise. And he wore a hat with his traveling clothes. So my thought is that he came to this town, changed into his suit for a business meeting, met his end, and was taken back and left off in another town, by the train line. Whoever did that tossed away his hat and his valise."

"It's a theory."

"Not long after that, Rachel Valera came to town to tell me something she did not want to send in writing. Robert Sandoval's family had found a letter from José Luna, which Sandoval left behind, one would assume, so that no one here would read it. The letter stated that if anything happened to Mr. Luna, someone could find a box of papers in the wall of his lodging house, behind a plaster-of-Paris painting of The Last Supper."

"Indeed."

"Yes. I had seen the painting. A large, heavy thing, screwed into the wall. It looked like a permanent fixture. Rachel went to stay at the house, and when we had a chance, we took down the painting and found the box. In it were mortgages and promissory notes, dated over a period of a couple of years, showing that Mr. Luna had lent about ten thousand dollars to Barton Melworth and had taken papers on various pieces of property as security. Oh, let me back up. The letter he sent to Robert Sandoval had said that he had been lending money in that way so that someone could pay someone else, but he didn't say who."

"But you did not see this letter."

"No. Rachel did."

"She told you she did."

"Well, yes."

"Just sticking to what you actually know. The same with the man who was found in Willett. These are things you heard. We can confirm them if we need to."

"As for what I know, I saw those documents with my own eyes."

"I believe that. Where are they now?"

"I have them in safe keeping with another person. To use a saying I once heard, I can lay my hands on them in an instant."

The deputy smiled. "Very good. We may want to look at them at some point. Let's move on to the recent deaths."

"I consider José Luna to be one of them."

"Oh, I see."

"And Robert Sandoval to be the next."

"If he turns out to be the one who was found, which very well could be. But go on. I'd like to get to the death of Mr. Edward Cunningham. I believe you were there."

"A hired man from another ranch found him. I helped bring him in. It didn't take me long to suspect that he might be the person who was blackmailing Melworth, but I didn't know why."

The deputy smiled again. "We'll leave that hanging in a cool place, like a quarter of beef. Did you tell Deputy Engel about the papers you found?"

"I decided to wait. He said he was going to talk to Melworth, and he made it sound as if they were friends. He didn't seem to care for other people's suggestions, and I was afraid he might tell Melworth that we had found the box where it was hidden. Among other things, that would make us vulnerable, not to mention the papers. By the way, Melworth had taken over the management of The Blue Iris and had someone staying there. I assumed he, Melworth, had searched the place and hadn't found the box."

The deputy shrugged.

"So I decided to find out what I could about Cunningham. I learned that a rather rundown-looking woman had come to visit him here on a couple of occasions, trying to dun him for money, and had been staying in Ashton. I was given her name as Beatrice. I went to Ashton and found her. She told me her last name was Lennox. She also told me an interesting story about Cunningham and Melworth, but since this is hearsay, I'll make it brief."

"We can always fill in the details if it is pertinent."

"Very good. She told me she knew Melworth by his original name, Tick Mason, and Cunningham by his original name, Tom Raymond. The two of them and a third man kidnapped the boy of a wealthy family in Chicago. Beatrice worked for the family and was conned into being an accomplice. They made a haul of money, something like ten thousand dollars, but things went wrong. The boy died, the third kidnapper was killed during an arrest, Cunningham was arrested, and Melworth made off with the money. Cunningham went to prison while Melworth came out here, assumed a new name, and became a cattle rancher. Cunningham spent quite a while in prison, never peached, and when he got out, he went looking for Melworth. He found him and bled him for money until it ran out, and he came here to pressure him in person. By then, Luna had quit lending money to Melworth."

"I believe it is in the report that you knew Edward Cunningham."

"I met him twice. Once when he was on a buggy ride with his companion Miss Capps, who, by the way, is back in town and is somewhere in the hotel."

"You don't say."

"I saw her. Anyway, the second time I met him was when he was out on a drive with Steven Reed, who works for Melworth at managing The Blue Iris in a minimal way. He was showing Cunningham the country. Looking back, I think Cunningham might have been getting an idea of what property Melworth had and how he could get his hands on it, not knowing it was mortgaged up."

"That's all speculation, but interesting. Let's go back to this woman who died. You went to see her in Ashton, and you brought her back here. Is that right?"

"Not in the same trip. I wanted to bring her here after I thought about it a little while, and I thought Rachel would be better at helping me persuade her, so

I went back to the ranch to work for a couple of days. That was last week."

"I'm following."

"And we had a big interruption, when we found Joel Wyman in the perfect setup of branding a calf, except that his rope was coiled on his saddle and his horse wasn't tied up as it would be if he was fixing to start a fire."

"We have that information."

"Right. And when the weekend came around, Rachel and I went to Ashton, talked to Beatrice Lennox, persuaded her to come back here, and got her a room under the name of Mary Hamilton, which she suggested."

"Did you give her any money? Mr. Sullivan helped me search the room, and we didn't find any money."

"I don't think she had any. We paid off her room rent in Ashton, and I told her we would buy her a ticket back to Illinois, but I didn't give her any cash. I don't like to admit it, but I think the money aspect is what convinced her to come, even though Rachel's presence helped. If she hadn't come here, this wouldn't have happened."

"The last part is certainly true. What did you hope to achieve?"

"I wanted to expose Barton Melworth, but I didn't want to give away the evidence I had until I was sure he wasn't told about it. And with Beatrice, I wanted a first-hand witness and not just my hearsay."

"I think you took a lot upon yourself."

"As I said before, Deputy Engel didn't seem to take suggestions or want to listen to people unless he was asking questions. In the end, I'm working for Robert Sandoval's family, and I wanted to know whether

Melworth or someone who worked for him caused his death or José Luna's. I wanted more than to know. I wanted the investigation to go that far, and I still do."

"At the moment, I'm most interested in the deaths of Edward Cunningham and Mary Hamilton—or Beatrice Lennox, as you gave her prior name."

"It may not have been her real name, either."

"We can find out. Is there anything else you can tell me, from your own knowledge or observation, about the deaths of either of these two?"

"Maybe one small thing. When I saw Cunningham in person, he was wearing a ring, an expensive-looking thing with a blue stone set in gold. Bill Ambler saw it, too, and said it might be cobalt. When we were helping with the body, I saw that the ring was missing. I told the other deputy."

"That may be in the report. I'll have to look."

An exchange of voices drew their attention to the reception desk, where Miss Capps was talking to Sullivan. Her new companion stood a couple of steps behind her, holding what looked like two glasses of white wine. She finished her conversation with Sullivan, motioned to the man in the brown suit and hat, and began walking in the direction of Delaine and the deputy. She had the same brassy air about her as before, and Delaine had the impression that while she was in town, she was reclaiming her earlier status.

She stopped about six feet away with her young man behind her. Bearing down on the deputy, she said, "We were on our way out to the porch, to take a refreshment, and Mr. Sullivan told me you are assigned to the case of Mr. Cunningham. I knew him when I was in town before, and I have just learned that he was killed. Is that true?"

"Evidence at the scene confirms it. He was shot."

"I'm sorry to hear that. My association with him had ended, but all the same—" She did not finish the sentence.

Deputy Corle picked up the slack, as if she had dropped the end of her rope on the ground. "I appreciate your concern. And of course we're doing all we can to try to find out who's responsible." He paused. "Among the things I have heard, one is that Mr. Cunningham may have been receiving money from someone in this vicinity. Do you know anything about that?"

She waved her hand, which had a couple of rings on it but nothing that looked like a wedding band. "Only in the most general way. You know how men are about their business. But I understood that there was a person who owed him money from an earlier business partnership."

"No names?"

"I didn't inquire."

Delaine sensed that she was keeping herself on a high level of language, to go along with the status she was asserting. He was sure that in a different setting, she could drop down a level or more.

"This is not the best place for these questions, anyway," said the deputy. "How long are you in town?"

"I leave tomorrow."

"Are you staying here at the hotel?"

"Yes. I have a person traveling with me, a gentleman, who has his own room."

The deputy's eyes went to the young man holding the glasses. "Very well. I may want to talk to you again. For the time being, thank you for your attention to my questions, and it's a pleasure to meet you. Just to be sure—your name?"

"Evangeline Capps. Miss Evangeline Capps."

"Very good, Miss Capps. Good day."

"And the same to you."

Delaine watched for a couple of seconds as she walked away and her gentleman companion fell in behind her. Delaine couldn't blame her for wanting to take what she could out of life while she could. Perhaps she felt that she had seen a great deal and had learned wise lessons, but he thought she might not have much awareness of where a person's life could lead. In that respect, she might have common ground with Sienna Wilson—or even an earlier Beatrice Lennox.

13

———

The deputy shifted in his seat, as he, too, had been watching Miss Capps walk away. "That wasn't very definite," he said, "but it seems to confirm some of what you have told me. It might be a good idea if we looked at the materials in that box you told me about. How far do we have to go for it?"

"Across the street to the café. I can ask for it there."

"Then we can go on foot."

"Oh, yes."

They walked out into the sunlight, across the street, and into the café. One table on each side was occupied.

"Let's wait here," said the deputy, as Delaine closed the door.

Teale came toward them with a look of expectation. "Is there some way I can help?"

Delaine spoke. "We'd like to have the metal box I left with you a while back."

Teale looked around at the two tables where customers were eating. "I think I can go out the back way and be back in a thrice. Would you like to sit here and wait?" He motioned with his hand toward a table.

"I wouldn't mind having a sandwich or something quick," said the deputy.

"I'll mention it in the kitchen on my way through." Teale glanced at Delaine. "You, too?"

"Oh, yes. I was hungry an hour ago."

"I won't be long. Sit where you'd like."

Deputy Corle selected a table on the right side and took a seat facing the door. He set his hat on the chair next to him. Delaine took a seat across from him and looked back over his shoulder.

The deputy put his hands on the table. "I'll tell you if anything interesting happens in the street."

Within a few minutes, a man in a stained white apron and a drab work shirt came out of the kitchen with two plates. He lumbered down the aisle in a forward-leaning walk and stopped long enough to set the plates in front of the two men.

"Thanks," said the deputy.

"You bet." The man turned and went back to the kitchen.

Each plate had a sandwich consisting of two thick slices of bread with irregular chunks of cold cooked beef.

"It's food," said Delaine, as he prepared to take a bite of the dry combination.

"No complaints."

Teale returned with the box and set it on the table. "Here it is," he said. "It should be just as you left it. I never opened it."

"Thank you very much," said Delaine.

"Glad to help. It looks like you could use some coffee. Two?"

The deputy nodded as he kept his mouth closed around a bite of sandwich.

Delaine was afraid he would open the box and find it empty. He swallowed the food in his mouth, braced himself, worked the latch, and opened the lid on its hinge.

The folded documents looked just as he had left them. He turned the box toward the deputy and said, "Have a look."

Teale arrived with two crockery mugs, poured the coffee, and left without comment.

The deputy ate the rest of his sandwich and drank his coffee as he gave his attention to one document after another. At the end, he stacked them and put them back in the box. "Like you said. Not that I had any reason not to believe you, but it's important to see these things for myself."

Delaine felt a wave of satisfaction. He sat up straight and said, "They're not mine. I think I should turn them over to you. I hope they can stay in safe keeping."

"I'll ask Sullivan to put them in the safe at the hotel. Let's finish up here. Oh. It looks like you're done and you're waiting on me."

———

IN THE HOTEL lobby once again, after leaving the box with the hotel proprietor, the deputy said, "It all looks probable in terms of what I'm investigating right now, but I wish I knew more about who knew that the woman was staying here. I've talked to people who work here at the hotel, and I'd like to talk to Reed. While I'm at it, I can see where you found the box with the documents, and I can even have a look at the place where José Luna lived and had his business."

Delaine found the comment encouraging. "Would you like me to go with you?"

"It wouldn't hurt. You know how to take down the painting."

Delaine felt as if he still had to prove his own testimony, but at least the deputy wanted to verify, and he seemed to be interested in Luna himself.

They walked the two blocks to The Blue Iris, passing the watch and jewelry shop and the curious gaze of Bill Ambler, who stood in his doorway.

The deputy had to knock twice to have someone answer. The door opened partway, and the Slender Reed blocked the gap.

"What is it?" he said.

"Are you Mr. Reed?" the deputy asked.

"I am. Steven Reed."

"I'm Deputy Corle from the Converse County Sheriff's Office. I'd like to ask you a few questions."

"About what?"

"Related to a couple of deaths that have occurred here in the recent past."

"I don't know anything about either of them. I knew Cunningham, but I don't know anything about how he died. And I didn't even know the young rustler."

"I suppose we could include him, but when I said 'a couple,' I was thinking of Edward Cunningham and the other death that was discovered at the hotel this morning."

Reed's facial features did not move, but an expression passed over him as if he had to suppress a turmoil in his bowels. "I don't know anything about that."

"Did you happen to pass on any information about someone who was staying there?"

"Nothing of the sort."

"Did you ever help Mr. Melworth look among the belongings of the late owner of this business, Mr. Luna?"

"Again, nothing of the sort. This place was vacant for a while before Mr. Melworth asked me to look after it. In Mr. Luna's interest."

"I see. Do you mind if we come in and take a look?"

"I don't see a need for it."

"Maybe you don't, but I have my reasons. If you don't want to cooperate, I can arrest you under suspicion of aiding and abetting, and then I don't need permission."

"Suit yourself." Still sullen, Reed backed up and opened the door.

The deputy walked in, and Delaine followed. As he moved around to the deputy's right, he saw a blank area where the painting had hung, with the gaping square hole in the middle. The light from the open door closed off. His eyes moved down, and he saw the painting resting on the floor.

"That's it," he said. "It looks as if someone thought to take it down at last."

"And that's not all," said the deputy. He stepped closer. "That wasn't necessary."

The light was dim. As Delaine moved forward, he saw where the deputy was pointing. Someone had smashed the painting a little off center, making a hole where a couple of white fragments hung on wires. Whoever had done the damage must have done so when the painting was leaning against the wall, for the square hole in the wall above was clean and empty.

Delaine looked around, and Reed was nowhere to be seen. Delaine went to the door, opened it, and looked out. "He's gone."

"No wonder he didn't want to let us in," said the deputy. He returned his attention to the painting. "This look rather peevish to me," he said, with emphasis on the *p*.

"For the person who did it," said Delaine, "I would guess Jim Rudy. I would bet his boss is in a worse state, though. He had a hunch these papers were somewhere, and now he has a good idea that someone else has them."

"I think I have enough to go after him." The deputy took a calm breath. "I still wish I had something more concrete to show that he was paying Cunningham. I don't doubt what you say the woman told you, or what Miss Valera said was in Luna's letter, or what Miss Capps said, which was vaguest of all. Just owing money is not a crime, even though two people may have died because of it. Or three, if you count Luna, which you seem to want to."

"Or more."

"Oh, you mean Sandoval. That could be, in an indirect way."

"I was thinking of another."

The deputy's face held still, and his blue eyes fixed on Delaine. "Who is that?"

"Joel Wyman."

"Wait a minute. I haven't forgotten about him. but I don't see the connection here."

"I don't have anything definite about the man

himself, but I heard a couple of things and saw something else."

"Well, go ahead and tell me. But let's not waste time."

"Let's go outside where we can be sure no one's listening."

The two of them walked to the corner of the main street, where the road to the left led out to the country and the broad street to the right led into the main part of town. The area around them was open and quiet.

Delaine said, "I imagine you have heard about the boy from Billings, Montana, who is missing and has a reward out for him."

"I've seen the posters, and we have the information in our office."

"I think Joel Wyman was interested in that case. When he stayed at the ranch, he mentioned it as a way that a person could make a nice sum of money. When he died, his lady friend said to Deputy Engel, in my presence, that he was trying to put together a stake so they would have something to leave on."

"Sure. Lots of people think that way. A reward is good money."

"And I've talked to another fellow who has also hung out in this area. He's a reward hunter, and he has mentioned the boy from Billings, and I think they might both have had a hunch that the boy is somewhere in this part of the country."

"In Wyoming."

"In this part of Wyoming."

"What is this other man's name?"

"He goes by Milligan. A rather large fellow."

The deputy shook his head. "I don't know him. I'm sure there's more than one person on the lookout for that reward, and I can imagine that more than one could be looking for that kid around here."

Delaine cast a glance to either side to be sure no one was near. "I think I found him."

The deputy held still again and stared with his blue eyes. "I don't know if I heard you right."

"I think I found him. Without trying."

"Where in the hell was that?"

"In a place called Broken Horn Canyon, in an area northwest of here called Broken Horn. Out on a pine ridge."

"I have a general idea of where that is. And how did you come to see this?"

"Out hunting horses and checking on cattle. I've seen the place twice. It's a line camp owned by Barton Melworth. The second time I saw the place, I watched it for a little while, and a towhead kid came out of the cabin, followed by a ranch hand named Sorensen, who hung around with Melworth's other men, but I hadn't seen him for a couple of weeks."

Deputy Corle frowned. "So you think Barton Melworth is holding this kid? You seem to want to heap a lot of blame on him."

"It took me by surprise. But it sure makes sense. He started out as a kidnapper, and he's never been that much of a cattle rancher. When Luna either couldn't or wouldn't lend him any more money to pay his blackmailer, he went back to one way he knew to raise money."

"You seem to have it pieced together pretty well. I would need more proof for some parts of it. Some of it seems petty, like destroying that painting, and some of it seems tenuous, like the death of Luna and the disappearance of Sandoval. But the things I know of are dead serious, and if you think that boy is out in Broken Horn, I've got to look into that, whether it's related or not." The deputy looked up at the sun. "I think we have time to go out there today."

"We? Do you want me to go along?"

"If you want to. You know the way, and I don't think I should go by myself. Even two isn't much against three or four. I think I should see about getting a third man to go along. Are you in?"

"Yes, I am."

"Good. Then let's not lose time. Ah, one other thing. I should tell Miss Valera she can leave her room."

Delaine fell into step. He thought it was inaccurate to refer to Rachel as "Miss," but he did not think it was worth mentioning at the moment, even to a person who valued accuracy.

When they returned to the hotel, Miss Capps's escort was leaning against a post on the veranda. The two of them had been sitting together when Delaine and the deputy went in with the box and left again for The Blue Iris. Miss Capps was gone, and the man in the brown suit and gambler's hat was chewing a toothpick as he looked over the dusty street.

He stood up straight and moved aside to let the two men pass. "Makin' progress?" he asked.

"I believe so," said the deputy. He came to a stop. "I'm about to form a posse. How are you on a horse?"

"Ah kin rad one. Don' know what's in it for me, though."

"Thanks anyway," said the deputy. He continued to lead the way into the hotel.

Delaine wondered if the deputy had taken the opportunity to exercise a wry sense of humor.

"Wait here," said the deputy when they were inside the lobby. He stopped at the desk to talk to Sullivan and then walked down the hallway.

After several minutes, Deputy Corle returned to the lobby where Delaine was standing. "Sullivan says Bill Ambler, the man with the jewelry store, has asked how he can help. Galen says he can go along with us, so I think I'll ask Ambler to stand watch 'n front of the deceased's room. I've talked to Miss Valera, and she said she'd like to talk to you before we go."

"My horse is ready. That's it tied up outside."

"Good. I need to go to the stable and get mine ready. Galen needs to do the same. We should be ready to go in less than fifteen minutes."

"I'll be ready."

The deputy left. A minute later, Galen passed through the lobby and went out. Delaine waited.

Rachel came out of the hallway with her room key in her hand. She did not stop to give the key to the man at the desk. She had a troubled expression on her face as she walked up to Delaine, but she spoke in a calm voice. "It looks as if things are beginning to move. Did you tell him about the papers in the box?"

"Yes, I did. I gave him the box, and he left it with Sullivan to put in the safe. He looked at the papers first. I told him everything I knew, including what you told me about the letter you saw."

"That's good."

"I also told him about something I saw yesterday, which I didn't get a chance to mention to you earlier, with everything else that happened."

"What was that?"

He lowered his voice. "There's a boy that's been missing from Billings, Montana, and I'm pretty sure I saw him where he's being held out in a cow camp belonging to Melworth."

Rachel took in a quick breath. "Oh, my. There's no end to it."

"There may be. This is the one thing the deputy didn't hesitate about. I think he's expecting resistance, so he's taking me and the town marshal along."

"If this man has done the things we think he has, it can be very dangerous." She glanced at the pistol in its holster. "You have to be careful. I see you are prepared."

"I have my rifle on my horse as well."

"Good. I hope you don't have to use it, but if you do, I hope you use it well."

He caught the mild scent of powder and perfume as she moved close, touched her lips to his, and drew back. "*Ve con cuidado*," she said. "Be careful."

"I will." As he stood back, he noted a weariness. He said, "I hope you can get some rest. Have you had anything to eat yet today?"

"No. That's what I'm going to do now."

"Good."

Her face softened. "Come back to me."

"I will."

<hr>

DEPUTY CORLE and Marshal Galen showed up together, each with a rifle in view as well as a pistol. The deputy said, "I'm sure Reed passed the word on to somebody, so I don't think we'll take anyone by surprise. Galen says he knows the way to Melworth's place, so we'll let him lead. Melworth's got at least three men working for him, so even if one of them is out at Broken Horn, he's got enough to make trouble. I'd like to say don't fire until we're fired upon, but if you see someone aiming a gun, don't stand on ceremony. This is a posse. Consider yourselves sworn in. I'm in charge, but use your own judgment."

The three men rode for more than an hour at a fast walk, not wearing out their horses. Galen took them past the turnoff to the Six Mile. The land had opened up into basins and swells of grassland, with cattle scattered here and there. Galen followed a trail northeast, and without slowing down, he led them over a crest and into a ranch yard.

Like many such places, the headquarters were built up against a ridge that gave shelter on the west. The buildings were stark and weathered, and not a tree or shrub was in sight. For as much as Barton seemed to have big holdings, his headquarters did not amount to much. There was not a ranch house, or big house, as some punchers would say, just a bunkhouse and cook shack that had been built in two parts, with a stovepipe sticking out of each half. A low stable served as a barn, with a shed perpendicular to it. A few horses looked out over the rails of a set of corrals, and a stack yard had the remnants of a winter supply of hay.

"The bunkhouse is on the left," said Galen. "I think we should try there."

The deputy said, "We'll all get down. Two of us can go in, and one of us can stand outside and keep watch."

They dismounted and tied their horses at the rail. Galen said he would wait outside. The deputy led the way to the door and tapped on the frame with the blunt end of his pocketknife. He tapped again, and a voice from inside said to come in.

The deputy led the way with his right hand near his pistol. In the dim light inside, a man in an apron sat at the far end of a table, smoking a cigarette.

"What do you need?" he asked.

"I'm Deputy Corle of the Converse County Sheriff's Office, and I came to speak with Barton Melworth."

"He ain't here."

"I see. Is anyone else?"

"I am."

"I meant a foreman, or second in charge."

"This is a workin' ranch. They're all out workin'."

"When do you expect them back?"

"When they git here. I don't worry about them, and they don't worry about me." The man tipped his ash in a sardine can.

"I'm sure that's a good arrangement." The deputy swept the room with his glance and went past the man at the table. "Are you the cook?"

"Just as you see me."

"I'd like to look into your kitchen."

"Make yourself happy."

The deputy said to Delaine, "Wait here." He walked to the doorway of the kitchen area, paused, and went in. He came out a minute later and said, "Thanks."

"No trouble."

"I'd like to look in the barn next."

"Be careful of spiders."

Deputy Corle led the way out. Delaine followed, and he did not like turning his back on the cook.

Outside, the deputy said, "I have a feeling there's someone else here. I think all three of us can take a look at the barn. Galen, I'll have you go to the door at the other end, and when I give the signal, we'll go in at the same time. Delaine, I'll have you stand near that shed and keep an eye on it."

The deputy waited at the near end of the stable while the other two went to their places. The deputy gave the signal, opened the door, and went in, leaving the door open. Galen did the same.

A minute later, two blasts of gunfire sounded from the end that Galen went in. Voices went back and forth between Galen and the deputy.

Delaine approached the door that Galen had left open. Inside, the deputy and the marshal were standing at right angles to one another, looking at the floor.

Delaine walked farther in. A man's body lay on the dirt floor. His pale scalp showed through thinning dark hair. He wore a brown cloth vest, and a hat of similar color lay on its side a couple of yards away. His right hand seemed to be reaching for a Colt .45 that gleamed where it had fallen in the straw and dirt.

"That's one of Melworth's men," said Galen.

"I recognize him," said Delaine. "His name is Vick."

Galen said, "I don't know what he thought. Maybe he didn't know there were three of us. Even two wasn't good odds."

Deputy Corle moved his head one way and another as he studied the man. "It's hard to know what he was thinking. Sometimes when a man feels trapped, he doesn't think much about the world beyond. I'd like to say they're like a rat in a feed box, but a rat doesn't have a choice."

The cook was waiting in front of the bunkhouse with a single-barreled shotgun leaning against the wall.

"You were wrong," said the deputy. "There was a man in the barn."

"I don't know what he was doing there."

"Neither do I. But you need to do something with him."

"Bart's not going to like this when he gets back. You don't just come onto his place and shoot his men."

"He shot first. He didn't have to."

"You didn't have to come here and hunt him down like you did."

The deputy let him have the last word. He motioned to the other two, and they all mounted up. As they rode up onto the ridge, the deputy said, "I don't know how much of a bluff this man is running, but I wouldn't expect Melworth to come back right away. I would bet that he and his foreman are on the way to Broken Horn."

14

DELAINE LED THE WAY NORTHWEST TOWARD THE PINE ridge. It was that time of day when the sun overhead did not seem to move, but it would be slipping into the latter part of the afternoon before long. He continued to see cattle in small bunches, and he felt that he should be taking closer notice, but his sense of a more pressing purpose kept him looking straight ahead. From time to time, he glanced at each of the two lawmen, and he imagined they had other responsibilities cross their minds as well. For all he knew, either of them could have a wife and a family, as well as other aspects of their work pending.

Half a mile from the base of the ridge, Delaine saw a light-colored horse to the right of the place he had in mind. He told himself not to take interest in horses, either. Rawlinson had all of his saddle stock in, anyway. Still, habits of mind persisted, and Delaine glanced at the horse more than once. After a couple of minutes, an inconsistency in the color of the horse registered in Delaine's mind.

"That horse looks like it's saddled," he said.

"It does," said the deputy. "And it looks like it's loose."

The three men rode on. When they were within a quarter of a mile of the horse, it turned and trotted a few paces toward them.

"Yella horse," said Galen.

"I think I've seen it before," said Delaine. He kept the group on course but searched the ground on either side for a man on foot or a spilled rider.

The light-colored horse took a few more steps in their direction.

"Over there," said the deputy, who was on the right.

The three men changed course. A clump of sagebrush receded. A form on the ground proved to be that of a man in drab clothes. He was lying on his back, and he was not a small man.

The deputy held out his left hand and approached by himself. When he came to a stop, he dropped his hand and waved, and the other two rode up even with him.

Delaine felt a wave of dread pass through him. The man was Milligan, as he had anticipated, but with a red spot in the middle of his large abdomen. The man's eyes were closed, and his blank, sallow face was turned upward toward the sky.

"Do you know him?" said the deputy.

Delaine spoke. "His name is Milligan. I mentioned him earlier as a man who was looking for the boy from Billings. He did this for his work, look for missing people."

"I saw him around," said Galen. "I thought I had seen that horse, but I didn't place it."

Delaine said, "I saw him ride it once." His eyes passed over the body. "He must have gotten too close." He had a familiar feeling, a sense that here was a person who would never see the world around him again. "The first time I saw him was in The Elkhorn saloon in Willett. Jim Rudy picked a fight with him. I don't know if he was looking for the kid yet or if Rudy had any idea that he was. It was almost as if it was some kind of instinct. I don't think Rudy and Milligan knew each other at that point."

The deputy spoke. "I have to think about what to do. I don't like to leave him here and the horse running loose, but I'd like to catch up with those others today if we can. And I don't want to leave one man here. There's still at least three of them." He pushed his lips together in a firm line. "Sorry, but that's the way it's going to be. We'll come back for him."

Delaine gave one last look at the man who had seemed so sure of himself, then reined his horse in the direction they had been headed before, toward the area called Broken Horn.

He recognized a couple of inlets along the pine ridge where he had scouted for cows and looked for horses. Before long, he came to the passage that led to the line camp and branched off to the spot where he had found his observation point. Rather than take the route to the left, he stayed to the right. From that point on, he did not know the trail, but there was enough wear from horse tracks that he was not concerned about losing his way. His main worry was the possibility of meeting one or more riders coming out.

The passageway opened up into the small canyon. The line shack sat in silence with no smoke rising from the stovepipe. The yard was vacant, and not a single horse stood in the corral.

"The place looks empty," said Delaine.

Galen said, "So did the last place."

"We'll see," said the deputy. "Let's all three be ready, like before."

They dismounted and tied their horses, and the deputy led the way up to the door. He rapped on the doorframe with his pocketknife, and the door opened.

Sorensen stood in the doorway, a man of average height and a sturdy build, wearing a dull brown shirt and vest and a pair of cuffed denim trousers. His light hair and thin mustache caught the sunlight as his face spread into a smile.

"Well, who do we have here?"

"I'm Deputy Corle of the Converse County Sheriff's Office, and these men are my posse."

Sorensen's light-blue eyes, set in his thick face, moved back and forth. "Did you come all the way out here to see me?"

"I came to see who's here. I want to look inside this shack."

"There's no one here but me, just as solitary as a sheepherder."

"Let me see for myself."

"By all means." Sorensen stepped aside.

The deputy walked in, with his hand on his pistol butt as he scanned the room. Galen and Delaine followed. The deputy said, "Watch him."

Sorensen still had a smile on his face when the deputy came back after searching the two smaller rooms.

The deputy said, "What kind of work are you doing out here, all by your lonesome self?"

"Ranch work."

"Without a horse?"

"He ran off. He's out grazing."

The deputy pointed a finger at Sorensen's chest. "Your bunch has something to hide, or your pal Vick wouldn't have been hidden out in the barn, quick to pull a gun. That was his mistake. Don't you make one."

"I don't have a gun on me."

"And you're not going to." The deputy took a pair of handcuffs out of his jacket pocket and said, "Put your hands behind you."

"What for?"

"For taking part in the kidnapping and sequestering of a child."

"Oh, go on."

"Don't make me lose my patience. Put your hands behind you."

Sorensen did as he was told, and the deputy put the handcuffs on him. The thick-chested man said, "I don't know a thing."

"I have an eyewitness who saw you and the kid here together, so don't play dumb. It looks to me like someone has been here and has taken the kid away on your horse."

Sorensen laughed. "You know everything."

"What I don't know, I'm going to find out. And that's where the kid is. Where did Rudy and Melworth go with him?"

Sorensen lolled his head and smiled.

The deputy said, "What do you know about a man named Milligan?"

"Not much. Just that he's about as tough as a dish of mashed potatoes."

The deputy did not answer. He seemed to be taking another measure of Sorensen. He said to Galen, "How would you like to stay here and watch this fellow?"

Galen nodded. "I can do that."

The deputy regarded Delaine and said, "Then let's you and I see if we can pick up the trail."

From his earlier point of observation, the canyon had looked to Delaine as if it might be a box canyon, but when they looked around, they found a trail leading out of the far side. The deputy said, "It looks like three or more horses have been out this way in the last while."

Delaine said, "The horse I saw here twice in the corral was a common-looking sorrel that I had seen Sorensen ride."

"Well, he's not going anywhere right now. If we can bring those others back, he might not have so much wind in his sails." After a couple of seconds, the deputy added, "He didn't seem to know anything about Milligan, but that could have been an act as well."

"He was with Rudy that day in the saloon in Willett. Like I said, I don't think they knew each other's names. They must have picked up Milligan's name since then. And Milligan didn't make a secret about what he was looking for."

"It's too bad he didn't do any better. He may have just given them more reason to take off."

They followed the trail through what seemed like a maze until it led to a long sidehill climb and took them out on top of the ridge. Pine trees grew all around like a small forest, but there was not much deadfall, and a path wound its way north through the trees. It looked like a cow trail, as had the trail they had climbed up the side of the ridge. Cow pies and scuff marks on fallen logs showed that cattle had been in there this spring.

The deputy had taken the lead, and now he stopped. He pointed down at the trail where a deposit of horse manure was turning from green to a darker shade.

"Not too long ago," he said. "I've got no idea if we're gaining on them, but if they've got that kid, they can't go all out."

The deputy continued to lead the way for a long while. Delaine did not know how far they had come, but he knew that a mile was a long distance in timber.

They came out of the tees, and the ridge appeared to continue north, although it was no longer timbered and it did not form as much of a divide, as it no longer rose as high above the land on either side. The terrain was rough grassland, with rocks dotting landscape.

The deputy stopped and said, "We've got to be careful not to lose their trail here."

Delaine nodded as he scanned the area around him. As clumsy as cattle seemed, they made trails as narrow and steep as game trails in high country, and they knew how to avoid rocks and pits and drop-offs in country like this. He said, "Like as not, they'll follow a cow trail. Let's look for one that's got recent horse tracks on it."

Cattle trails led in various directions, and the two men did not pick up horse prints right away. They rode in circles until Delaine found a trail where horses had stepped on one another's tracks.

"Hard to tell how many," said the deputy. "But it looks like more than two."

The trail led northwest to wide open country. Delaine said, "I don't know of any towns out this way. Do you?"

"No, I don't. I think that if you rode in this direction for a week, you'd come close to Billings. I don't think they're going there."

"I don't think so, either. My guess is that they're going to a place that Rudy knows of."

The deputy looked at the sky. "I hope we can gain on them. The sun's moving on us."

The trail took them through a broad bottom and up to a crest. As always, they took it slow as the land ahead came into view.

Specks showed against the pale landscape about two miles away. The deputy said, "I don't know if that's them or if it's even three on horseback."

"It looks like three," said Delaine.

"Let's do this. It doesn't look like they're moving very fast. We'll let them go over the next ridge, and then we'll try to catch up with them."

Delaine slid off and walked his horse back down the hill a few feet. The deputy joined him.

"Waiting is the hardest thing to do. Knowing that they're getting farther and farther away, and you don't know what the land looks like on the other side of the next ridge."

After a few minutes, the deputy walked to the crest and came back. "They haven't crossed yet."

A few minutes later, he tried again and called over his shoulder. "I think they went over. I don't see them anymore."

Delaine turned his horse so that the animal was standing downhill for an easier mount. He stepped into the saddle and rode to the top.

The deputy rode up and stopped beside him. "I doubt that they saw us, but you never know. They might be waiting for us to come over that next ridge. If they shoot, we shoot. But whatever you do, don't shoot that kid."

"I won't."

"Then let's go."

They rode down the slope at a walk, and when the ground leveled out, the deputy put his horse into a lope. Delaine stayed behind him as they crossed the basin. Sagebrush and rocks flowed by. The horses grunted, but they kept a steady pace.

Deputy Corle slowed as he neared the next crest. His horse came to a stop, and he swung down. Delaine stopped behind them. The deputy pushed his flat hand downward, and Delaine waited. The deputy walked to the top and came back.

"We've gained on them, but not enough. We're going to have to try it again. No need for both of us to look over. Just gives them more to see. When they've gone over the next rise, I'll tell you."

After a couple of observations in which he did not hurry or say anything, the deputy returned. "They're out of sight again. Let's give it a try."

They went up and over and began to lope while they were going downhill. They rode through the bottom and up the other side, again slowing before they cleared the rim. The deputy swung down, motioned with his hand for Delaine to stay back, and inched his way up. He stood for a long moment and motioned for Delaine to join him.

The stretch of land ahead of them did not dip down but was more of a level plain for a mile all around. No horses or humans were in view.

The deputy said, "This is like chasing antelope. I don't know which way they went. We might as well keep going in the same direction. We've been following them more than a trail."

The deputy set the pace, and Delaine stayed with him. The horses moved at a trot. In country like this, a person had to wait to see what the next change in terrain was like.

They came to the edge of the level area and saw that the land fell away into deeper draws, not shallow basins. A thin trail led down into an area where a bluff rose on the left and cast a broad shadow.

The deputy said, "This is the most likely way. We have to be careful and not ride right up on them. At the same time, if they see us from a distance, this is a place where they could lose us."

Delaine had not seen a tree for an hour. The land was all grass and low sage and prickly pear, with protuberances of broken clay sticking up in random spots. Dust and the scent of sage drifted on the air.

The deputy led the way, following the faint cattle trail as it made a curve around the base of the bluff. They came to an area of deep draws crossing in front of them with the land rising in levels to the northwest on the other side.

Deputy Corle drew rein. "If they're just on the run, they'll go straight. If they know where they're going, they'll go one way and another over some of these ridges so as not to make such a steep climb. I'm still worried about popping over the top of a ridge and having them waiting for us."

"If we're going to cross at an angle, I think it's better to go uphill than down. Stay above."

"I think so, too." The deputy pointed to the right.

They rode down into a grassy bottom and took a diagonal up the side of the ridge. The next draw was empty, so they went down to the left and up to the right, still staying near the top of those draws that fingered down into a drainage.

"It looks like there's one more," said the deputy, "and then a climb out of here, unless they go out that way." He pointed to the southwest, where the vista opened up into broad sunlight on lower rolling hills. "But my sense is that they're going in this direction. I don't know why they didn't go around on the right, but maybe there's more of the same there."

They crossed the next draw and began to climb out of what now appeared to be what plainsman called a hole. Delaine had seen places like this before, where coyotes strolled on terraces inaccessible by men on horseback and where badgers climbed down rocky little cliffs into their dens. Again, it looked like good deer country, where the bluish-grey animals with dark features would stand stock still in autumn shadows. But today no animals moved, and no change of color showed against the pale tones of sparse vegetation with earth showing through.

"Son of a bitch," said the deputy. "There they are."

Delaine snapped to attention. Straight across to the northwest, on a steep hillside, three riders crept up the trail in shadow. The shades of color were perceptible. Jim Rudy, with his dark hat and vest and a red shirt, was riding in front on the dull-colored bay. A shorter rider with hair that showed almost white in the shadows, was riding a medium-sized sorrel. Taking up the rear was the solid form of Melworth, with a pale hat, grey shirt sleeves showing against a brown vest, and a dark-brown saddle on a buckskin-colored horse. All three riders had their backs to Delaine and the deputy, who would have been in plain view if anyone had turned to look. But the climb was steep, and the three on horseback had good reason to watch the trail ahead.

Deputy Corle let out a long breath as the riders went around a low bluff and out of sight. "I don't want to follow straight up behind them," he said. "If they stop to rest, they'll hears us coming up."

Delaine nodded. He could almost hear the noise of huffing horses, thudding hooves, rustling leather, and jingling spurs. "What do you want to do?"

"I think if we go up and around on the right, we might come out on a level with them, and they can see us. If we go around on the left, we can come up out of this hole and get a peek at them. So let's cut across this bottom."

Cutting across entailed a few ups and downs, but the rises were not steep in the bottom. On the other side, a deep gash led north, and a cattle trail showed that there was a way out on top.

Delaine felt his horse's neck. It was warm and damp. The day was not hot, but a horse could overheat if it was pushed too hard. Delaine was glad to see the deputy pick up the trail at a fast walk. Dust rose in clouds a foot high, and the dry scent of dirt was in the air. The horse hooves thudded in the loose earth but not loud.

The two men dismounted and rose up out of the top of the cleft on foot, raising the line of vision an inch at a time.

"I wonder where the hell they are," the deputy whispered. He led his horse up onto level ground, and

Delaine did the same. They were on high ground again, where the plains leveled out, but there were always dips and rises. "They seem to be bearing northwest all this time. If they know where they're going, they should be looking for water."

Cattlemen had been in the country long enough to build small earthen dams that now had small trees growing out of the banks, but Delaine had not seen one on this route. There was always a chance of coming across a windmill as well, but that would be on private land, often fenced.

The deputy led the way north by northeast, to cut the imagined trail of the other party. In less than half a mile, he stopped and pointed at a trail where cattle had ground the soil and horses had left their prints. "Looks like they went this way."

The Laramie Mountains were well to the south, and no tall land formations loomed in the west, so the sun did not seem to be sinking. But it was slipping.

"We're a long ways from anything," said the deputy. "If they get away from us in the dark, I'm afraid we'll just have to go back. Let's try till dusk. We don't want to be taking any chances with gunfire after that, anyway. We don't want anything to happen to that kid."

"I agree. Someone will catch up with those two, sooner or later. The kid matters most—to us. I don't think Melworth is as concerned about the kid's welfare as he is for himself. As I understood it, he let the boy from Chicago die, though I don't know how."

"We just have to be careful. If we don't find them by dark, we'll go back and send telegrams out."

They rode on, and the land began to roll again. Delaine kept an eye out for a line of trees that would mark a watercourse. At last he saw one, angling toward the trail they were on.

"What do you think of that?" he said. "It looks like it might be a creek."

"It does. If they've stopped, I don't want to ride up on them. So let's be on the lookout as we get closer."

The land sloped down to the creek on each side. Deputy Corle took a detour to the right to stay behind a lump in the land, and they came to a creek bed about a quarter of a mile from the point where the trail crossed it. The creek bottom was about forty yards across, grassed over, with box elders and a few small cottonwoods. It did not look as if it ran much water at any time, and at present, a trickle less than a foot wide ran through it.

The deputy said, "Wait here and hold the horses. I'm going to take a look." He took off his spurs and hung them on his saddle horn, and he pulled his rifle from its scabbard. "I'll be back."

Delaine waited for what seemed like a long time, but the sun did not move much in its descent. The deputy came back and said, "They've stopped there. This is our chance. I think I'll go on one side, and you can go on the other. Let's tie our horses here. If they get on their horses and take off, I guess that's it. But we don't want to shoot and hold onto our horses at the same time, and I think at least one of us may have to shoot."

"All right." Delaine took off his spurs and was about to hang them on his saddle horn, when he decided they would be quieter and more secure if he put them in his saddlebag. He tied his horse to one of four thin trunks growing out of a cottonwood stump, and he pulled his rifle.

Deputy Corle spoke in a low voice. "I'll try to keep track of you. When I see you on the other side, with them between, I'll call out to them. I don't expect them to give up, but I'll try. Again, if you shoot, be damn sure of where you're aiming."

"I will."

Delaine could feel his heartbeat in his chest and in his temples as he picked his way along. He kept the hump of ground between him and the crossing for as long as he could. He thought about how far they were from Galen at Broken Horn Canyon and from town. He agreed with the deputy on not expecting the two hard cases to give up.

He kept back from the edge and could not see into the creek bed. He kept walking, one careful step after another, and he did not see the trail until he crossed it. He backed up and approached the edge of the creek. Little by little, the scene came into view.

Melworth was standing in mottled shade, smoking a cigarette and holding his buckskin horse with the brown mane and tail. The light-haired boy was lying on his back on the ground. Rudy in his red shirt and dark vest was bent over looking at a hoof on the sorrel horse. His dull-colored bay stood a few yards away with its reins on the ground.

The deputy's voice rang out. "Melworth. This is Deputy Corle from the Converse County Sheriff's Office. I've got men on both sides of the creek here. The best thing for you to do is to give up."

Rudy dropped the hoof of the sorrel horse, pulled his pistol, found his aim in the deputy's direction, and fired. A rifle shot roared back.

Melworth threw his cigarette on the ground and scrambled to grab the kid as he was getting up.

Rudy fired again, and a rifle shot came back. Rudy dove for the ground.

Melworth came up with the kid struggling at his waist. The hard-looking man had his left arm hooked across the kid's chest and under both arms. He drew his gun with his right hand. He called out, "You'd better back off, deputy. It would be a shame if this kid gets it."

Melworth snapped up and back as the rifle blasted again. His hat fell away, his left arm swung loose, and his pistol dropped from his right hand. The boy slumped in a heap.

Rudy sprang up, and running in a crouch, he caught the kid as he was beginning to crawl away.

The deputy appeared to be searching for Rudy, who must have been below his line of sight. The man was on all fours, as if he had caught a lamb or a pig. He transferred his catch from his right arm to his left, and he was drawing his six-gun when Delaine fired a rifle shot over his head.

Rudy twisted around, and the kid squirmed away. Rudy rose in a crouch, searching to place a shot in Delaine's direction. He held the pistol in both hands, and his shadowy eyes found a target. As he thumbed back the hammer, Delaine settled the bead in the notch and fired.

The shot caught Rudy high in the chest, and his arms flew out to the sides as his pistol fell away. He landed on his back.

The boy was crying and screaming as Delaine and Deputy Corle crashed down into the creek bottom from each side. Between sobs, the boy hollered, "Don't shoot me! Don't shoot me!"

The deputy took him by the wrist and said, "Don't

worry, son. I'm a deputy sheriff. I'm with the law. These two don't have you any more."

The boy turned his face up and rose to his feet. His face was flushed and dirty, and he looked as if he was about to cry again. A dark spot showed where he appeared to have wet his pants.

Deputy Corle said, "Don't worry. Calm down. I'm with the law. You're safe now."

The boy's breath heaved in and out.

"Can you tell us your name?"

The boy burst as if he was going to cry again, but his mouth opened, and a pair of buck teeth showed as he said, with a tone of impatience, "William Harris Banks!"

15

———

A FAINT LIGHT WAS SHOWING IN THE WINDOW OF THE line shack when the group rode in. Deputy Corle helped the boy down from the sorrel horse while Delaine held reins and lead ropes. The deputy knocked on the door with his knuckles, and when Galen appeared, the deputy told him to bring the prisoner out with a lantern.

The deputy took the lantern and held it up to illuminate Sorensen's face. He said to the boy, "Do you know this man?"

The boy said, "Yes," in a drawn-out syllable, and added, "he kept me here."

The deputy turned to Sorensen. "Then let's quit pretending we didn't do anything or know anything. Come over here." He held the lantern as Galen ushered the handcuffed man toward the two bodies tied onto horses. "I think you can see where things stand. This whole enterprise is done, along with anything else your bunch was up to. But this boy is alive and well, and he will talk. You stand to face some drastic punishment, and you can decide for yourself how much you want to cooperate."

Sorensen did not answer, but the smirk was gone from his face.

The deputy spoke to Galen. "The boy can ride with me. We'll handcuff the prisoner in front, and he can ride the horse he's used to riding." The deputy had cut Rudy's manila rope into lengths for lead ropes, which Delaine held. The deputy motioned with his head. "You can lead his horse. Delaine will lead the other two. I still have to do something about Milligan and his horse tomorrow."

———

THE GROUP STOPPED at the town jail, a log building about ten feet square. Galen took out his keys and opened the door. When Sorensen had his feet on the ground, he said, "You're right, deputy. They kidnapped that boy."

"And you held him. Don't think you can put the whole blame on the others, now that they're gone. But you can make it easier on yourself." He paused. "Who shot Cunningham?"

"I was out at the line camp, so I didn't see it. But I understood that Jim did it."

"Jim Rudy."

"Yes."

"And how about Wyman?"

"The same."

"Did Vick help him on these jobs?"

"I think so, but I wasn't there."

"Why did they do in Wyman?"

"They thought he knew about the kid. He was

snoopin' around, and they heard someone had him pegged for a runnin' iron artist, so they laid him out that way."

"How about this woman who was stifled in her hotel room? An older woman, who knew enough to inform on Melworth."

"I don't know anything about that."

"How about José Luna?"

Sorensen seemed to gather his thoughts. "Oh, that was Jim. He did it with a needle. Same as with the other Mexican. Jim was good with a needle. He knew a lot of things."

"Who helped him?"

"Dorr."

"Who's that?"

"Dorlyn. Vick. They always worked together. Rode together."

Delaine said, "I saw you and Rudy at The Elkhorn in Willett on a Sunday afternoon. When he picked a fight with Milligan."

"That was just once."

The deputy said, "And you never did anything."

"You know I can't lie. The kid will tell you. As for this other stuff, I told you what I know. I was out at the line camp most of the time. And what I don't know, I told you that, like this woman you mentioned, whoever she was."

"Did Rudy know how to get into a hotel room?"

"Oh, yeah. He knew a lot."

The deputy glanced at the body tied onto the bay horse with the dark hat crushed under the lash ropes. "And a lot of good it did him."

After leaving Sorensen in the jail, the group went to the hotel. The deputy said, "Delaine, we'll get you a room for the rest of the night. If you can help Galen leave off the bodies and put the horses in the stable, your room will be waiting for you. I'll take the boy in now. He can stay with me, and I'll send a wire to his father in the morning."

———

DELAINE WAS EATING breakfast near a window in the café when Miss Capps and her escort left the hotel and set out toward the train stop. The man was carrying the bags.

Teale poured another cup of coffee. "Life goes on," he said. "All of us are like ants crawling over the face of the earth. Sooner or later, every one of us comes to an end, and life keeps going on around us. It's too bad someone couldn't have stopped these others a little sooner."

"I agree with you there."

Teale brushed at the lapel of his dull tweed jacket. "I've always got a stock of philosophy. When something happens, sometimes a person can go back to a point when he could have done something different, but in this case, I just didn't know enough. And I was nobody. But I wonder if I could have done something."

"You did. You helped me."

"Yes, and you did something."

"Almost in spite of myself. But I got out of it all right."

"I suppose you and Rachel will go back to Overton."

"Well, yes. We have to report to the family. And pick things up where we left them."

"If you ever come through, look us up. We can go on a picnic together."

"That would be good." Delaine imagined sitting on a canvas blanket, with Teale rolling cigarettes with his little machine and serving beer out of a bucket, and he thought that being alive was not a bad way to be.

———

BACK AT THE HOTEL LOBBY, William Harris Banks was slumped in a chair, scrubbed clean and wearing new clothes. Rachel was sitting in a chair nearby. Delaine took off his hat as she stood up to meet him.

"Elmira and I helped him get a bath. She's having his old clothes washed. He wore the same things the whole time."

"I assume the deputy has notified his father."

"Oh, yes. He sent a telegram to Billings. The father is on the way."

Elmira appeared from the direction of the dining room. She was carrying a tray with a dish and a spoon visible. She said, "Here's some ice cream, William. We just made it. It's kind of soft, but it tastes like ice cream."

The boy had his elbow on the armrest and his fist pushed against his cheek. "I don't want any."

"That's all right. It won't go to waste." Elmira spoke to Delaine. "Thank you for your part in this. You made an extraordinary contribution."

"I didn't do everything right. I feel responsible for what happened to Beatrice."

Elmira's face fell, and she drew herself up. "You did your best. You're just a regular citizen, and you rose to the occasion."

"Such as I had to. But we can't even prove who was responsible for what happened to her, even though I'm sure we know."

"Justice isn't perfect. Well, Edwin would say that is a platitude."

"Where's the deputy?"

"He went out with the coroner to bring in the other body."

"I imagine the coroner got here yesterday and saw what there was to see."

"Yes. He also did some work this morning and found a ring with an expensive blue stone in Jim Rudy's pocket."

"That should help. Maybe I'll cross paths with them. I have to go out to the ranch to get my things and to collect what little pay I have coming."

"I guess no one gets to collect the reward."

Delaine glanced at the sullen boy. "Law enforcement can't collect a reward, and I was part of a posse. I was working on something else, anyway."

Creases showed by Elmira's eyes as she smiled. "I hope to see you again before you leave, but if I don't, I wish you the best. Come and see us again."

"Thanks. I'll look forward to it." He turned his hat in his hands. "I guess I'll go to the stable to get my horse."

Rachel said, "I'll walk to the door with you. I said I would stay here with William until Deputy Corle comes back."

She walked with him to the door and onto the porch. "You must be tired," she said.

"Not as much as I might expect. I just wish things had turned out better."

"Like Elmira said, justice isn't perfect. And as I've

seen for myself, life isn't always fair. We've done the best we could. I'm sorry for her, too, but we can't do anything about it. Let's be glad for what we did."

"Thanks." They brushed their lips together, and he met her dark eyes. "I'll be back in about three hours, and we can plan on how to make our separate ways back."

"That will be fine."

He went out into the sunshine and turned left toward the livery stable. He walked in the street, conscious of the pistol at his side.

Quick footsteps behind him caused him to turn.

Dan, wearing his cloth cap and work clothes, was hurrying along with his donkey.

"Mr. Delaine."

"Yes, Dan. What is it?"

"Do you mind if I ask you a question?"

If it had been Reed, Delaine might have said, "You just did. Would you like to ask another?" To the boy, he said, "Go ahead."

"Are you a Pinkerton man?"

Under a broad sky, standing in a dusty street in a small town with the vast plains all around, Delaine glanced at the donkey and met the boy's eyes. The words came to him. "No, Dan. I'm a regular citizen. Like you."

A LOOK AT BOOK THREE
FORGOTTEN ROSE

Out in the open range, the greatest threats lie hidden…and one cowboy must risk everything to bring them to light.

Jess Delaine arrives at a modest ranch near Sayers, Wyoming, ready to guide hunters and face the hard labor of a roundup. But his routine life is upended when Tiburcio Martínez, a man searching for his missing daughter, is found dead. As questions multiply, Delaine uncovers dark secrets stretching across the rangeland—secrets tied to ruthless criminals exploiting women for profit.

When more bodies appear, including that of Martínez's nephew, Delaine finds himself locked in a desperate struggle against a hidden network of traffickers. After receiving a tip from a spirited saloon woman, he teams up with Deputy Blackmur and follows a trail that leads to shadowy ranchers, mysterious visitors, and a group of women held against their will.

Facing ambushes, betrayals, and a chilling conspiracy, Delaine must decide how far he's willing to go to protect the innocent and deliver justice to the guilty. In a lawless land, will he be able to expose the truth—or become its next victim?

AVAILABLE APRIL 2025

ABOUT THE AUTHOR

John D. Nesbitt is the author of more than fifty books, including traditional Westerns, crossover Western mysteries, contemporary Western fiction, retro/noir fiction, nonfiction, and poetry. He has won the Western Writers of America Spur Award four times—twice for paperback novel, once for short story, and once for poem. He has won the Western Fictioneers Peacemaker Award twice—once for novel and once for short story. He has been a finalist for the Spur Award twice, the Peacemaker eight times, and the Will Rogers Medallion Award eight times. He has also received two creative writing fellowships with the Wyoming Arts Council—once for fiction, once for nonfiction—and he has won the fiction award four times with the Wyoming State Historical Society.

www.johndnesbitt.com